In Pursuit of the Dead

The rediscovered cases of Sherlock Holmes Book 5

Arthur Hall

Paperback 978-1-78705-417-2
ePub ISBN 978-1-78705-418-9
PDF ISBN 978-1-78705-419-6

MX Publishing
335 Princess Park Manor, Royal Drive,
London, N11 3GX
www.mxpublishing.com

Cover design by Brian Belanger
www.belangerbooks.com and www.redbubble.com/people/zhahadun

Arthur Hall was born in Aston, Birmingham, UK, in 1944. He discovered his interest in writing during his school days, along with a love of fictional adventure and suspense.

His first novel "Sole Contact" was an espionage story about an ultra-secret government department known as "Sector Three" and has been followed, to date, by four sequels.

Other works include five "rediscovered" cases from the files of Sherlock Holmes, two collections of bizarre short stories and two novels about an adventurer named Bernard Kramer, as well as several contributions to the regular anthology, "The MX Book of New Sherlock Holmes Stories."

His only ambition, apart from being published more widely, is to attend the premier of a film based on one of his novels, ideally at The Odeon, Leicester Square.

He lives in the West Midlands, United Kingdom, where he often walks other people's dogs as he attempts to visualise new plots.

The author welcomes comments and observations about his work, at: arthurhall7777@aol.co.uk

Also by Arthur Hall:

The Bernard Kramer series:
The Sagittarius Ring
Controlled Descent

Anthologies:
Facets of Fantasy (A volume of fourteen short tales)
Curious Tales (A volume of five bizarre stories)

Rediscovered cases from the files of Sherlock Holmes:
The Demon of the Dusk
The One Hundred per Cent Society
The Secret Assassin
The Phantom Killer

The "Sector Three" Series:
Sole Contact
A Faint and Distant Threat
The Final Strategy
The Plain Face of Truth
A Certain Way to Death

CONTENTS

Chapter One – An Uninteresting Letter

At the time of the occurrences which I have described in the following account, the intimacy between Sherlock Holmes and myself had increased greatly. It had reached the point, in fact, where I would be invited to accompany him on almost all the cases that presented themselves for his consideration. Such was the situation between us when, some months before the dreadful affair that altered our lives, my friend received a letter that began a strange sequence of events.

"An unexpected invitation, Watson," my friend said as he passed the contents of the envelope across the breakfast table.

I took it and began to read, as he opened the rest of his post with a butter knife. The letter was written in a strong hand, which suffered from a slight tremble when forming capital letters.

My Dear Mr. Sherlock Holmes,

I find myself in a desperate position. The local police are unavailable to me, for reasons that I will confess to you if you consent to help me escape from my predicament. You are known, even here, to be interested in situations of an unusual nature, and certainly none could deny that such is so in this instance.

Have you, I wonder, ever encountered circumstances where a dead man returns to life to become a plague to those he formerly knew? I would wager that you have not, unless by trickery, and that positively cannot be so here.

I feel that I shall take leave of my senses if these hauntings do not cease, for I am at my wits' end with nowhere else to turn. I beg you to telegraph me, saying you will take a fast train to render me your assistance, to give me some little hope until you arrive.

Yours most sincerely and in gravest anxiety,

Squire Harcourt Foley.

"From Foley Grange, near Bowness, Cumberland," I observed.

"Indeed," Holmes tossed the postcard he held onto the pile of discarded correspondence near the coffee pot. "It will of course be one of those seemingly supernatural situations which have, in the end, a solution that is only too ordinary. Someone who wants to share in the Squire's wealth in one way or another, I expect."

"Do you intend to pursue it?"

"Not at all. If you have read the letter, pray add it to the pile."

"The man does sound desperate, Holmes, as he says."

He scowled at the paper, which was still in my hand. "The only mystery, as far as I can see, is why he cannot consult the local official force. His anxiety may be as a result of some crime he has himself committed. No, there is little that is unusual enough to be interesting, here."

"Is there anything else then, among your correspondence, that is worthy of your notice?"

I saw his expression change at once. My implied sarcasm had not escaped him. "I fear there is not. I may spend the day bringing my index up to date."

There was something in the way he said those words that served as a warning to me of the coming onset of the black depression that often possessed him in the absence of a case. My worst fear was that he would resort to the cocaine bottle once more.

"It may turn out to be something quite different, you know."

"This Cumberland affair? It is true, I suppose, that some of my most memorable cases appeared as nothing more than mundane at first," he conceded.

"At the worst, it could turn out to be nothing more than a problem you could solve with ease, and you have mentioned that there is little that awaits your attention."

He turned to look through the half-opened window, down onto the sunlit pavements of Baker Street. His eyes held a bored expression which suddenly changed, as a faint smile lit up his face.

"I see your situation clearly, Watson. Your wife is staying with her sister, convalescing after a long bout of influenza, while you have taken some time away from your practice in the hope that we might share some experience that you can sell to your publisher. "He stretched his arms lazily above his head. "It is, after all, a beautiful day and does not appear likely to change soon. Very well then, if a day or two near the English lakes appeals to you, send a telegram to this Squire Foley and, if you will be so good as to hand me my Bradshaw from the bookshelf, I will ascertain which train will take us there."

#

The journey seemed interminable. Holmes would stare, seemingly in a trance-like state, from our carriage window for long periods, alternating with sudden bursts of conversation about topics as diverse as the dietary habits of Mongolian shepherds and the hitherto unknown creatures discovered during a recent South American expedition.

As for myself, apart from wondering how my dear wife's condition was improving, I was content to watch the rapid passing of areas of woodland. The new leaves had not yet lost their spring freshness, and the bluebells among the grass were harbingers of the warm months ahead. The train came to rest at stations that grew increasingly sparse in their amenities and population, as we headed north and further away from the capital. Presently the villages,

3

speeding by in a flash, became less frequent, and the view a sea of endless green.

At last I felt the engine speed decrease, and saw that fields of cows or sheep now surrounded us on both sides. The wheels screamed briefly against the metal tracks and we came to a slow stop, as Holmes emerged from his reverie.

"I believe we have arrived at Windermere Station, Watson."

Carrying our travelling-bags, we left the train and peered up and down the platform. A few others disembarked with us and quickly dispersed, some of them having been met. We gave up our tickets to a fellow who seemed to be guard, porter and station-master, not unusual in country stations, and passed through a tiny waiting-room to stand in a leafy lane beyond. Several dog-carts and traps waited to bear some of the arriving passengers away, but from a landau with two splendid black horses a man emerged and strode to confront us.

"Pardon me, gentlemen. May I ask if you are Mr. Sherlock Holmes and Doctor Watson?"

"Indeed, we are," my friend replied.

The man's slight frame bowed towards us. "Good sirs, I am Underton, Squire Foley's coachman. If you will please accompany me…"

Underton took our bags and placed them aboard the coach. Holmes and I settled ourselves and enjoyed a short ride through beautiful countryside, beneath overhanging trees and with pleasant meadows near the roadside. The sun shone brightly through the luxuriant leaves, dappling the road with shapes and patterns.

After more than a mile we reached the town. Near one of the rather quaint buildings, Holmes directed Underton to stop, and left the landau in a sprightly fashion. He entered an imposing inn, which I saw from the sign was called 'The Weary Traveller.'

"Have you reserved rooms for us?" I asked him as he resumed his seat opposite me.

He nodded. "The Squire did not indicate that he could accommodate us. Doubtless he could and would, but I prefer to stay some distance away where I can gain a somewhat different perspective."

I was not sure what Holmes meant by this, but I imagined it to be something akin to the old saying of being unable to see the wood for the trees. My attention was arrested then however, by the view of Lake Windermere that was revealed as the landau began to climb a gradual slope. The water was as blue as any sea that I have ever seen, with gentle waves across its surface. I could see small boats scattered here and there, and the tiny figures of folk walking on the far shore.

It was no surprise to me that Holmes appeared indifferent to our surroundings, sitting with his chin upon his chest. He changed his posture as our coach suddenly left the road to enter a long drive with leafy boughs overhanging from either side. Quite soon, the path ended and we found ourselves in a square courtyard. The house that confronted us had obviously once been much larger, since most of both wings had become a ruin and only the remainder showed signs of habitation. Underton brought the landau to a gentle halt before a massive iron-studded door, which opened to allow an elderly man in butler's attire to walk in stately fashion down the steps towards us.

Holmes and I alighted, and Underton placed our bags beside us before leading the horses away.

"Gentlemen," the butler beamed, "welcome to Foley Grange. The Squire awaits you in the library." He then lifted our luggage with amazing strength, for a man of his years.

We were led along a stone-flagged passage that was a little the worse for wear I thought, then ushered into a cavernous room where leather-bound volumes lined the walls. The butler announced us and the door closed softly as he left. Looking out of the tall window directly ahead stood a huge man, his back to us.

After a moment he turned to face us. With the sun streaming through the window, I was able to see him well.

"Mr. Holmes and Doctor Watson." We shook his outstretched hand in turn. "Welcome. I am already in your debt. I read of you some time ago in a London newspaper and pray that you can relieve me of the burden of guilt and anxiety that I bear. Please, gentlemen, be seated and drink a glass of brandy with me."

When we were settled around the empty fireplace with full glasses, I took the opportunity to scrutinize Squire Foley. I had already seen that he was as tall as Holmes, though broader and thicker-set. His square, schoolboy face had a red tinge to it, which could have been the result of excessive drinking, or simply from the embarrassment that some feel in the company of strangers. His hands had a slight tremble, and his eyes held an expression of great uncertainty.

"I must apologise," said our host, "for not making it clear in my letter that there is little accommodation for guests here. However, if you consent to stay after hearing of the events leading up to the present situation, I will gladly make arrangements for you both to be made comfortable in one of the inns in Bowness."

"Thank you." I put down my depleted glass. "But we have already secured rooms at the Weary Traveller."

Holmes glanced around the room, before turning to our host. "May I ask, is this your ancestral home?"

"It is indeed. It was built by an ancestor who is said to have been at the court of King Henry VIII. It is now in a deplorable state, as you will have observed, since several of my more recent forebears were poor speculators. Most of the family fortune was lost through their unwise investments, with the result that the upkeep and maintenance of the place is quite beyond my means. But still," he said more lightly, "I have a roof over my head and can live fairly well."

"You do not then, keep a large staff?"

"There's Jenson of course, and Anne Warwick the cook, and two maids. Between them and the coachman, Underton, they care for my needs well."

I allowed my eyes to roam over the faded portraits that hung from every wall. The house was quiet apart from the distant toll of a church bell and the Squire's rather laboured breathing.

Holmes broke the silence suddenly, "Perhaps you would care to relate to us the extraordinary events that you alluded to in your letter. While the notion of the dead returning to life is intriguing, I must tell you that my experiences suggest that it is impossible. Watson here will tell you that our brushes with the supernatural have never failed to have a very ordinary explanation, in the end."

"Most certainly," I confirmed. "Without exception."

Squire Foley seemed to have gone a little pale. "Then I hope, gentlemen, than any investigation you make here will have a similar conclusion. I accept that I am at fault to some degree, and my conscience has not been clear since."

"Pray tell us all," Holmes interrupted to slow down the Squire's quickening narrative. "But from the beginning. I must have a complete account if I am to be of any assistance."

"Of course, I apologise for letting my anxiety get the better of me. I should mention that I am engaged to be married to Miss Priscilla Todbury, a charming girl."

"Confine yourself to the facts of the case, I beg of you."

"But she is the very basis of the case, Mr. Holmes. We have been promised to each other for a year, now. There were no clouds on our horizon until, six weeks ago, a scoundrel calling himself

7

William Lance appeared and began calling on her. She rejected him of course, and after the second time told me of his advances. I then made certain to be in Miss Todbury's home at the time he said that he would call again, the following day. When he arrived I confronted him at the door, and told him in no uncertain terms that he was unwelcome. At first he was insolent and then he laughed in my face, at which I gave him a sound thrashing. He ran off shouting curses and threats, and I thought we were rid of him."

"But he turned his attentions to you?" I ventured.

"He did indeed. For the next two weeks I was plagued with letters containing death threats, and once he appeared in front of the house in the middle of the night. I instructed Jenson to fire a shotgun over Lance's head, whereupon he fled, and when I heard that he had disturbed Miss Todbury similarly, that was the last straw."

"But why did you not report these incidents to the official force?" Holmes asked. "I noticed the police station in Bowness earlier, as we arrived."

"For one reason Primpton, the local magistrate, is my enemy. He has hated me since our schooldays, when I bested him in a trivial dispute. He is unlikely to put himself out to help, despite the requirements of his office. Also there is another reason, which I alluded to in my letter, which puts official assistance beyond my reach."

Holmes leaned forward in his chair. "You have committed a crime, then?"

"I challenged Lance to a duel, and killed him."

Chapter Two – The Boatman's Tale.

Holmes looked at Squire Foley curiously.

"Duelling is frowned upon," I interjected. "Though I cannot be sure how the law stands now."

My friend ignored this. "Yet you believe Lance still lives?"

"I have seen him since, and the letters have continued."

"Most interesting. Pray continue with your narrative."

Squire Foley fixed his eyes on the patterned carpet, and spoke in a sombre voice. "Because of his persistence, I walked around Bowness at different times of day, until I set eyes on the blackguard. I struck his face with a leather gauntlet and told him that I would be waiting, as tradition demands, at midnight in the high field beyond the meadow at the far end of Bowness. His reply was a multitude of oaths, but he said he would be there. As I left him, he shouted after me that he chose pistols, that he would be bringing no second and that he would certainly take great delight in my death."

"So the arrangement was that the two of you only would be present?" Holmes enquired.

"Most unusual," I observed.

"Indeed," the Squire agreed. "But that is how it was to be. The field was of course in darkness when I arrived. I was armed with a duelling pistol that had been used by my forbears, and lit a coach-lantern to guide Lance when I saw him approach. Naturally, I thought we would be observing the rules as gentlemen, that is standing back-to-back and pacing the required distance before turning to fire, but he discharged his weapon on sight and I heard the echo before I felt the ball pass my face. I immediately fired in return, but realised that my aim was off, so you can imagine my surprise when he cried out and flung up his arms before falling on his face."

9

"Did you then approach the body?" Holmes asked then.

"Of course. I could not leave there without knowing whether Lance was dead or wounded. I was prepared to help him to a physician, regardless."

"And what did you discover?"

"The results of a lucky shot, if one can put it like that. His face was a mass of blood, and I saw by the light of my lantern that my shot had struck almost the centre of his forehead. He was as dead as a man can be, so how in God's name can he still walk the streets of Bowness and threaten me with his writings?"

"What became of the body?"

"I left it there and returned home. The following day I read in the late edition that a farmer had found it, and it had been taken to the mortuary. Later, the local coroner recorded a verdict of death by person or persons unknown, if that is the phrase. Lance was buried in a pauper's grave in a nearby cemetery, and the police – I know not if they were local or called in from elsewhere – began an investigation that was soon discontinued."

"But no connection with yourself was ever discovered?"

"None. I was afraid, more than anything, of what Primpton might make of it. Certainly, I told no one"

"Yet you now freely confess to us?"

Despair filled our host's face. "What choice do I have, gentlemen? In order to be free of this man, or his ghost, I have to tell you all that there is to tell regarding this matter. To do otherwise would be tantamount to tying your hands, would it not?"

"Quite so," agreed Holmes. "If some of my previous clients had but pursued such a path from the beginning, their problems might have been more quickly solved."

I had noticed that my friend had made no judgement regarding the Squire's actions of taking a man's life during a duel, or of abandoning the body afterwards. This was far from the first time that I had seen him ignore or circumvent the law, if doing so aided his enquiries.

"You mentioned that you have seen Lance since his death," he reminded the Squire.

He nodded. "Twice, Mr. Holmes. Once he threatened me from a passing coach, and once called to me from a high window in a building near the lake shore. I entered the place and climbed several flights of stairs, but he was nowhere to be seen. Also, there were more letters."

"You are quite certain it was he?"

"As certain as I can be. After the duel, I was never able to see him closely."

"And the letters?"

"I have them here."

Squire Foley opened a drawer in a side-table and withdrew several crumpled sheets of paper which he handed to Holmes. My friend looked at each in turn but seemed to allow them little importance. When he passed them to me I saw that they were written in a childish scrawl and that the message was repetitive. All threatened death or torture by monstrous means. These were the words of a hideously cruel man, or one who is out of his mind, and yet there was a strange melancholy about them.

"By any chance," said Holmes, "have you retained the envelopes? Often, more can be learned from them than their contents."

Our host shook his head. "That did not occur to me. I can, however, recall that they were quite unmarked except for my name, which was written in the same hand."

"That was so with all of them? They were all delivered by hand?"

"Without exception."

"Their content is tediously consistent, nothing more than threats and curses." Holmes produced his pipe with the amber stem. "I trust, Squire Foley, that you have no objection to strong tobacco?"

"None whatsoever. I do not smoke myself, but I find the fragrance pleasing."

I took out my pouch as my friend had done, and we both smoked for a few minutes while he contemplated the situation.

"Very well," he said at last, "I have but one more question. Since Lance's apparent death, has anyone else seen him in the town or elsewhere?"

The Squire nodded, I thought reluctantly. "There is a man called Nathaniel Barley, whom I chanced to meet in Bowness immediately after Lance called to me from the coach. I did not mention him until now because his reputation is that of a habitual drunkard, and I therefore assumed that his testimony would be confused or worthless. He is a boat-builder, working at one of the small lakeside concerns. It is an easy place to find, since it is the closest to the bandstand, across from the Town Hall. His remark to me was 'That man in that there coach wishes you ill, sir. I would not cross his path, for I know him of old.'"

"A most fortuitous encounter. Had you any acquaintance with this fellow, previously?"

"I have a vague recollection of seeing him in the streets of Bowness, and of observing him being thrown out of a tavern or two, but that is all."

"Did he say anything more, concerning Lance?"

"Nothing. He merely staggered past me. The incident appeared to amuse him."

Holmes breathed out a cloud of smoke as I, having finished with my pipe, looked through the high window across the lawn to an ornamental pond. Here the tranquillity was disturbed only by a swan beating its wings, I thought to repel a rival for the affections of a female, and by the strange cry of a peacock.

At that moment the door opened. I glanced over my shoulder to see a tall woman enter, her poise and elegance immediately evident.

Squire Foley stood up at once, as did we.

"My dear, these gentlemen are Mr. Sherlock Holmes and Doctor Watson, who have come to find a solution to our problem. Gentlemen, this is Miss Priscilla Todbury, my fiancée."

The introductions were quickly over, and we all sat. While I was impressed by Miss Todbury's elfin features which were ensured by her high cheekbones, soft blonde hair and blue eyes, Holmes remained indifferent. As usual with the fairer sex he was the soul of courtesy, but his interest lay only with the problem that confronted us.

Squire Foley briefly reiterated our discussion to Miss Todbury, who nodded her head at intervals, while my friend and I looked on. When he had finished he turned to us, intending to make some remark, but Holmes forestalled him.

"Tell me, Miss Todbury, have you, yourself, received any further communication from this man Lance since his supposed death?"

"Nothing has come to me." Her eyes were full of strain, or fear. "How could I, if the man is dead?"

"Quite. And for the same reason, you could not have seen him?"

"Obviously not."

"What do you know then, of his death?"

Miss Todbury's expression hardened, and I began to suspect that beneath her pleasant exterior lay a quite different personality.

"Only what has appeared in the newspapers. He was found shot, but it is not known why or by whom. Surely you must have learned this already, if you are to investigate."

Squire Foley gave her an embarrassed glance, but before he could apologise to us for her forthrightness, my friend got to his feet.

"Thank you, Miss Todbury. I think we have learned enough for today, Squire Foley. Watson and I will now adjourn to our lodgings to consider the matter. Please allow that we may call upon you unannounced during this investigation, for I feel that such may be essential to its progress. For now, we bid you both good day."

#

The Squire was good enough to allow Underton to retrieve our bags and return us in the landau to the inn in Bowness. When we were settled, we met in the dining room by arrangement. The red-faced, much overweight landlord was a jovial man who, to both Holmes' and my own relief, did not ask questions about where we hailed from or anything else. He did, however, provide us with a satisfying meal of boiled ham with parsley sauce, and it was after finishing this that we retired to a corner seat with a pint of good ale.

"What are your impressions, Watson on what we have seen and heard this afternoon?"

He had been silent for most of the journey back from Foley Grange, and this was his first reference to our visit.

"I think that the Squire has a certain disregard for the law, and possibly a nervous affliction. Miss Todbury's manner of answering your questions was a little harsh. One does not speak in that way to those who have been called to furnish assistance."

"Quite so. But we must keep in mind that she apparently knows nothing of Squire Foley's duel with Lance, nor of its result. Also, if she is as close to the Squire as he believes, she will share his anxiety at Lance's return and persistence."

I nodded. "Perhaps. My last memory of them before we left, was of him comforting her with his embrace. His large stature dwarfed her, and she is a tall woman."

"Indeed. We are given to believe that she knows of Lance's persecution of her fiancé but nothing more, save the advances to her person prior to his 'death'."

"So tomorrow, do we comb Bowness until we find this Lance or some explanation as to why he appears to have risen from the dead?"

"I think," Holmes replied as he took out his tobacco pouch, "that we will be much better employed if we seek out Mr. Nathaniel Barley."

#

We rose early the following morning. After a hearty breakfast, we made our way to the lakeside. As we left the last shops and houses behind, a large steam launch left the landing stage, some of its passengers visible through the open-sided seating area.

"Beyond those sheds is a structure containing boats in various states of repair," Holmes indicated. "I will wager that the man working on that upturned craft is Barley. If not, he is sure to know where to find him."

My friend was soon proven correct. We approached a hunched, unshaven man who worked on a small boat that was turned upside-down and supported by trestles. As we drew closer I saw that he had become aware of us, and his expression became guarded.

"Good morning," Holmes began. "Can we trouble you for the whereabouts of Mr. Nathaniel Barley, if you know them?"

The man put down the wood plane he was using, and turned to face us. That he had been drinking recently was evident from his tainted breath.

"What if I do? What has he to do with strangers?"

"Perhaps the opportunity to earn a shilling or two."

"I am Barley." He went still, and ran his tongue over his lips. "But I already got a job. No time to do anything else."

"Even if it consists of nothing more than answering a few questions?"

Barley's eyes switched from Holmes to me, and back again. "I don't talk to the police. I want no trouble."

"But we are not the police," Holmes assured him. "We are investigating a curious matter on behalf of Squire Foley. It can do you no harm to listen to us, and I have already indicated that it might bring you some reward."

He gave us both a wary glance. "Speak, then."

"I understand that one William Lance, who is known to you, recently died hereabouts. A conflicting account states that he has since been seen by yourself, among others. Can you furnish an explanation for this, if it is indeed what happened?"

Barley's eyes narrowed, and I wondered whether he was concocting something, or if we were about to hear the truth. "I saw Squire Foley recently. He seemed upset after a man in a passing coach called to him. The trouble is, my eyes aren't so good these days so I couldn't see the man. Come to think of it," he added slyly, "I don't hear good either."

Holmes produced a coin from his pocket. "A half-sovereign if your sight and hearing improve within the next few minutes."

"Well then sir, I suppose I could remember some more, if I put my mind to it. I knew Lance some years ago, when we both lived in Carlisle. A more cunning scoundrel God never put breath into, I can tell you. Thief, burglar, liar, blackmailer, he was all of these things, and everyone was surprised when he married a beautiful local girl named Grace Turley. He wasn't bad looking himself though, but it didn't take him long to gamble and drink away what money his new wife brought with her. About that time I had to leave the town, but we won't go into that, and I came to live here. Sometime afterwards I got talking to a fellow who brought his boat in here to be scraped, and we found that we both knew Lance. He told me that Lance was serving time for trying to rob a Post Office, and I heard nothing more until the news came that his body had been found up on the hill there," he pointed vaguely to a point behind us, "and that's about all I know."

"Except for the incident with the coach," Holmes reminded him.

"Ah, that. I heard him threaten to kill Squire Foley, that's all."

"Did he give a reason?"

"He said the Squire had something of his that he wouldn't be allowed to keep."

"Most interesting. Can you say with certainty, that the man in the coach was the man you knew in Carlisle?"

Barley hesitated, perhaps waiting for his payment to increase.

"Assuming," I interjected, "that this was an occasion when your eyesight had improved somewhat."

"Oh it had, that day." He fixed his eyes on the coin, as Holmes held it nearer to him. "Lance was wearing the tall top hat he always wore, and anyway I saw his face as he turned to shout to the Squire. It was him all right, so the reports about his death must have been false."

"Indeed they must have been," confirmed my friend as he gave him the half-sovereign. "Thank you, Mr. Barley."

I glanced over my shoulder as we walked away. Barley was leaning against the boat, watching us.

"Really, Holmes," I said. "How much can we rely on that man's account? I believe he was half-drunk just now, and would have made anything up in order to get his drinking-money."

"Without a doubt you are correct, old fellow, but notice how his version of events agrees with that of the Squire. Both men believed that the man in the coach really was Lance, and not an impersonator, and that he threatened the Squire. Also, friend Barley supplied us with some useful information about Lance's earlier activities."

We strolled away from the lakeshore, past the bandstand and further into the town.

"It is already midday," I observed as the Town Hall clock chimed.

"By which I am sure that you mean it is time for your lunch."

"I was merely stating…"

"Come now, Watson, I have known you for too long. But I see that there is a coffee shop across the road, next to the bakery. I am sure they can supply you with enough sustenance to last until our evening meal. As for me, a cup of strong coffee will suffice."

After I had eaten, with Holmes brooding over his coffee, we returned to The Weary Traveller. No sooner had we arrived than Holmes sought out the landlord and arranged for us to borrow the trap that was kept in the yard at the rear of the building.

"Where are we bound for, Holmes?" I asked as I seated myself next to him.

"To see Squire Foley again, of course. There are still questions to be answered."

I drove at a moderate pace, for the horse was no longer young. My friend made various remarks about our surroundings throughout the journey, refraining from lapsing into his usual silence. As we neared Foley Grange he was in the midst of identifying the various birds we had seen, and explaining their nesting habits, when he broke off abruptly.

"Did you see that, Watson?"

"I saw nothing except the flash of the sun's reflection on a window."

"The second storey, directly above the entrance?"

"Yes. Did you see something more?"

"Perhaps. I am not certain."

He said nothing more until we stood again in the same room with Squire Foley, having been relieved of the trap by Underton.

"Have you come to report some success already, Mr. Holmes?" The Squire enquired with some impatience. I saw at once that his mood today was quite different. He seemed to be suffering some nervous discomfort.

"That would be a little premature, I think. Nathaniel Barley has been interviewed, however, and his statements proved interesting. Apparently, this man Lance is not long out of prison."

"I am not in the least surprised!" Our host's hands clenched into fists. "He can be nothing else but a villain. My life has become fraught with anxiety as I await his next assault upon my senses."

"Have you received any further communication?"

"I am thankful that I have not."

"Barley was prepared to swear that the man who called to you from the coach was indeed Lance. He disclosed to us that he knew Lance in Carlisle, where he was married. Is it possible that you also knew this?"

Squire Foley stood very still, his boyish face trembling.

"Have I not already said that I have told you all? No, I knew nothing of this." He began to pace the room with an aggressiveness that he had not shown before. "But I tell you, Mr. Holmes, the notion that I am haunted without reason, and by a dead man, is trying my patience too much!" He glanced as us with much tension in his expression. "I will have no more of this. If you gentlemen will be so good as to attend Highwall Cemetery at midnight tonight – I believe that to be the traditional time for such gatherings – we will ascertain, once and for all, that Lance lies in his grave."

"My good sir," I interrupted, "it is unlawful to exhume a body without reference to a magistrate. You must have permission to proceed."

"Primpton can go to hell!" He shouted, his entire body shaking. "I would never get his blessing, regardless. If we are to resolve this, we must act of our own accord."

"Squire Foley, I have a request to make, which may well throw some light on our predicament," Holmes said then.

The Squire shook his head and answered more calmly, as if awakening from a dream. "What is it, Mr. Holmes?"

"I would like your permission to ascend to the second floor of this house, and look out through the window."

Our host's face went blank.

"I do not understand you," he said.

"It is quite simple. As we approached, I noticed some fellow with a telescope who may have been observing Foley Grange from the road. I would like to see him from a more advantageous point, so that I may be certain."

"Why did you not mention this before?"

"I was preoccupied with our discussion."

"Very well. Clearly there is no time to lose. I will accompany you."

Holmes moved towards the door. "Pray do not trouble yourself. Watson and I can manage."

"But you have never seen Lance. If it is he, then I can identify him."

"Of course. I had quite forgotten."

We hurried up the ancient, creaking staircase. At the first landing stood a leafy aspidistra, leaning precariously from its pot. From the top of the second flight Holmes looked out, across the grounds to the deserted road.

"There is no one," the Squire observed.

"He seems to have gone," agreed Holmes, "but it is no great loss. From the glimpse I had of him, he appeared too old to be Lance. It was merely a possibility." He gave me a quick sideways glance and smiled. "Although of course, he could have been an agent of Lance."

"Perhaps, but it is irrelevant, now," the Squire remarked as we descended.

"Pray tell me," Holmes asked when we had re-entered the drawing room, "is Miss Todbury here today?"

The Squire looked surprised. "No, she is not. As far as I am aware, she is at her home. Why do you ask?"

"It occurred to me that there is a question that could be asked of her. No matter, it is of little importance. But now I fear that we must leave you, until our rendezvous tonight."

"Yes, indeed. We will see then, the truth of this."

#

Underton had brought the trap around and we had left Foley Grange behind us, before Holmes spoke.

"You may be wondering why I asked about Miss Todbury, Watson. The answer is that I am beginning to believe that the roots of this affair may lie in her past."

"How did you arrive at such a conclusion?"

"You will recall the guarded way she treated my questions, as if I might discover something that she would rather remain hidden. Also, it was Lance's attention to *her* that began this entire sequence of events."

I glanced across the wide fields surrounding us, remembering that my friend had once said that such innocent countryside often concealed more evil than the lowest parts of London. "Perhaps you are right. I am puzzled however, by our excursion to the second floor of the house. I saw no one with a telescope, as we arrived."

"Ha!" Holmes exclaimed. "I would have thought that you would realise that it was but a ruse. You will recall the flashes that we saw from the window as we arrived. It was imperative that I examine the place from where they appeared to originate."

"But there was no mirror on the second floor."

"No, indeed. But there was, you will recall, a large copper gong."

"It was, I imagine, once used for summoning the family and guests to the table. Now, it is probably no more than a decoration."

"There is a little more to it than that, I think. The flashes that I saw were too regular, as our angle of view changed, to be random or accidental. Someone was sending a message or a warning. The gong had nothing to do with it, since it was placed inappropriately and, as I ascertained, was quite immovable. Note though, the cleverness of whoever was signalling. The place was chosen well. A possible explanation, in the shape of the gong, was provided for us, should we be curious about the flashes. I think we have a worthy adversary here, Watson."

I felt foolish, as I often did after Holmes" explanations. "Was there anything else I should have noticed?"

He waited until the trap steadied after passing over an uneven patch of road.

"Only the Squire's curiously altered mood."

"I confess that his anger struck me as uncharacteristic, judging by our previous encounter with him."

"There is some small mystery there too, I think. But we will see what tonight brings, by all accounts it should prove interesting."

Chapter Three – At Dead of Night

We ate a late dinner at the inn. Holmes said little about the affair that we were engaged upon, but I could tell that it filled his thoughts.

As for me, there were many questions without answers. What, for example, had Holmes deduced about Miss Todbury's past? Was the Squire persecuted by Lance's ghost (Holmes would have remonstrated with me for considering this) or someone assuming his identity for his own purposes? What, in fact, were those purposes? Who was it, in Foley Grange that signalled a message or warning, for what reason and to whom? My head began to spin and I retired to my room as soon as dinner was concluded, after arranging with Holmes that we should meet later.

At a few minutes past eleven, long after full darkness had fallen, we met in the corridor near the dining-room. My friend explained that he had, to the landlord's dismay, arranged to borrow the horse and trap again for the evening, and obtained directions to Highwall Cemetery. How he had achieved this without attaching some suspicion to us, is still a mystery to me.

We drove through streets that were silent except for the raucous sounds from the taverns. I avoided a man who staggered drunkenly across the road, and soon all lights and buildings were left behind. Now trees formed a continuous arch above us and the only sound was the occasional bleat of a sheep or the lowing of cattle. After but a short distance a dark building appeared atop a hill.

"To the right, Watson, there is the gateway. I saw a flicker of light near the church."

I turned onto a wide path, dimly aware of the lynch gate not far off. As the horse slackened its pace for the slow rise I made out the light of two burning torches, Squire Foley's landau and a dog-cart. With the trap brought to a halt, we left it secured and made our way towards them.

"Good evening, gentlemen," Squire Foley called from the shadows beyond. "My thanks to you for coming. As you see, we are close to setting this matter to rest, once and for all."

Holmes and I approached, leaving the gravel path and passing beside a succession of vaults, stone angels and crosses, as well as more moderate monuments to the dead, before reaching the grassy patch where the Squire and Underton stood before an open grave. Behind them, more clearly illuminated, two burly men worked with shovels. The piles of earth to each side of them were high and increasing quickly, from which I concluded that their work was almost completed.

Holmes came to a sudden halt, peering in the torchlight at the headstone which leaned at an angle, a little away from the gravediggers.

"This grave has been disturbed before. The stone is chipped and these are marks made before now."

"That is unlikely," Squire Foley said after examining the headstone where my friend had indicated. "There could be no reason for such interference."

"Perhaps it appears like that, because of the poor light," Holmes allowed, "but we shall see before long."

The Squire moved towards us a pace, the torchlight casting his shadow across the wall of a nearby vault.

"I have received a further note, this evening."

"Do you have it with you?"

"No, but it was much like the others."

"Nevertheless, I should like to examine it."

"Come again to The Grange tomorrow, and you shall." The Squire's eyes moved restlessly, in the manner of a man engaged upon something secretive or unlawful. It was easy to see, despite his earlier outburst, that this night's work troubled him.

A moment later we heard the ring of a shovel against a solid surface, and one of the men shouted that they had reached the coffin.

"Bring it up," Squire Foley cried excitedly, "and open it!"

The men's arms and faces glinted with perspiration in the torchlight. After a last few shovelfuls of earth had been removed they kneeled at the side of the grave and, grunting and cursing loudly, heaved the casket upwards and onto the surface. It occurred to me then, as I am sure it did to Holmes, that Lance's funeral had been a makeshift, cheap affair. Otherwise, the grave would have been a full six feet in depth.

"Drag it over here, into the light."

They did so, and looked up at the Squire for further instructions.

"Open it. What are you waiting for?"

The gravediggers looked fearfully at each other. These were men not without fear of the dead.

"We cannot," one of them replied. "It is sealed."

Squire Foley raised his arms in exasperation. "Then break it open! Use your shovels."

Blows rained upon the coffin lid, but it took almost ten minutes, by my estimation, for the wood to split. Strips and pieces were torn away. At Squire Foley's urging, the men attacked the casket like savage animals.

Finally, their work completed, both men shrank back from the grave. Squire Foley immediately hurried to it, with Holmes and I close behind.

"So, he is dead," the Squire said in a voice that held both relief and wonder. "So who then, is plaguing my life and Miss Todbury's? We can be certain now, Mr. Holmes, that the dead, or anything beyond this world, is not concerned here."

"I never doubted that," Holmes agreed.

Through the shattered coffin lid the body of a man could be seen in the waning torchlight. The Squire, apparently satisfied, moved away sufficiently for us to draw closer. Holmes and I produced handkerchiefs simultaneously, to hold over our faces against the appalling smell.

"Pray bring the torches closer," Holmes called to the men.

When they had done so with some reluctance, we saw that the body was fully dressed, rather than clad in a shroud. Its face was disfigured more than could be attributed to deterioration, the features all but gone. A tall top hat was crumpled upon its chest.

"What do you make of it, Watson?"

"Some agent has been applied, to enhance decomposition." I touched the body with distaste, then rubbed my fingers together. "It is likely that quick-lime was used, although as to why I could not say. This treatment is usually reserved for the remains of condemned men."

"Precisely. The condition of the face suggests some other application also, possibly a corrosive acid. It seems that my observation that the grave had been reopened after burial was correct, after all."

"Someone must have hated Lance intensely, to have gone to the trouble to desecrate his grave in such a manner."

To my surprise, Holmes gave a short laugh as we turned away. "When is a corpse not a corpse?" he mused.

"But Holmes, we have just seen a body. The man is dead. There can be no doubt."

"No, indeed."

By this time the Squire, after ordering the men to replace the coffin and leave the grave as it was before, had returned with Underton to the landau. The moon emerged from a dark cloud at that moment, and as we approached I saw that our client was still in a state of excitement.

"Well, gentlemen, we can now be certain that Lance is no more. However, who it is that has taken his place as my nemesis, if he can be called such, is still not known to us. I trust you will continue your investigations and keep me informed of your progress."

"You will recall that we are to meet tomorrow at Foley Grange," my friend replied. "You may expect us in the afternoon."

"Very well, then." He leaned forward to speak to Underton. "Drive on. Our beds await us."

The landau disappeared into the darkness with a final wave from the Squire. Looking back I saw that the men were rapidly filling in the grave in the reduced light of the remaining torch. Holmes hesitated, and I thought for an instant that he intended to return to the graveside, but he merely shrugged and climbed into the trap.

"Back to The Weary Traveller, Watson," he intoned in a rather light-hearted fashion. I feel that for one night I have learned enough."

#

We rose late the next morning, but the innkeeper was ready with a hearty breakfast as we entered the dining room. Holmes had almost finished his second round of toast when he became suddenly still, looking past me through a half-open window.

"There are some peculiar fellows approaching, Watson. They are dressed as undertakers, yet they are not as they seem. They lack the solemn bearing and measured tread."

I peered past him, into the broad grassy passage that ran alongside the inn. I could see a four-wheeler, not a landau or coach, pulled by a black horse that was adorned by black ribbons. It stood waiting as four young men supported a long box between them, in the manner of a coffin, and carried it towards a side door. Holmes was undoubtedly correct in his observation, since the use of the four-wheeler and a box to replace a hearse and coffin gave the spectacle something of a ridiculous appearance.

"I believe they are coming in here," I said.

"Undoubtedly. Unless I am much mistaken, they are bound for us."

I shook my head. "Holmes, what on Earth is happening?"

"We shall discover that soon, I think."

The first of the young men, presumably their leader, entered then, his eyes passing over the other diners until they settled on us. He beckoned to his companions, and joined them in bringing in the box. They approached our table and he bowed courteously after they had set their burden down upon the floor.

"Mr. Sherlock Holmes and Doctor Watson, I presume?" The leader asked.

"You presume correctly," my friend replied.

"Sir, we have been commissioned to deliver this box and its contents to your good selves. I was told to tell you that it is to be regarded as a message."

"What does the box contain?" I asked him.

"Our client said only that it was something you would understand."

"Did he give you his name?"

"He declined to do so, again saying that you would know him."

"How much did he pay you for this spectacle?" my friend enquired.

The young man hesitated, as if unsure as to whether he and his companions had committed an unlawful act. "We each received five shillings, and the horse and trap were paid for by the client."

Holmes nodded. "And which firm of undertakers do you represent?"

This caused some little embarrassment. All four of the box-bearers averted their eyes momentarily, and their faces reddened.

"We are not undertakers, sir. We are actors from a local repertory company. Occasionally we do special work, for certain celebrations and commemorative dates."

"Have you had dealings with this client before now?" I asked.

"Not ourselves, but I can recall seeing the man at the theatre on a previous occasion. Our colleague, Mr. George Crendall, a performer of fine talents, dealt with him some weeks ago. I know not the nature of the commission, but it was undoubtedly well-paid for none of us have seen Mr. Crendall since."

"Was that not unusual," Holmes interrupted, "for him to leave his employment so suddenly?"

The young man shrugged his shoulders. "No one at the theatre thought anything of it, since Mr. Crendall talked constantly of his ambition, which was to perform on the London stage. If his reward was sufficient, that was exactly what we would have expected of him."

"Very well," Holmes turned to the box, his eyes glittering. "I think the time has come to open this rather bizarre gift, if that is what it is." He went down on his knees, but looked up at the young men before making an attempt. "Pray remain, while I remove the lid. Perhaps the landlord will provide a crowbar if it proves necessary. It may be necessary also to entrust you with a reply, though I doubt your client will be available to receive it."

The diners at the few other occupied tables had finished their meals. Every head craned towards us, as their curiosity had been aroused by what they had seen and overheard. The landlord had stopped, as if frozen, in the act of pouring coffee. A deathly hush descended upon the room.

Holmes examined the box from all sides, tapping it here and there with his pocket-knife. He ran his fingers around the edges and appeared satisfied. After a moment of thought he cut through the twine and lifted the lid. To the surprise of everyone, it came away easily.

He placed the lid away from the box and inspected the contents, which appeared to be a bundle of filthy sacking. He peeled this away and went very still. I was distracted for a moment by the exclamation of alarm that spread through those watching, but as I returned my gaze to the box I became instantly transfixed.

The face of Nathaniel Barley stared sightlessly up at us. Around his neck was a length of rough cord, bloodstained from where it had cut into the flesh. The evident extent of the constriction would have meant that he died quickly and, and from his expression, in horrible agony.

Many of the others left the room then, several of the ladies crying. One or two men remained, frozen in ghoulish fascination, but Holmes ignored them and spoke directly to the landlord in a perfectly calm voice.

"Pray summon the local force. A detective, rather than a constable would be desirable."

The man became suddenly reanimated, spilling coffee as he called for a boy to take the message. I replaced the lid and turned to the onlookers.

"This is now a matter for the police. I suggest you leave at once."

They complied, and I turned to my friend, who had extracted a piece of paper from the corpse's fingers.

"What is it, Holmes? What does it say?"

"He handed it to me, as he rose. "This adds a new perspective to this affair, I think."

The message was written in a bold hand:

Mr. Holmes – Leave well enough alone.

#

"Some of us have heard of you, Mr. Holmes, even here. We have friends at Scotland Yard. I am not so foolish as to disregard your methods or your reputation when I, myself, am quite new to my post."

"You are indeed young to have risen so far," my friend acknowledged.

Inspector Grey, I judged, could not be more than thirty years of age. He stood almost as tall as Holmes, but broader, and his manner was that of a man keen to prove himself. His clothes were of a dark tweed and his hat of soft felt, all of which appeared to be of good quality. As I studied him, I noticed that his eyes were never still. They were eyes determined to miss nothing.

"If you are agreeable, perhaps we could, to some extent, join forces, inasmuch as that would involve an exchange of information. You have said that you and Doctor Watson are here at the request of Squire Foley, and it would seem that our separate enquiries are bound to converge at certain points."

"Inevitably," said Holmes. "For my part, I will be glad to share with you anything relating to Barley's murder that presents itself during my investigation."

"And I, in turn, will reveal information on the man you have spoken of, William Lance, should I come by any in the course of my duty."

"Excellent, but I see that two black-coated fellows have arrived, no doubt to remove the body to the mortuary. I trust you will let me know of anything of significance resulting from the coroner's examination?"

The inspector nodded. "As we have discussed. I must now continue my interviews with the landlord and the other witnesses to this event, including the four fellows who brought the box."

Holmes glanced at them briefly. "They look as if they expect to carry the blame for this, but they were as shocked as everyone else when I removed the lid. I advise you to treat them considerately, Inspector, since I have found that more can be gained this way."

"I will indeed. I am never too proud to learn."

With that, he bowed respectfully and began his work. Holmes took my arm and steered me out of the inn before I could ask what his next intentions were. Fifteen minutes later we were walking along the lakeside, away from the bustle of the town.

"Inspector Grey seems a bright young man," I remarked.

Holmes nodded slowly. "If he is as good as his word, his enthusiasm will take him far. I remember well the treatment I received from the likes of Lestrade and Gregson, in the early days.

Grey appears more enlightened and to possess the sort of imaginative trait that has proven so useful in solving such cases. However, regarding our own investigation, we now have definite confirmation of something I have suspected since we were last at Foley Grange."

"The flashes from the window?"

"Precisely. If there were any doubt that they were a warning or a message, there can be none now."

"I confess that I can see no connection between that and Barley's death."

"The note, Watson, the note. Did you not see it?"

I shook my head. "It held no mention of Foley Grange."

"True, but it was sent to me, by name. How could the sender have known it? You will recall that Inspector Grey said that the official force had heard of me *even here,* so my identity or my profession is hardly common knowledge otherwise. Yet Lance, or whoever is behind this, knew with whom he was dealing."

"I cannot follow you."

Holmes hesitated, I suspect while he controlled his impatience. "I recall that, during our first meeting with Squire Foley, both our names were spoken, but more importantly the name of the inn was brought up. Now, if Lance's confederate or agent was listening to our conversation, he doubtlessly relayed this information by the use of the mirror or by some other means."

"Hence he knew where to address the box, and its intended recipient," I agreed.

We walked in silence for a while, Holmes with his head upon his chest in contemplation while I let my attention focus on the various small boats moored upon the lake and the sunlit ripples that flowed gently towards us.

"I must make a purchase," he said at length, "then we will have lunch. After that we will make our way to Foley Grange, as was arranged last night."

We left the lake at the next short flight of steps that led to the pavement. Holmes glanced around him and apparently settled on what he sought, and we awaited the passing of several carriages before crossing the road. He made for a hardware shop and I for the tobacconist, where I bought replenishments for my pipe before rejoining my friend.

"Did you find what you need?" I asked.

"Oh yes," he indicated a large paper bag tucked beneath his arm, "but that is for later. Let us now return to the coffee shop of yesterday, and fortify ourselves."

The jovial proprietor recognised us at once, and we were soon served with pork pies and hot tea. Holmes said little as we ate, as was usual for him while his agile brain was occupied with unravelling a case. Later we returned to the inn to once more hire the horse and trap and were presently within sight of Foley Grange.

"We must proceed carefully, Watson. The Squire seems rather unstable, at times."

"So I have observed, but what are we dealing with here? We know of no adversary except Lance, whom we saw in his grave. I feel that we are in pursuit of the dead."

"We are up against more than one enemy, I think," he replied as I drew the trap to a halt, "and we have yet to learn their purpose."

Jenson met us at the door and we were soon in the Squire's company once more. As we entered the room he looked up from his book and rose.

"Gentlemen, welcome. Since our discovery of last night I have felt like a man reborn. Lance cannot be my tormentor for we have seen his dead body with our own eyes, so it must be some other local scoundrel who is responsible. I have heard nothing more since we last met, but how is it with you?"

"I will tell you presently," Holmes said as we were seated, "but first show me the note that you mentioned at the graveside."

Squire Foley produced a scrap of paper like those before, and passed it to Holmes who examined it with his lens.

"The paper is of the cheapest quality and is the same as the others, as are the handwriting and the meaning of the message. Do you not immediately grasp the significance?"

Our host's face went blank, and his posture appeared unsteady. "I cannot say that I do."

"Since the death of Lance, you have seen him briefly twice in Bowness, but since the opening of the grave, you have concluded that it must have been an imposter, is that not so?"

"I can conceive of no other explanation."

"Nor can I at present, but consider – you have received several of these threatening notes since he was interred."

"That is so, as you are aware."

"Then the imposter must be a most proficient forger, since he is able to perfectly reproduce the handwriting and style of the letters that were sent by Lance before the duel."

Squire Foley became still as the implication of Holmes' words came home to him. With a quick movement, he reached for a full glass of port from a side-table and drained it in one swallow.

"What can be the meaning of all this? How can a man be dead and still live?"

His rosy, youthful face was now full of fear, and I noticed that his eyes had a vagueness about them. He rose and walked around the room, stumbling often and shaking his head in confusion. With clenched fists he resumed his seat, sitting down heavily.

"Pray calm yourself," Holmes said quietly, "and dismiss all thoughts of risen ghosts and the supernatural from your mind. Watson and I have heard from our adversary this very morning, in a way that demonstrates well that he can be nothing else but flesh and blood."

Holmes related to him the events of the morning at the inn. Seeing the man's state I would have advised against further excitement, but I knew of old that to attempt to dissuade Holmes when he was set upon a course was useless.

"Poor Barley," the Squire said in a dull tone after my friend had concluded his revelation. "I did not know much of the man, only that he drank to excess and was something of a troublemaker, but I swear that I would not have wished such a fate for him."

"Barley did nothing to invite this but answer my questions. Doubtlessly his murderer extracted their content from him. For your own sake then, please resolve to obey my instructions to the letter, now that our enemy has demonstrated the lengths he is prepared to go to succeed in his as yet unknown purpose."

"There appears to be no other course open to me. I will do as you suggest."

"Excellent!" Holmes leaned forward in his seat, his jaw set. "For now, I have but two requests."

"Very well. You have only to name them."

"Firstly, I must ask. Do all of your staff live at The Grange?"

"Every one."

"Capital. Pray ensure then, that no one ventures out of the building, no one as much as passes through an outside door, until I return tomorrow morning. This must be your rule from the moment I leave here today."

The Squire nodded. "And the other instruction?"

"That you allow Watson to remain here tonight."

"Of course, he is most welcome, but…"

"Please allow that there is purpose in this."

Holmes caught my eye, and I nodded my assent.

"I will tell Jenson, who will issue the orders to the others." Squire Foley got to his feet unsteadily. "But now I must ask you gentlemen to excuse me, for I am feeling quite unwell."

With that he left us abruptly. As soon as we were alone Holmes snatched up the Squire's empty glass. He held it carefully, while smelling the residue.

"Here, I think, is the explanation of the Squire's rather unpredictable behaviour." He passed it to me. "Can you identify this substance, Watson?"

"I fear that I cannot," I concluded after smelling the glass as he had done before rubbing a smear between finger and thumb. "The texture and aroma are unknown to me. I can tell only that there is no opiate content, and that I suspect a drug of foreign origin."

"Thank you, old fellow, that is as I suspected."

I was about to make a further remark when the door opened to admit an attractive middle-aged lady wearing a spotless white apron. She appeared surprised at our presence.

"Gentlemen, I apologise for the intrusion. I was looking for Squire Foley."

"He is indisposed," I informed her. "You are the cook, I presume?"

"I am, sir. My name is Anne Warwick. I sought the master's choice for evening dinner."

"Doubtlessly the Squire will discuss it with you later."

"Of course, I apologise again for disturbing you."

She was gone in an instant, and Holmes listened until her footsteps faded.

"Her expression on finding us here was most revealing," he said. "The puzzle acquires an added dimension."

Chapter Four – An Unseen Appearance

I gave my friend a puzzled look.

"What have you seen, Holmes?"

"Only that she is rather more than the Squire's cook, whether he realises it or not."

In a moment, I had it. "You believe that she cares for him?"

"It was in her eyes, quickly extinguished when she saw that he was absent."

"And you said this has some bearing on the case." I considered for a moment. "So you are perhaps thinking that this lady might be connected in some way, because she is jealous of Miss Todbury?"

"I never get your measure, Watson," Holmes smiled. "You arrived at that conclusion in the same breath as myself. It is, of course, merely a possibility as yet, but one worth keeping in mind, I think."

"As for the drugged port, this reinforces your theory that Lance has a confederate within the house."

"It does indeed, and after tonight we may know more about this."

"Is this the reason why you want me to remain here?"

"Partly, old fellow, but primarily I want you to witness the delivery of any new message or note. We have not seen Lance nor whoever is impersonating him, and I would be glad of a first-hand impression."

I nodded. "And I am to protect Squire Foley?"

"I hope that will not prove necessary, but should that be the case I know I can rely upon you."

"As ever." I felt a flush of pride, at having Holmes' confidence.

"You have your service revolver?"

"It is seldom far from me."

"Capital! Now I will leave you. It is vital that you ensure that no one leaves the house, as we agreed with the Squire. Also, he should drink only from sealed bottles of wine at dinner. This should prevent any repetition of his erratic behaviour, although our unknown adversary may find a different way to administer the drug. Guard your charge in every way you can."

With that, Holmes took his leave. I saw through the tall windows that he was examining the area near the entrance for some little time, before disappearing from sight. Shortly afterwards I watched as Underton brought the trap around, and my friend departed. Feeling rather dejected, I found a volume of obscure tropical diseases among the Squire's books and settled myself in an armchair to read. When he reappeared for dinner I became conscious that I had brought no evening clothes, not having been forewarned of my extended stay.

We consumed an unexceptional dinner, served by Jenson with the assistance of Elizabeth, a maid of silent and sombre disposition. The other maid, Mary, was mentioned twice during a short conversation between the Squire and Jenson, but never appeared.

The Squire proved to be a dull companion and a poor conversationalist. His knowledge of local affairs was sparse and his grasp of life in the capital almost non-existent although he claimed to have visited London several times that year. Moreover, his opinions on political matters were rather indeterminate. By the time the dessert plates had been cleared away he had lapsed into a sullen silence; after repeatedly trying to pry a response from him I eventually abandoned further attempts.

"I would imagine you have accompanied Mr. Holmes on many occasions," he said suddenly, his schoolboy face shining from the wine.

I nodded. "We have known each other for some years."

"I have heard that he has been responsible for the capture of some dangerous criminals."

"He is respected for it, even by Scotland Yard."

Jenson brought cigars, which I refused in favour of my own pipe. I was prepared for our rather mundane conversation to continue, when Elizabeth burst into the room.

"Begging your pardon, sir," she began breathlessly, "Mary has seen a man in the grounds."

"Where?" I asked at once.

"At the back of the house, near the stables."

I was on my feet in an instant, the Squire beside me.

"Lead the way, but we must not leave the house," I cautioned him.

"But surely, if we can apprehend this man?"

I shook my head as we entered a narrow passage. "Holmes does not take precautions without purpose. If we are fortunate we will observe the intruder and know him again, but we must not approach him".

Squire Foley grunted something in reply as we entered the kitchen. A girl with a rather vacant expression pointed to the window and we rushed to it. I peered into the darkness but could see nothing.

"Extinguish the lamp!" I called to the girl.

She did so, giving me a view unspoiled by our reflection, and I craned my neck to see as far as I could in both directions. A light rain fell and the silhouettes of a row of trees moved gently in the breeze, but I could see no sign of life.

"He is gone."

"If he was ever there," Squire Foley whispered to me. Then, more loudly, "Light the lamp Mary, please."

"He was there, sir, I saw him run past holding something in his hand," the girl assured us as she lit a taper from the fire.

"It is of no importance. Do not distress yourself, but continue your duties."

Mary curtsied as we left the kitchen. The warmth and cooking smells were behind us, when the Squire spoke again. "Dr. Watson, I feel I should explain, lest you believe that I am making light of the matter."

"Not at all. We are in your house."

"Nevertheless. Mary has been with us only a few months. She had apparently been befriended by her predecessor, Jane, on whose recommendation she was employed. Mary is in some ways a simpleton, which is why I put so little store in her observations, but she is an excellent maid and works in the kitchen also. I think that we can attribute this incident to her imagination."

"Possibly," I allowed. Then I remembered Holmes' practice of leaving no aspect of a situation without examination. "Your previous maid, Jane, can you recall why she left your service? I would have thought such positions difficult to come by, in these parts."

"Indeed they are, but Jane left us after her husband had secured a position in Cornwall. I believe he is to join his brother as a fisherman."

I nodded. "And what were the circumstances surrounding Jane's befriending of Mary?"

"Mary, a newcomer to the district, joined an embroidery class that is run by our local church, if I recall correctly. Jane, who had attended regularly for some time, noticed her difficulties in learning the craft and was of some assistance. This was only a short while before Jane left Foley Grange."

By this time we had gained the corridor leading to the drawing room. We turned a corner to see Jenson waiting by the door. He carried a tray which he held out to the Squire with a courteous bow.

"I believe this has just arrived, sir."

The Squire took the paper and glanced at it. "Again! Damn the man to hell!"

He held it so that I could see. The sighting was explained - it was indeed another of Lance's notes.

#

I spent an uncomfortable night, in a room above the kitchen. Sleep proved elusive and my mind churned with what I knew of this curious affair, until I finally dozed. Then I was roused by the ring of pots and pans from below, and decided to abandon all further attempt at rest. I left my bed to shave with cold water and dress.

Holmes arrived early. After Underton had taken the horse, my friend immediately examined the area around the doors and windows. Finally, just after the breakfast things had been removed, Jenson showed him into the drawing-room.

Greetings were quickly dispensed with, and he stared at both of us expectantly.

"I see from your expressions that something has occurred since I left yesterday. Watson, pray be so kind as to elucidate."

With an occasional addition from the Squire, I related the events of the previous evening. "I hope I acted correctly, by not giving chase."

"That was exactly in accordance with my instructions, old fellow." He shifted his thin form in his chair. "But of course I had already ascertained that."

Squire Foley shot him a puzzled look, and Holmes smiled.

"No, there is no mystery about it. Before I left yesterday I laid lengths of the fisherman's twine that I bought for the purpose across the areas surrounding the doors and windows. These were undisturbed when I retrieved and discarded them on arrival just now, save for where a single set of footprints approached a rear service door. The soil was softened somewhat by the rain, and so the impressions were clear."

"So no one within the house colluded with the appearance of Lance's imposter?" I ventured.

"I have not said that. The picture is far from complete."

"In my house!" the Squire exclaimed. "What is this you are suggesting?"

"I beg you not to distress yourself," Holmes replied soothingly. "Watson merely mentioned one of a number of possibilities that I have explored."

Our host glanced at him sharply. "But nothing came of them?"

"I have discovered nothing of the sort, as yet."

"Neither will you, I am certain."

"Pray allow me to examine this latest message," Holmes requested, I thought to change the direction of the conversation.

The crumpled sheet was produced and given to him.

"Little variation," he commented. "The writer is not articulate, I think."

"Whoever he is, the man is mad," Squire Foley said as he resumed his seat. "Who but a lunatic would seek to imitate a dead man and issue threats in his name?"

"Someone with a purpose that is unknown to us, as yet," I pointed out.

"Indeed," Holmes assented, "but that may be revealed before too long. For the moment, we must consider our next course of action." He was silent for a moment, then: "Squire Foley, what do you say to a walk around your pleasant town in the company of Watson and myself?"

"Is that advisable, with this threat hanging over my head?"

"It may prove enlightening, if we chance to meet our adversary. As you yourself have remarked, neither Watson nor I has ever seen Lance's imposter, and it would of course help us greatly if we were familiar with his appearance. He cannot approach to threaten or harm you while we are with you and, at the very least, the fresh air will be beneficial."

I could not tell if Holmes had some reason of his own for this proposal, but less than half an hour later found us strolling near the lakeside. We passed various fishermen mending their tackle and several boat-builder's sheds where repairs were taking place or a new craft was under construction. Midway across the water, the two ferries passed in opposite directions, with passengers on both boats waving good-naturedly.

"The lake is a dull place today," the Squire said, breaking a short silence.

"Only because it reflects an overcast sky," I observed. "But you appear to be of a morose disposition today, despite our reassurances."

"I am thinking of Miss Todbury, Doctor Watson. I have not seen her since the day you arrived."

"Possibly this affair has upset her more than was apparent. I recall that Lance made objectionable visits to her, before he turned his attention to you."

"He did indeed. Perhaps you are right, and her absence from Foley Grange amounts to no more than that."

We crossed the road, away from the lakeside. A wide paved alley confronted us, with tall lamp-posts spaced at regular intervals along the centre. At the far end, I knew, the shops and businesses that clustered around the centre of the town began.

The Squire began to talk of the history of the town, pausing to glance into a shop window where several models stood mutely resplendent in fine clothing.

"My tailor," he explained. "He appears to have some new tweed in stock."

Holmes, who had said little for some time, produced his pocket-watch and consulted it. "Ah, but I see that the time for coffee approaches. I confess to feeling the need for some fortification. What say you, gentlemen?"

"An excellent suggestion," I agreed, thinking that this was for Holmes quite unusual while in the midst of a case.

Squire Foley raised his eyebrows as if reluctant to comply, before pointing along the street as we gained the end of the alley.

"There are several coffee-houses nearby. The choice is yours, Mr. Holmes."

Nevertheless, it was I who led us to an establishment with a rather flamboyant sign that stated that coffee from all over the Empire was served there, a shop with an exceptionally large plate glass window through which customers could be seen sitting at tables while enjoying steaming beverages.

"It is modelled on Edward Lloyd's premises," Holmes observed.

"Lloyd? The insurance people?" The Squire queried.

"The same. The marine insurance company began in such a place."

I believe that the subject would have been pursued further, but Holmes suddenly steered us away and took us around a corner to another, less grand, coffee-house.

In answer to our surprised stares, he said: "Inspector Grey was in there, and would undoubtedly have made his way to our table. At this stage, his intervention could only impede my investigation."

Over coffee, which was a little bitter for my taste, Holmes reverted to the matter in hand.

"It occurs to me, Squire Foley, that I have insufficient information as to the physical appearance of Lance. I saw his corpse in darkness, and we have no reason to believe that the imposter resembles him, but for my files and possibly for Dr. Watson's future benefit, I would like to know if he had any special peculiarities. Did he, for example, have red hair?"

"Not at all, but," he put a hand to his forehead as if something had just entered his mind, "his hair had a streak of premature grey down the left side. I must apologise, Mr. Holmes, for I had quite forgotten this until now."

"It is relatively unimportant. There is only one more thing, I think, that I must ask of you before we go our separate ways."

"I am at your disposal."

Holmes hesitated, perhaps to consider how to choose his words. "Before my investigation can continue, there is something I must know. Often, a person conceals information because he does not recognise its importance. I am convinced that this is the case here."

"Very well. What is it that you wish to know?"

"The address of Miss Priscilla Todbury. It is imperative that I see her alone."

There followed a few moments when the only sounds were the clanking together of crockery as the waitresses collected cups, saucers and plates from the tables, and the quiet hum of conversation from the other customers. Remembering the strange behaviour of the Squire previously, I found myself hoping that the drugged wine was the only cause of this. I could not help but be apprehensive about his reply.

Clearly, he was unsure about his own standing with the lady, despite their forthcoming marriage, for an expression of grave doubt and fear crossed his face. His eyes went from Holmes to myself, and back again.

"You may see her, but I must be present."

"That would be unwise, I think. The nature of my investigation precludes the presence of a third party, to avoid embarrassment."

The Squire gave my friend a harsh glance. "And how, pray, would the presence of her future husband embarrass Miss Todbury?"

"Surely you are aware that a lady has things she must keep to herself. Any physician would understand this instantly. It is similar with my profession."

I do not believe that the Squire understood Holmes' reasoning here, more likely that he feared being seen as possessive or weak.

"So be it then," he finally conceded. "She lives at the far end of Bowness, about half a mile from the red-roofed house that overlooks the lake. Her home is known as Iris Cottage."

Shortly afterwards we left the Squire, who returned to the waiting landau that had conveyed us here from Foley Grange.

"I am afraid we will have to forego lunch, Watson," Holmes said. "There are no cabs hereabouts so we are obliged to walk to Iris Cottage, and I will be surprised to find an eating-house on the way."

It was indeed a tiring trek. We came eventually to the red-roofed house described by Squire Foley. The darkening sky promised rain and, with the breeze that had sprung up, the lake was full of white-capped waves.

"We can see a fair distance ahead, around the shore," Holmes observed, "and there is nothing but trees and the road. That wide track leading inland would appear to be the only alternative."

"I see no other way, Holmes."

We then struck out away from the lakeside, along a lane wide enough to accommodate a two-horse conveyance. High bushes lined either side and birds flew up noisily as our passing disturbed them. After a sharp bend we came upon an ivy-encrusted cottage of sturdy brick, surrounded by a colourful flower bed. Holmes unlatched the gate set in the low surrounding fence and we approached the door, but not before the movement of the curtains came to our notice.

My friend was about to knock at the door, when it was quickly opened. Miss Todbury confronted us angrily, her expression set and her eyes blazing.

"I was not expecting you, Mr. Holmes, and I see no reason for this visit. I have no connection to your investigation."

Holmes allowed a moment of silence to pass before replying. "I must apologise for this intrusion, Miss Todbury. I fear however, that Squire Foley's difficulties have most definite roots in your past." She stared fearfully at us in silence, and he continued. "I must tell you, I know all."

I saw in her a sudden transformation, as the resentment in her manner faded. She appeared lost and unable to find any words of defence before her expression changed to one of resignation.

"Please come in, gentlemen," she said in a quiet voice.

We entered a pleasant room with carved wooden furniture and low beams. A brass warming-pan hung above the fireplace and freshly-cut flowers filled the air with fragrance. She indicated that we should each take an armchair while she sat facing us, offering tea which we declined. Holmes waited until we were settled before he finally spoke.

"I think it best, for the sake of your future and that of Squire Foley, that you make a clean breast of it. I will say nothing to him of your secret, provided that you speak to him when an opportunity presents itself. We have more yet to look into, which gives you time."

"Very well." She turned away for a moment, looking through a window with a crestfallen expression. "How did you discover my part in this?"

"You yourself demonstrated it."

She stared at both of us in astonishment. "But I was careful, I could not risk Harcourt finding me out."

"Did you not meet William Lance, in a coffee shop in Bowness, this very morning?"

I heard Holmes' assertion in amazement. He was saying that Lance still lived!

Miss Todbury went very still. "And so," she shook her head hopelessly, "all is lost."

"That may not be. I cannot see that you have committed a crime, only that you have kept your past from your prospective husband. When this matter is cleared up, he may yet forgive you."

"William and I were not happily married for long. I discovered him to be the conscienceless blackguard that he is, and then all his pretensions of goodness fell away. My life became filled with horrors."

"You then," I interrupted after recovering somewhat, "were formerly Grace Turley?"

She nodded. "And I changed my name again, from his, when I moved here from Carlisle. After he was released from prison he discovered my whereabouts somehow, and followed me."

"To conduct a campaign of persecution against you?"

"It was much worse than you can know."

"Was his objective to compel you to return to him?"

"That was his stated intention. He claimed to have again become the attentive man I married."

Holmes fixed her with a disapproving glare. "But, as I understand it, you are now to marry Squire Foley?"

"We are engaged."

"Are you then, divorced from Lance?"

She stared at the floor, not meeting our eyes. "Not as yet."

"Then you intended to commit bigamy?"

"Not at all. At first, I was told that Lance had died in prison, leaving me a free woman." Slowly, she raised her head. "When he appeared here I was by this time engaged and it was a terrible shock. After I said I wanted nothing more to do with him he began to taunt me and later Harcourt, who had thrashed him. Yesterday I received a note, arranging the meeting that you witnessed earlier. I kept the appointment to inform him of my intention to obtain a divorce."

"How was this received?"

"He said he would allow nothing to come between him and what is his, and left without another word."

"But he made no mention of his reason for summoning you?"

"Only a repetition of what had gone before. He said he would see both Harcourt and myself dead before he would release me, and that he would see me again tomorrow."

Holmes was silent for a short while, during which Miss Todbury moved nervously in her chair. Finally he rose.

"Thank you Miss Todbury, your narrative has cleared away several aspects of this affair that I was unsure about. We will leave you now, but I must reiterate that I expect you to reveal the truth to Squire Foley, before too much time has passed."

She replied with what I took to be her assent, in humble tones, and we departed.

"So the sighting of Inspector Grey in the coffee-shop was false? It was a ruse to distract the Squire from his fiancée's presence?" I enquired as we began the walk back to Bowness.

"The risk of him seeing her with Lance was too great. I recognised him by the streak of grey in his hair. The attitude of intimacy between them was unmistakable – it has become a habit, even though their marriage is over. With the Squire we must exercise care, for although he is now without the drug he was unconsciously taking, he has an unpredictable nature."

"And Lance is not dead after all? I confess to being confused, Holmes. Who was the body in Lance's grave?"

To my surprise he laughed shortly. "One question at a time please, Watson. Unless I am much mistaken the grave was occupied by one George Crendall, an actor who you may remember was mentioned by the young man who delivered Barley's remains to us at the inn."

"I recall that he was believed to have departed to London to seek his fortune there."

"Instead, he has found his final resting place in Lance's stead. Remembering that Squire Foley expressed surprise when his shot found its mark, the rest is quite easy to reconstruct. Lance would have paid Crendall to take his place at the duel, probably telling him that there was no danger as it was all some sort of drunken prank without live ammunition. He would then have concealed himself nearby in advance of the arrival of the other two, and shot Crendall from close up almost at the same moment that the Squire discharged his pistol. You will recall that the Squire mentioned hearing *the echo*."

"So that the Squire believed he had killed Lance."

"Precisely. Lance is cunning and no stranger to deception."

"And he is married to Miss Todbury, still?"

"So we have established. Now we see the reason for his persecution of her, and also for that of the Squire, her intended."

"That, at least, has become clear," I agreed.

"There are one or two points still to be clarified. One of them is Lance's attitude to Squire Foley."

"His resentment of a richer man as a rival is understandable, surely?"

Holmes shook his head. "That is not what I meant. Consider, Lance has done little more than issue threats, send cryptic notes and make brief unwelcome appearances to the Squire, since supposedly returning from the dead. Yet almost immediately after you and I enter the fray we are presented with a severe warning in the shape of the corpse of Barley, who furnished us with information about Lance. Obviously that interview was observed and Lance took steps to ensure that it would never be repeated, demonstrating again that murder is not outside his intentions or capabilities. From what we have learned of his history, I never doubted this, but it makes his relatively mild intrusions into Squire Foley's life seem peculiar."

"Perhaps he wishes the Squire to remain unharmed in order to witness Miss Todbury's return to her husband. Lance has referred to her as his property, several times."

"That is a possibility."

We left the red-roofed house behind and walked in silence for a while. Holmes wore a thoughtful expression, with his head upon his chest. After a short time a coach, driven at high speed, overtook us and I heard a sharp report as something rushed past my face. The road was quickly empty again after it disappeared around a bend ahead, and my friend scrutinized me carefully.

"Are you hurt, Watson? I see that you are trembling."

"I felt the bullet pass, nothing more. I have been a target, before now."

"We were fortunate, doubtless the motion of the coach made his aim difficult. I fear that Lance's interest in us has intensified."

"We may be able to trace the driver."

"For the present, I think we will leave things as they are. I am anxious that you should spend another night protecting Squire Foley, for tomorrow I am going to Carlisle."

Chapter Five – Some Explanations

I did indeed spend a further night at Foley Grange. The Squire made no objection to my request, since Holmes was adamant that it was necessary to maintain his protection. My friend returned to the inn, and after several short-lived attempts at conversation I left the Squire, who seemed even more preoccupied than usual, to his port. Again, I slept fitfully.

The following morning brought a brief visit from Miss Todbury. I believe that she had intended to make the disclosures to the Squire that Holmes had insisted upon, but she had not expected my presence. Her embarrassment became increasingly evident, although she attempted to conceal it with rather hollow humour as she played the piano briefly while the Squire sat enraptured. She cut short her stay quite suddenly, to return to her home in the borrowed dog-cart she was using.

The day passed slowly. I spent much of it reading, but was never far from Squire Foley who grew increasingly restless. He paced the rooms aimlessly, gazing through the tall windows at the surrounding countryside. Evening arrived and after dinner a hansom drew up in the courtyard. Holmes leapt to the ground and was with us in an instant.

"Good evening, gentlemen," he said quickly as Jenson ushered him into our presence. "Squire Foley, I am pleased to be able to say that my investigation is proceeding. There have been several new developments, but we must now take our leave of you. I apologise for such a brief visit, but Watson and I will be back in the morning. Then you shall know all."

The Squire appeared unconcerned, wishing us goodnight with a vacant expression. Given his unsettled nature, I found myself concerned that the strain he had endured might be taking its toll. As the hansom rattled along the drive I could wait no longer to hear of my friend's progress.

"Holmes, you implied to the Squire that you have solved this curious puzzle."

In the darkness I could sense his secretive smile, as he sat upright in his seat. "And so I have, in part. At least, I know a great deal more of the situation than previously. I do not think the Squire is in much immediate danger, but I thought it wise to suggest to Jenson that he take over your role for the present with the aid of a shotgun from the gun-room. Incidentally, old fellow, did Miss Todbury make an appearance today?"

"Indeed, she did," I braced myself as the hansom rocked during the tight turn onto the road, "but she failed to acquaint the Squire with the information she gave us yesterday. She did no more than say a few words and play a mournful tune on the piano. Her demeanour was, I am sure, due to my unexpected presence, and I will be much surprised if she does not visit him again soon."

"Capital! It will be as much of a shock, no doubt, as what I shall tell him tomorrow."

"Am I, also, to wait until then?"

"Not at all, but I have spent the day interviewing solicitors, seeking out various old acquaintances of Lance and poring over local records. You must forgive me if I sound somewhat weary, Watson."

"After such vigorous activity, and the railway journey, you must be exhausted."

"Nevertheless, I will tell you tonight. We will soon be back at The Weary Traveller and, after the landlord has supplied us with a glass each of his best brandy, we will find a place of privacy."

#

It was some while later that we sat on opposite sides of a battered round table, away from the customers at the bar. Holmes took a sip from his glass and leaned forward so that his voice would not carry.

"I have discovered all but one of the answers to our little puzzle," he began in a low voice. "Firstly, you will recall that, compared with Lance's reaction to our appearance here, his treatment of Squire Foley has been relatively mild."

"As you said previously, his murder of Crendall and Barley and later attempted murder of ourselves seem at odds with his actions against the Squire, which can do little more than frighten the man."

Holmes nodded. "I found it rather inconsistent. However, I have now discovered the reason, and it is twofold. The first should have been obvious from the beginning: it is simply that Miss Todbury, or Mrs. Lance as she truly is, begged him to do the Squire no serious harm. As Lance was eager to be reunited with his wife, he reluctantly complied."

"The simple solutions," I observed, "are sometimes the last to be considered."

"Quite so, but the second reason is more complicated, and took more research to discover. I first suspected it when I glimpsed Lance with Miss Todbury in Bowness."

"You recognised him?"

"Not in the sense of having seen him previously, although the streak of grey hair was significant. I became aware however, of his resemblance to Squire Foley."

"I saw no such likeness."

"It was not readily noticeable. The tilt of his head and his way of using his hands to express himself as he spoke suggested it to me, as did his habit of hunching his shoulders."

"You amaze me, Holmes, to have deduced all that from what could have been no more than a momentary glance!"

"I am experienced in observation, as you are aware."

"But does this mean that Lance is related to the Squire?"

"So I discovered in the archives of births and deaths, in Carlisle."

"This is astonishing!"

"The Squire is unaware of it, of course. Lance is the result of an indiscretion between the Squire's father, Henry, and a barmaid working at a Carlisle hotel. I was unable to discover how he discovered his true heritage."

"But he is nevertheless the Squire's half-brother and this, if Lance has any such sensitivities, may be an additional reason for his restraint. But now the reason behind all this becomes apparent," I said confidently, "Since Lance will surely seek what he sees as his share of the family inheritance."

To my surprise, Holmes laughed. "My dear fellow, how many times have I reminded you of how easy it is to jump to conclusions? Does it not occur to you that it would be an amazing coincidence if Lance came here from Carlisle to reclaim his wife, only to find her betrothed to his brother who is unaware of his existence? Yet that is almost the truth. It seems that Lance came here after his release from prison with the intention of gaining some menial employment on the Squire's estate, while he assessed the situation with a view to eventually making a claim. The shock he received at his wife's reappearance (probably an accidental encounter, before he could put his plan into action) must have been considerable, but there is yet more to this."

"I recall Squire Foley saying at our first meeting, that his family fortunes had long been exhausted."

"Precisely. I realised, therefore, that Lance's motives could not be to profit from the Squire's remaining wealth. I soon ascertained that he had gone to considerable lengths to trace his wife before leaving Carlisle, succeeding only in establishing the general area of her new residence. He also discovered something quite unexpected. A relative on her mother's side, the owner of a factory making weatherproof rubber boots I think it was, died some time ago, leaving a not inconsiderable amount of money to Mrs. Lance, or as we know her, Miss Todbury. I do not know if she is yet aware of this."

"So that is Lance's true motive for wanting a reconciliation?"

"Doubtlessly. But in view of his behaviour up until now, it seems likely that his wife would eventually become disposable."

"There is one question that remains unsolved," I reminded him.

"The identity of Lance's accomplice within Foley Grange? I had not forgotten that aspect of the case, Watson. Fortunately the possibilities are few. It can be none other than Underton, Jenson, Anne Warwick or one of the maids, Elizabeth and Mary."

"Then it is to this you will now turn your attention?"

"Not immediately, but soon."

#

We talked for a while longer and then retired. When I entered the dining-room the following morning Holmes had, judging by his empty coffee cup, consumed his breakfast not long previously.

"Today," he said when I had seated myself and ordered breakfast, "we will finally meet Lance. Then we will understand more of the reasons behind his extraordinary conduct."

"How can you be certain that we will meet him?"

"You will recall that he told Miss Todbury that he would see her again today."

"He did, but he did not say where and at what time."

"There was no need to say where, for she understood him to mean at her home. But that is hardly conclusive. On arriving back from Carlisle, I called at the local hire company in case Lance had booked a cab in advance for a second journey to Miss Todbury's home. I found that he had, at nine this morning. It would be as well, I think, to get there early and wait."

We set off soon after. Again, we walked along the lakeside until we reached the track which took us within sight of Miss Todbury's cottage. Holmes looked around us and selected a clump of thick bushes to conceal us.

"This grassy slope will, I think, provide us with comfortable seating until Lance arrives."

I consulted my pocket-watch. "We have half an hour to wait."

"If we remain silent and listen, the sound of his approaching coach will warn us. We should also watch carefully, in case he chooses to arrive on foot."

And so we were still and quiet for the short vigil. Only the sounds of the birds and insects disturbed the peace of the place. There was no sign of life or sound from the cottage.

I had begun to doubt Holmes' conclusions, when Lance emerged suddenly from where the bushes were thickest. I gripped my service revolver and felt my companion tense immediately.

"Not yet, Watson." I felt a restraining hand on my arm.

Lance stood very still, looking from side to side before venturing further. He was shorter than I had imagined, almost squat, and wearing an unseasonably long coat and tall top hat. We watched as he advanced furtively towards Miss Todbury's cottage.

"Good morning, Mr. Lance." Before our adversary reached the door Holmes stepped out of concealment with his gun levelled, and I did likewise.

Lance stared at us for a long moment and then moved quickly, producing what looked like a long-barrelled pistol from beneath his coat and firing almost instantly.

"Down, Watson." Holmes pulled me to the ground beside him.

Behind us, leaves and twigs were torn away from the bushes. We struggled to our feet but Lance had already disappeared. I could hear his retreating footfalls as a movement seen from the corner of my eye attracted my attention. I had a momentary glimpse of Miss Todbury at her window, before I turned and raced after my friend in pursuit of our quarry.

"Take care," Holmes called to me. "He may conceal himself and fire again as we approach."

But, careful as we were, we saw Lance no more. We reached the end of the track and crossed the lakeside road, pausing to look along the shore. In the distance a figure approached, a uniformed constable walking his beat or returning to his home at the end of his shift. I saw that one of the ferry boats had adopted a parallel course along this part of the shore, making its way to the nearby dock while avoiding a craft that had slipped its moorings. Beneath gathering clouds and a grey sky, the dark waters stirred as a breeze sprang up.

"He is nowhere to be seen, Holmes. Yet I would swear we have not passed him."

My friend's keen eyes swept the shoreline. "Possibly he knows some sort of short cut. We will wait awhile and watch."

For four or five minutes we stood beneath an overhanging tree. The constable, his uniform now plain to see, drew closer. The ferry boat now turned from the shore, to approach the dock. I could see a growing queue in the distance, waiting to board the ferry for the return journey.

"There, Watson!" Holmes indicated a place about a hundred yards ahead, where a man emerged from the shelter of a group of small stone sheds. "If we are quick, we will catch him!"

The figure, which I could now identify as Lance, saw us at once and began to flee, only to be confronted by the approaching constable. He hesitated, then assuming himself to be trapped, took his only remaining way out. He scrambled down the slope to the shoreline and tore away the mooring-rope of one of the small group of boats which nestled there. In seconds he had seized the oars and was rowing furiously.

The constable stood still, unsure of the situation. Holmes pointed at the departing boat to alert him, but this was misinterpreted by Lance who dropped the oars and stood, raising his pistol to fire again. We took shelter behind a stone bench, but this proved to be unnecessary since the distance was now too great for the weapon's range. The constable blew his whistle repeatedly, but I thought it doubtful that there would be an immediate response this far from Bowness. Holmes and I watched as Lance, still standing in the boat but without direction, lost his balance in the swaying craft and plunged into the water.

"No!" cried Holmes. I saw that he shouted not to Lance but to the constable who had stripped off his tunic and was already running to the edge of the lake. The officer came to an abrupt halt, possibly because he had realised the reason for my friend's warning. The ferry boat could not swerve or stop, making a collision with the thrashing figure of Lance inevitable. A hideous scream was torn from his throat, before the waters closed over the body.

Many passengers cried out in horror, as the ferry continued towards the dock as if there had been no incident. The distance had increased, but on board the vessel I thought I saw several women swoon. The constable, buttoning his tunic, rushed up to us.

"What's going on here, sir? Did that man steal a boat?"

"He did indeed, officer," Holmes confirmed. "But there is much more to this. Inspector Grey is conversant with the details. I suggest that you fetch him while we remain here. You may tell him that Sherlock Holmes awaits him."

The constable, on hearing my friend identify himself, saluted smartly and made off.

Inspector Grey arrived within the hour in a police coach. Holmes had spent the time speaking little, but his keen eyes never left the water. He was apparently satisfied that Lance was no more, for he immediately launched into an account of the events that had brought us here.

"Thank you, Mr. Holmes," the inspector said at the end of my friend's narrative. "It all seems quite clear. I have arranged for the crew of the ferry to be interviewed, and we will send out a boat in case there is anything to be found."

"I have been watching. There is nothing afloat, certainly."

The official detective nodded. "You have no doubt that this is the man responsible for the murder of Nathaniel Barley, and the persecution of Squire Foley and his intended bride?"

"None whatsoever. Nor are those the extent of his crimes."

"I must ask you gentlemen to attend the station, where a full report must be made by each of you."

"When do you require us?"

"Now that this is concluded, is it your intention to leave Bowness immediately?"

"Not for a day or so." Holmes glanced at me for assent, and I nodded.

"Then let it be at your convenience, within that time."

#

Shortly afterwards, we left Inspector Grey to his work. Our walk back to Bowness was unhurried, and although my friend did not enter into one of his silences I formed the opinion that his mind was still much occupied with this morning's events.

"We will take luncheon here, I think, if you are agreeable."

The street we had entered had a strong aroma of food, and Holmes indicated the pie shop that was its source.

"Certainly."

While we drank tea and awaited two steak and kidney pies, I asked him to confide his immediate intentions.

"There are still the matters of the mirror flashes at Foley Grange, the drug in the Squire's wine and my undisturbed twine to be considered."

"These are all the work of one person, surely," I ventured.

"Unless there is more than one accomplice."

"Is that likely?"

Holmes shrugged. "We will see what can be discovered, this afternoon."

At that moment two steaming pies were brought to us, and I was glad to see Holmes eat with unusual appetite. Afterwards, we sat over more tea as we observed the cavalcade along the street.

"The dark side of life," I said philosophically, "robbery, murder and the like, occasionally reveals itself even in a quiet and pleasant place such as this. In the capital we have come to expect it, to an extent, but here it seems oddly out of place."

My friend put down his empty cup. "You will no doubt recall, Watson, that I have remarked before now upon the evils of the countryside. They are the equals of anything that occurs in London, I assure you."

"Humanity being little different, anywhere?"

"Precisely. Now I think we will return to the inn and borrow the landlord's trap for what I expect to be our final visit to Foley Grange."

We rose as one, and made our way back to The Weary Traveller.

The landlord greeted us cheerfully. "The package has arrived, Mr. Holmes."

My friend was silent for a moment, before replying. "Do you know from where?"

"It came from Foley Grange of course, sir. The maid who delivered it asked if the room was made up and then if she could leave it there, as it was of a private nature. I didn't understand what she meant by that, but I gave my permission. I hope I did right, sir?"

Holmes nodded. "There is probably no harm in it. Did the maid leave her name?"

"I didn't ask. I thought you were expecting the package."

"No matter. When did she leave?"

"Couldn't rightly say, sir. I was busy at the bar and serving lunch, so I didn't see."

"Something from the Squire," I remarked needlessly. "An appreciative bottle or two of wine, perhaps?"

"That is unlikely, but possible." He turned back to our host. "Landlord, is there a ladder here, tall enough to reach an upstairs window?"

"Why, yes," the man looked bewildered, "the boy who uses it to clean the upper windows leaves it against the wall near the stable. Is everything quite all right, sir?"

"I am sure it will be. Come, Watson."

We retraced our steps through the front entrance and walked around the building to the rear. The trap had been left nearby, while the pony busily emptied its food-bag in the open stable. The ladder was where the landlord had described, and we carried it to the front of the building.

Holmes looked up thoughtfully, at the half-open window of his room. I ensured that the ladder was firmly lodged and gripped it with both hands as he began to climb. He reached the top and peered through the glass for a few moments, before opening the window further and vanishing inside. I could hear nothing but the sounds of passing traps and hansoms as I stood there waiting. An eternity seemed to pass, then a hand fell upon my shoulder.

"It is quite safe now, old fellow, we can return the ladder to where it belongs."

"Holmes!" I retorted, greatly surprised. "What has happened? What was left in your room?"

"After we have returned from the yard and each downed a pint of the landlord's excellent ale for restorative purposes, I will tell you. Say nothing within his hearing, for now."

"But what was it? Was there some sort of trap up there?"

"There was."

"When did you suspect?"

"The moment that the landlord mentioned that the maid had asked if the room had been made up."

"Because she wanted to ensure that the room would be left undisturbed, until your return?"

"So it would appear."

Presently we again sat on opposite sides of a table, the furthest from the bar.

"Holmes, will you now kindly explain," I asked, impatient because he had delayed the explanation by taking a long drink.

"I will say only that Lance and his associates seem to delight in the discharging of firearms."

"I heard no report!" I exclaimed in alarm. "Was the maid lying in wait with a pistol? Good heavens, Holmes!"

He put down his tankard and laughed. "No, dear fellow, there was no one there. I would certainly have been fatally injured nevertheless, had I entered my room through the door. The maid, or whoever she was, had erected a tripod, supporting a shotgun with a cord attached to the triggers. It would have been discharged by means of small pulley-wheels, which she had affixed strategically. As she left, she slipped a loop over the door-knob."

"That was what the package contained?"

"The wrappings were strewn across the floor."

"The woman must be a fiend."

"At any rate she is quite professional, to have left such a device. She could easily have fallen foul of it, herself."

"Who can she be?"

"Perhaps we will find out, later."

"Have you rendered the gun harmless?"

"I could not risk the landlord or anyone else entering, so I immediately removed the charge and packed everything as I imagine it was before. Then I simply descended the stairs and came out to you, after concealing the package to await the attention of Inspector Grey, later."

We finished our drinks but remained talking for some time. Holmes appeared to be in no hurry to attend Squire Foley, and I wondered at this. It occurred to me that the prospect of finding Miss Todbury at Foley Grange might be distasteful to him, in the circumstances.

"Well, Watson, I suppose we must conclude our business here," he said when the conversation lapsed for a moment. "I will ask the landlord if we may borrow the trap one final time."

My friend rose as a constable, younger than the man we had met at the lake, appeared in the doorway. The landlord immediately approached him and, in answer to his question, pointed to us.

The young officer approached us, a little breathlessly.

"Are you gentlemen Mr. Sherlock Holmes and Doctor Watson?"

"The same," said Holmes expectantly.

"A message from Inspector Grey. He requests your presence at Foley Grange."

"We saw him earlier," I remarked. "What has happened since?"

"The inspector, together with myself, went to see the Squire to give him news of a poor fellow known to him who has drowned in the lake. After this was done we set out to return to Bowness. We had travelled more than halfway back when the inspector ordered me to turn the coach around, saying that he had suddenly remembered

70

something of importance that he had forgotten to tell the Squire." The constable paused to collect himself. "When we reached Foley Grange for the second time, the place was afire. Inspector Grey remained there, although I could not see how he could gain entry through such an inferno, and sent Constable Brigden, who was with us, for the fire brigade. I was to ride with him and to notify yourselves."

Holmes mumbled something that sounded like, "I should have realised." And called to the landlord. Less than five minutes later, we were on our way.

Chapter Six – Another Direction

We stood at a safe distance, while Foley Grange blazed.

"There can be no survivors," Inspector Grey observed. "I tried to gain entry when we discovered the fire, but it was impossible."

"No man could approach such intense heat," I said, as a burning rafter crashed to the ground.

"Is this an accident do you think, or a deliberate act?" the inspector asked Holmes.

"It is likely this was no accident."

"How have you reached that conclusion, Mr. Holmes?"

"We cannot be certain, but the blaze appears to have spread rapidly, and it appears that there was no time for anyone to escape. I believe it probable that some easily-ignited material was placed, probably hidden, at various points around the building in advance."

"But why? Who would do this?"

"Watson and I have already ascertained that Lance had an accomplice here, although we have as yet made no identification. We were, in fact, preparing to visit the Squire on just such an errand when your constable summoned us. If anyone escaped from this inferno, it is likely to be she."

"'She'? How can you be sure of that?"

"I have yet to tell you of an incident at The Travellers Rest."

"But why would this accomplice destroy the Squire's home?" the inspector asked again.

"There are at least two possibilities. I believe that this woman, whoever she might be, had some scheme involving the Squire that he was unaware of, and she sought to destroy evidence of her intentions after realising that our enquiries had brought her close to discovery. She may well have had accomplices working from without. Also, we must not overlook that she could have some connection to Lance, perhaps by blood or by affection. Also, as the news of Lance's death had already reached here, then it is possible that setting the fire to destroy the building and its occupants was an act of revenge."

"But the Squire had nothing to do with Lance's demise."

"I did not say that the action was logical, nor the product of a sound mind."

"You believe we are dealing with a madwoman?"

"That is a possible conclusion."

"Which would account for her apparent disregard for her own safety."

"Perhaps. But insufficient data results in theorizing, far too easily."

"It may be that we will learn more tomorrow," the inspector said.

#

We remained a short while longer, with Holmes wearing a deep and thoughtful expression, before we returned to the inn. He left me abruptly and I spent the remainder of the afternoon reading a medical treatise on Black Fever disease in the African colonies, one of such articles that I had brought with me, in between listening to my friend pacing in his room.

This affair was now over, it remained only for us to attend the police station for an interview with Inspector Grey before taking a London train. Lance was dead and, most regrettably, the Squire and his household had shared a cruel fate also.

Yet something was wrong. The whole situation had an air of incompletion, and Holmes knew it.

He said little over dinner and we retired early. By next morning, such sleep as the night had brought him seemed to have done little to lighten his mood. Breakfast, too, was a sombre affair.

"Are we to pursue this further, today?" I asked him as I pushed away my plate and folded my napkin.

"I shall be surprised if Inspector Grey is not doing so."

"Will we be joining him?"

Holmes nodded. "I think it best to go a little further. If you have finished your breakfast, Watson, we will drive again to Foley Grange."

We left the trap some distance from the remains of the house, as the horse had begun to show signs of uneasiness. Smoke drifted across the ruin, and many embers still glowed with a fierce heat. Here and there the blackened remains of a wall or doorway stood precariously, and the smell of destruction was evident.

Inspector Grey, in conversation with two constables, dismissed them and approached us.

"Has anything new been learned, Inspector?" Holmes enquired.

The local detective sighed. "Only that the extent of the damage is even greater than we feared."

"But the bodies?"

"Within the remains of the kitchen we discovered a tangle of human bones. The flesh of course had been completely burned off them, and it was impossible to tell how many perished. Our pathologist and his assistant removed them as soon as they were cool enough to handle."

"A pity, I would have liked to have made my own examination. Do you attach any significance to the remains being found in the same room?"

"It seemed as if the Squire and his household took shelter together, probably because the fire had driven them there. Or it may have been that they expected the thicker walls of the older part of the house would protect them."

The ghost of a smile passed quickly across my friend's face. "Of course, that must be the explanation."

"The fire brigade left some time ago," the inspector volunteered. "Perhaps you would care to inspect the site now. I believe some of it has cooled sufficiently."

"I would welcome the opportunity to do so." Holmes keen gaze took in the scene, the smoke, the steam and the desolation, before we accompanied the inspector through the charred remnants of the house.

I watched as Holmes peered into corners, measured distances and carefully scrutinized the wreckage of the interior. The inspector watched his every move in an attempt, I thought, to learn something of his methods.

"This area then, contains what is left of the kitchen?"

"Yes," Inspector Grey shook his head sadly, "and the wreckage of the upper stories that collapsed inwards."

"Quite. You are certain that the remains of all the bodies were together in this place?"

"I believe the pathologist said they were."

"Aha!" Holmes" face lit up, as if with understanding. His eyes glittered.

"Have I missed something, Mr. Holmes?"

"Probably not. I am wondering why the remains were not further apart, each person seeking his or her own way out."

"Fear kept them together, no doubt."

"That must be what happened."

After another half an hour, we left the inspector after confirming that we would call on him at the station to submit our statements later. This we did as the afternoon wore on, having settled our account at The Weary Traveller. We caught the early evening train to London, and I was glad to discover that it had an excellent dining coach. Holmes, still preoccupied with what he apparently considered to be uncertain elements of the affair, ate disinterestedly while I enjoyed a well-presented rainbow trout.

Finally, when my empty plate and Holmes' half-eaten meal had been removed, I asked the question that had not left my thoughts for hours.

"Holmes?"

He looked up from his coffee cup. "You are curious about something in my conversation with Inspector Grey."

His expression told me that it was not a question. He had deduced, probably from the fact that I had made no comment until now, that some aspect of the events at Foley Grange remained uncertain in my mind.

"As always, you are correct."

He glanced out of the carriage window, at the rural scene speeding by, before he answered:

"The only observation I made that is worthy of mention was about the position of the remains of the unfortunate Squire and his servants. Doubtlessly that is what you wish me to clarify."

I nodded. "It is."

"I am perplexed by the fact that all the inhabitants appear to have congregated in one room. I have so far formulated six possible theories, none of which I find satisfying to any degree."

"Could it be that they assembled together because the kitchen seemed the safest place, and that Squire Foley stood with them in an attempt to convey encouragement?"

"That is very similar to one of the situations I surmised," he mused. "But I cannot dispel the feeling that we will hear more of this."

#

For seven months it did not seem so. During this time, Holmes was active with such curious affairs that I have chronicled elsewhere as 'The Misfortunes of Mr. Elias Erstein,' 'The Adventure of Canal Reach' and 'The Adventure of the Frightened Architect.' The sad end of Squire Foley occupied my thoughts less as the weeks passed, except for a single reminder in the shape of a letter from Miss Priscilla Todbury, stating that she had almost recovered from the distress of losing her husband-to-be and thanking Holmes for what she now realised was his significant contribution to ridding the Squire of his tormenter.

Holmes was to be proven correct however, in his assumption that all was not ended, although we were not to realise this for some time. One Monday morning, when rain had just ceased to beat against our window to let the sun emerge from heavy clouds, we sat smoking after-breakfast pipes in the comfort of our armchairs when the door-bell rang, shattering our peace.

"A new client, do you think, Holmes?"

"If so, then it is a lady. I heard her footsteps as she approached our front door. If you have finished with your pipe, Watson, let us put them away so that we can concentrate completely on whatever she has to tell us."

We had no sooner done that than Mrs. Hudson stood in the doorway.

"Mrs. Evangeline Cutts to see you, Mr. Holmes."

Our housekeeper was about to withdraw when Holmes called for tea, which she acknowledged and closed the door.

As he conducted our visitor to the basket chair, I attempted to emulate his methods in a study of her. She was of above average height and slim, wearing a blue costume of the style of a year or two ago. Her hair, which appeared dark and lustrous, fell from beneath her bonnet in a rather long and unfashionable style. Her age, I thought, would be about thirty and the beauty of her youth had not yet begun to fade. I concluded that, although her clothes indicated that she had once been financially better disposed, she was far from the poor house and probably the wife of a merchant or shopkeeper of moderate means.

Holmes introduced me, saying as he always did that she could speak to me as to himself, and she looked at us both with some nervousness. At that moment Mrs. Hudson returned with the tea and I took the tray from her. When we were all settled Holmes addressed our client, wearing his most charming smile.

"And now, Mrs. Cutts, how may we assist you?"

She put down her cup and spoke in an unexpectedly cultured voice. "Let me ask first if it is true that you undertake to unravel strange affairs, for I have no crime to relate. In truth, I cannot tell if what happened to me was some sort of practical joke, but in extremely poor taste." She sighed. "Although who would do such a thing is quite unknown to me."

Holmes and I placed our own cups aside at almost the same instant, and I saw the curious interest in his expression.

"It is easy to see," he said, "that you have recently suffered a distressing experience. Take a moment to put your thoughts in order and then tell us all that you remember, leaving out no detail. Be assured that Doctor Watson and I will do all within our power to put matters right."

She nodded. "Thank you, gentlemen. I know you will be patient with me. I have been widowed for six months and have a daughter. Hannah is almost eight now. Every Sunday we attend church, St Matthew's in Kensington, although yesterday I did so alone because Hannah is staying with my sister in Hammersmith.

"For the past few weeks I have struck up an acquaintance, although it would be more accurate to say that she struck up an acquaintance with me, with a woman called Miss Rebecca Daal. I noticed that she seemed always to occupy a seat next to us and so we eventually took to having some small conversation after the service. I suppose I must have inadvertently divulged too much about our lives to her; it is easy to do when your friends are few, but I wish now that we had never met. It was she who threw a dark shadow over our lives."

I saw that Holmes had rested his chin on steepled fingers and appeared half-asleep, but I knew he was weighing her every word carefully.

"How then, has this woman caused you harm?" I asked Mrs. Cutts.

She stared at the floor for a moment, obviously still upset by the memory, before answering.

"Yesterday, after the service came to its conclusion, I filed past the vicar with the others as I left. I noticed that she followed closely as I walked further from the church. Miss Daal caught up and

79

spoke suddenly, startling me. I can recall the subsequent conversation exactly.

"I am not what you believe, you know," she began.

"Whatever do you mean?" I asked.

"You think of me as someone who goes to church on Sundays and works otherwise as a secretary or companion."

"I assure you that I had given it no thought."

"Nevertheless, I will tell you. I am a businesswoman."

"That is not at all unusual. There are several ladies known to me who run their own shops very well."

She has quite piercing eyes, and their expression grew sharper then. "But there is more to it. My business is not like that."

"Are we playing a guessing game?" I said, slightly confused. "Do you wish me to know your affairs?"

"My business is not with goods. It is with people."

"You become more mysterious," I said. "If you wish me to understand something, then speak."

"I will do so, plainly. The subject of my business now, is your daughter."

"Hannah? What can you mean?" I suddenly felt cold. "What are you trying to tell me?"

"That we have your daughter, she is with us. Unless you accompany me now, you will never see her again."

For a moment, silence filled the room. Holmes never moved.

"As you may imagine, gentlemen," Mrs. Cutts said to us, "I was shocked and appalled. I threatened to go straight to the police."

""We will know if you do," Miss Daal replied. "We have our own people at Scotland Yard. The result would be the same. I assure you that her body will never be found."

"That may or may not be true," Holmes interrupted. "It is a common device to prevent victims seeking police help. Most probably, there is nothing in it."

"I am sure of the truth of that, Mr. Holmes, but you must see that I could not put my daughter's life at risk."

"Naturally not. You went with this woman, then?"

"I felt I had no choice, for I could think of no way to alter the situation. We walked hurriedly in a direction she chose, and after a while I became aware that someone else followed us closely. I turned to look back and saw a tall man with a full beard, dressed in a morning-coat and top hat. His gaze met mine and – I am sure I did not imagine this – his eyes were pitiless. He continued to walk a few paces behind us until we turned a corner, to be confronted immediately by a waiting coach. Miss Daal ordered me to board it and followed, while the bearded man climbed up beside the driver. The horses then set off at a fast trot."

"Were you able to see anything of the surroundings, as you passed?" I enquired, noting an approving glance from Holmes.

"Nothing whatsoever, since drawn shutters covered the windows at all times. I did feel, eventually, that we had left the city streets and entered some sort of area where gangs of men worked, for I could hear loud groans and oaths as they strained at their labours. When the coach came to rest Miss Daal produced a large handkerchief and blindfolded me, issuing a reminder of what would be Hannah's fate if I refused. I was then guided onto uneven ground and made to climb a ladder after a few paces. A door closed and I had the impression of walls around me as I was forced into a chair and my hands tied behind my back."

"What were you able to hear at that point?" Holmes asked.

Mrs. Cutts raised her hands and shook her head in a helpless gesture. "At first there was absolute silence, then I heard someone approach. I thought it was the bearded man, but I could not be sure. I felt hands in my hair, rearranging it, then a thick paste was applied to my left arm. It was cold at first and I must have shivered, for a man's voice said, "Keep perfectly still, until the compound sets. Make no attempt to remove it when your arms are freed." I did as instructed and endured another wait of about half an hour, then I heard footsteps again and the voice told me that my arms were to be released and my blindfold removed. The ropes were cut and my left arm was raised and inspected, apparently with approval, then my eyes were unbound roughly. Still I learned nothing, since I was in almost complete darkness! The shape of the man standing close was hardly discernible, and he spoke again to tell me that I must sit up straight with my arms lying along the arms of the chair. All I had to do, he said, was to keep absolutely still. I could close my eyes if I wished, but on no account was I to make any sound."

"Your hair was rearranged?" Holmes repeated.

"He bound it with a scarf or length of fabric."

"But it was not actually cut, or covered completely?"

"No, merely pulled away from my face."

"Most interesting. Pray continue."

"I decided that I would keep my eyes open to learn what I could, and presently a strip of light dispelled the darkness for a moment as the door was opened and more than one person entered. After it was closed again I heard voices, two more I thought, one of a young man and the other of a man quite old. It was this elderly man who slowly approached me after a short conversation. I felt myself grow very tense as he stood beside me, and more so as he ran his hand over the side of my face and my left arm. His breathing became rapid, as if he were feeling extreme excitement, and then to my relief he returned the way he had come. In reply to a question, the elderly man spoke in the affirmative before leaving. It was then that I heard words that terrified me. The bearded man then told someone else, possibly Miss Daal, that we had been in the company of the devil!"

Holmes raised his eyebrows. "What did you understand by that?"

"I could bring no meaning to it. The man who put his hands upon me felt as human as anyone else."

"And so he was. If you have allowed any supernatural elements to influence your understanding of these events, Mrs. Cutts, I urge you to dismiss them at once, for they will do nothing but increase your fears needlessly. Watson will tell you that we have met many strange situations before now, none of which have defied rational explanation for long."

"Thank you, Mr. Holmes, but I had entertained no such notion. Many times, I have been described as a down-to-earth person, even by my late husband."

"Excellent, and I congratulate you on your powers of recollection, but please continue your story."

"There is little more to tell. The door opened once more and the silence resumed. I had thought I had been left alone, but then again I heard more footsteps coming towards me. The voice of the bearded man, further away now, told me that I must not move from the chair until I had counted to five hundred, that if I disobeyed I would be shot by an accomplice who waited outside with a pistol. Then I saw his shape briefly as he opened the door and left."

"What did you hear, immediately after?"

"Only a coach, presumably that which brought us to that place, being driven quickly away. After counting, I stood up and made my way through the darkness to where I thought the door was. I opened it and found myself at the top of a ladder leading down to a deserted area near the dockland. I had been held prisoner in an abandoned warehouse."

"What did you do then," I enquired.

"After descending the ladder I realised that I was lost, for I had never seen this place before. Frantically, I tried to get my bearings. I considered asking some of the working men for assistance, but they looked a rascally crowd and I had no desire to increase my difficulties. My overwhelming need was to discover whether the kidnappers had kept their word, whether my daughter had been released, so when my wanderings took me near a Post Office I despatched a telegram to my sister after informing the postmistress that I would remain close at hand to receive a reply."

"The answer was encouraging, I hope?"

"It was as surprising as any of the events of yesterday. My sister had been to Regent's Park with her children and Hannah for most of the day. Nothing unusual had happened to them!"

Holmes nodded his understanding. "So it was all deceit. Your daughter was never in any danger. That at least must have been a comfort."

"Indeed, so much so that I almost swooned. It was all I could do to summon a passing hansom afterwards, and so return to Kensington."

Holmes was still and silent for what seemed a long time. Mrs. Cutts sat patiently, as if she sensed that my friend was already seeking a solution to her strange experience. The window was half-open and I could hear the curses of the driver of a hansom or four-wheeler held up by the traffic in Baker Street, and the movements of Mrs. Hudson in the rooms below were audible also.

"Have you any explanation of your own, as to the events of yesterday?" Holmes asked at last.

Mrs. Cutts shook her head. "Not unless, as I said earlier, it was some sort of jest. I can think of no one of my acquaintance who would treat me so."

He looked at her with curiosity. "Did you discover the significance of the compound that was placed on your arm?"

"I could see no reason for it. My flesh had the appearance of sustaining a deep wound, a gash, before I was able to remove the encrustation. It seemed to me quite without purpose." At this, she rubbed her arm as if she felt pain from it. "I am left with a red blemish from the application, but it will fade."

My friend leaned forward in his chair, until he could see the mark. "There are a number of curious features in this tale," he concluded. "I think these events will bear some looking into." He turned to me. "Are you free for a trip to the docks, Watson?"

I nodded my assent.

"Mrs. Cutts, you will please accompany us?"

"Most certainly," our client replied.

Chapter Seven – Warfield House

Beginning at Kensington, Holmes instructed our cab driver to take a random route around the area, expanding it continuously until we came upon a place that Mrs. Cutts recognised.

"There is the post office from which I sent the telegram to my sister," she said after a long and watchful silence. "Two left turns and three to the right should bring us to where I was held."

"Again, I congratulate you on your memory and powers of observation," Holmes said.

He so directed the driver, and we soon arrived at an area where several warehouses overlooked the docks. It may, I reflected, have been less so yesterday, being Sunday when our client was held prisoner, but now the place was filled with unceasing activity. Men, alone or with others, carried their burdens to the wharf, while still others unloaded the vessels moored further away. The air was heavy with oaths, grunts of effort and the occasional cry of pain. The smell of unwashed humanity was appalling, but neither Holmes nor our client seemed aware of it. She pointed to a particularly dilapidated structure, directly ahead.

"That is the place."

"Are you certain?" I asked.

"I am sure that I will never forget it."

Mrs. Cutts had indicated a wooden building, or the remains of one, with a ladder that looked far from stable leading to an upper storey. Beneath this was the area where cargo would have at one time been stored to await collection. I doubted it would ever be used so again, such was the condition of the place.

"Let us ascend," said Holmes after a moment of visual examination, "but singly, I think."

I asked the driver to wait for us as my friend climbed slowly and uncertainly from rung to rung. Mrs. Cutts went next and I wondered why Holmes had not suggested that she remain at the foot of the ladder, although I realised that her presence might be significant to his investigation. I followed cautiously, as the wood creaked ominously with every step.

Before we caught up with him Holmes had tested the door and, finding it unlocked, opened it slowly and carefully. Until we joined him, he stood still near the threshold, before peering in every direction. Finally, he stepped inside and we followed.

"It seems that there has been no disturbance here since you left, Mrs. Cutts. Everything is exactly as you described it."

At his request, we did not move from our position near the door. I noted that the dust lay without blemish nearby, unlike the area that Holmes was already examining after producing his lens from his pocket.

"You were quite correct," he said to our client. "These rather smudged footprints reveal that there were at least two men here, as well as a lady besides yourself." He moved to the single piece of furniture, a chair, and scrutinised it minutely. "Here is where you were tied. Witness the severed ropes strewn across the floor, the congealed drops of whatever compound was applied to your arm and the strip of ribbon that was undoubtedly tied around your head, since some hair has adhered to it. My examination is now concluded, and you would oblige me greatly by sitting in the chair once again and placing your feet over the imprints in the dust nearby."

Mrs. Cutts did as he requested, with Holmes helping her into the chair. As he did so he became very still for an instant, and I saw his eyes grow wide with surprise. I could not imagine the cause of the astonishment written on his face.

He looked critically at our seated client, before once again allowing his gaze to travel around the room and to sweep across the floor.

"Very well," he said finally. "I cannot see that there is anything more to be learned here. I suggest that Mrs. Cutts take our cab to return to Kensington while you and I, Watson, make our way back to Baker Street."

We then filed out and descended the ladder. Mrs. Cutts was installed in our waiting cab before Holmes spoke to her with assurance.

"I have learned much here today, good lady. It will not be too long, I think, before you hear from us."

She expressed her thanks and we watched the cab depart, leaving him with a satisfied air and myself in the midst of confusion.

#

I waited until we were back in our rooms, before I could bear his reticence no longer.

"I am aware, Holmes, that you saw something of significance during your examination of the warehouse. Your changed expression told me as much when you bade Mrs. Cutts be seated. Would you care to share your findings?"

He took an envelope from his pocket. "Presently, Watson, when I am sure of my ground. I have here a sample of the compound used on her arm, a scraping from the remains on the warehouse floor. An analysis should prove revealing, I think. If you wish to visit your practice, or perhaps sit here and read for an hour or so, I may by then be able to arrive at some sort of explanation."

With that he immersed himself among his chemical apparatus. He leaned his thin form half-across the table that held his retorts and test tubes and his flaring Bunsen burner, and after a while the air became tainted with unfamiliar smells. I opened the window and looked up from my book several times, to see him watching carefully as heated liquids changed colour. Finally he emerged, but with dissatisfaction written on his face.

"What have you discovered," I asked him.

He shook his head absently. "Very little. The compound is a mixture of theatrical make-up and a thick substance resembling glue. I can discern no purpose to affixing this to Mrs Cutts' arm, nor can I imagine what it is intended to represent."

"How then, can we proceed?"

"A possibility did occur to me," he lowered himself into an armchair, looking thoughtful. "Mrs Cutts spoke of her captors referring to the man they apparently brought to the warehouse as 'the devil.' I immediately thought that curious, since there is no mention of black magic or the like contained in the threat they held over her or anywhere else in this affair. I then began to consider that she might, given her likely emotional state at that time, have misheard the remark altogether. If you would be good enough to hand me from the bookcase the fourth volume from the left on the second shelf from the top, which is a recent copy of *Who's Who,* it may be worthwhile looking there before consulting my index."

I did so and watched, as he hurriedly turned page after page. Mrs. Hudson knocked and put her head around the door to ask about our requirements for lunch, but he shouted to her without taking his eyes from the book that we would need none. That good lady's footfalls on her descent of the stairs had hardly ceased, when he gave a harsh bark of triumph.

"Aha! Listen to this, Watson, on the subject of General Charles DeVille, who served at...., I will omit his military history, who has been retired for some years and resides at Warfield House, near Gillingham, Kent."

"I can see how our client could have mistaken the name," I responded, "but there must be others also called DeVille."

"Indeed there are. Many live in the north of England, several in the list are ladies and all others mentioned there are young or middle-aged men. You will recall that Mrs. Cutts was quite certain that the man who ran his hand over her face and arm was elderly, since she heard his voice briefly and noted his slow movements."

I nodded. My friend's eyes glittered and I knew he had caught the scent of things and would try unceasingly until he had the answer to these strange events.

"Perhaps a telegram would suffice, at least to confirm that General DeVille is the man we seek?"

Holmes shook his head but made no reply, leaped to his feet and strode to the bookcase. He replaced his *Who's Who* with one hand while pulling out his Bradshaw's with the other, before quickly resuming his seat.

"We are in luck," he announced. "A train for Gillingham leaves within the hour. If we are quick, we will catch it."

#

Of the journey I recall only that Holmes talked constantly of unrelated subjects, as was sometimes his habit. I had no objection to this but listened and commented frequently, preferring this situation between us to the deep silences to which he often resorted.

The fields and foliage were interrupted quite suddenly by Gillingham Station, and we alighted in the company of several burly men whose trades Holmes had already identified. A fellow with a cage of racing pigeons emerged from the guard's van as we gave up our tickets and hired the dog-cart of a local man who waited for that purpose.

"How far is it, Holmes?" I asked as we set off with the horse trotting well.

"According to the map I consulted before we left Baker Street, no more than three miles."

He said little else as he drove through tree-lined lanes, and others bordered by fields. Cattle lay lazily beneath mighty oaks, and

I wondered if the belief that this behaviour indicates an impending storm had any substance.

"Ha!" exclaimed my friend at length. "I see a rather old and dilapidated sign, nailed to that tree."

Shortly after he turned into a wide drive, with tall and dense hedges on either side. After about five hundred yards the horse slowed, and I saw that we were approaching stables and a few out-buildings. An elderly man emerged, an unlit pipe in his mouth. Without a word, he took the reins and would have led the horse away to water, had not Holmes asked the direction of the house. I concluded that the man was mute, since he silently pointed in the direction of an apparently empty field without attempting to speak.

We took the path beyond the stables and saw that, unusually, the house stood some distance away. A decaying church loomed to our left, partially roofless and with the light of day shining through its empty windows, and it struck me that its situation might explain the position of the house.

"I am sure you are correct, Watson," Holmes said. "The drive was probably here to serve the church originally, long before the house was built. There may have been some dispute over access rights, in the past."

"My dear Holmes!" I retorted, yet I should have felt little surprise. He had, by his powers of observation and logic, seemed to read my thoughts many times before.

"There is really no mystery to it," he laughed. "When I see you peering with such a puzzled expression at the drive, the church and the house, and given the relative positions of them, what else am I to think?"

I declined to answer, but instead remarked upon our surroundings. "If we follow this path beside the stream, it should lead us directly to the main entrance."

"So I believe. Unless there is another approach, it seems certain that the inhabitants venture out infrequently, since the grass and weeds do not appear to have been trodden down for some time."

Soon after, we found ourselves in a gravelled courtyard. The red-bricked structure that confronted us looked to be of the Georgian style, with stone pillars at the front and wings that stood at right-angles to the main body of the house. We mounted the steps to a stout door with iron hinges. Holmes rang the bell and we waited.

Presently the door opened. The butler who stood before us was probably middle-aged, but appeared much older due to his excessively sombre expression.

"Please be good enough to take my card to your master," Holmes began before the man could speak.

The man bowed. "Very well, sir, but I must ask – who is it you wish to see?"

"Mr. Charles DeVille. Is this not his residence?"

"I regret to inform you gentlemen, Mr. Charles passed away yesterday evening."

My friend and I exchanged surprised glances.

"Then we must offer our condolences," I said then, "to his successor, or whoever remains."

"That would be Mr. George, sir. Please wait while I see if he is receiving guests."

The butler gestured that we should enter and remain in the hall, before turning and walking stiffly down a long passage. Crossed swords adorned the walls above the doorways, while medieval armour stood in the corners. The walls themselves were dominated by portraits of a handsome woman, in the last years of her youth.

"An ancestor, perhaps?" I ventured, glancing at Holmes who was scrutinizing the portraits.

"The clothes suggest someone of more recent times," he replied thoughtfully. "Although the lady's hair is of a rather old-fashioned style."

At that moment the butler reappeared and approached us.

"Mr George will see you now, gentlemen."

We followed him along the corridor and through a door near the end. He announced us to a dark-haired man of average height, whose age I would have imagined to be about thirty-five. He wore a grey tweed suit, with a black armband and tie.

"Good morning Mr. Sherlock Holmes and Doctor Watson," he said in a much lighter tone than I would have expected. He looked at Holmes' card again, before placing it in his pocket. "I have heard of you of course, and enjoyed reading of your exploits."

"Thank you, Mr. DeVille," my friend acknowledged. "We have only just learned of your bereavement. May I express our sincere condolences?"

To my surprise, our host smiled faintly. "My thanks to you both, but I always think these events are so much worse when they are unexpected. As it was, my father had been a broken man for years, and there has been little sign of his condition improving. And of course, he was blind."

"So you have, to some extent, been able to prepare yourself?" Holmes enquired.

"As much as one can, in such circumstances. My father had adopted a philosophical attitude to death, and he often urged me to do the same. The truth is," he paused and glanced towards the door, as though he expected the butler to be listening, "that Bidmead has taken it to heart more than I. Very long service, you see."

"It is often the case," I remarked, "with faithful retainers."

"Quite," Mr. DeVille indicated that we should sit, and we all three rested ourselves in the armchairs that surrounded the ornate fireplace. "Will you now take a glass of brandy with me, before we discuss whatever matter has brought you to my door?"

We assented and he called for Bidmead, who promptly withdrew to obey his master. Holmes enquired about the history of the house, and as our host answered I let my eyes rove around the room. It was furnished richly, and in excellent taste, but what arrested my attention immediately were the portraits that hung on every wall. They were all variations on those we had already seen, with the same subject.

Bidmead reappeared and served us, and I recognised the taste of good Napoleon brandy. As we replaced our half-empty glasses on the tray, Holmes sat back in his chair, his hands clasped in front of him and his eyes on our host who waited expectantly.

"We are here, Mr. DeVille, seeking the solution to a most curious affair."

"I cannot imagine what has led you to believe that you will find it here."

"There seems to be a good chance of it. If it will not distress you too much, I would be obliged if you would describe to us your father's movements of yesterday, as best as you can remember."

Mr. DeVille shook his head slowly, adopting a puzzled expression. "I cannot see how his movements could be a part of any investigation, for they were quite normal. As I recall, a friend arrived in a brougham, just after breakfast. My father seemed in an extraordinary state of mind, more optimistic and light-hearted than I have seen him for many a year. He waved goodbye to me as I emerged from the dining-room, and was gone in an instant."

"Was his companion someone of your acquaintance?"

"Not at all, but that is not unusual. Several of my father's friends to whom he has never seen fit to introduce to me, call for him here quite regularly. I believe they are from the Old Comrades Club, in Gillingham."

Holmes nodded. "Was there anything about this man that struck you as odd?"

"I can think of nothing." Mr. DeVille paused to reflect. "Though I did think he knew my father previously because of the way he helped him into the carriage. He was apparently aware from the first that he was in the company of a blind man."

"And you saw nothing more of Mr. Charles until late afternoon, or evening?"

"Nothing. He did not return until then. The coach had gone by the time Bidmead helped him into the house. My father was in a state of great excitement, and had a strange story to tell."

"If it will not upset you too much," my friend repeated, "pray tell us."

"I begin to see how these events could have a bearing on something deeper," our host said after a moment of thought. "To understand the significance of my father's tale, you must know a little of our family background." He paused to drain his glass, and I did the same. Holmes sat silent and statue-like, waiting. "Our family fortune arose from an interest in a Cornish tin mine, which was established during the last century. My father and grandfather, while regularly receiving dividends, rarely had any connection with the running of the place. The others in the partnership were men of experience and, although the yield was slowly declining, the arrangement functioned well. About five years go my father received word that a new lode had been discovered, sufficient to ensure employment for every worker for years to come. This was deemed to be cause for a celebration, and my parents set off to participate."

"This, of course, was their first visit?" I ventured.

"It was, and also their last. My father was invited to descend into the mine and readily agreed. My mother, always an adventurous woman, insisted on accompanying him. The cage was lowered, containing also three men with lanterns. My father said later that they had not reached the site before the tunnel collapsed, killing everyone except him. He was rescued with great difficulty, having suffered some injury. Several physicians have since explained that the gases released were almost certainly the cause of the deterioration of his sight which culminated in total blindness.

"From that time, my father's memory and soundness of mind began to fail. He could not accept the loss of my mother and was unreasonably convinced that she still lived and that she would one day reappear in his life. As time went on, this became an obsession and he spoke of little else. When he returned yesterday he was overcome with joy, shouting as soon as he entered that my mother had been found! I was able to calm him somewhat, until he was coherent enough to tell me that he had been taken to see her, and had actually touched her! He was adamant that it could have been no one else, since the signs were there."

I saw in Holmes" eyes that he had reached some understanding. He regarded Mr. DeVille with a keen stare. "And what did you conclude from that?"

"You cannot have failed to notice the many portraits of my mother, in this room and elsewhere in the house. Most were painted after her death, from a single picture, and are a testament to my father's devotion. He had them painted just as she appeared in life, including the large birthmark on her left arm, because he wished to remember every detail of her. This of course, was while some of his sight remained."

"Much is now very clear," Holmes said then. "But, having found your mother, why did your father not return with her?"

"It was at this point in his narrative that I realised that he was the victim of a cruel trick. When I asked him that very question, he replied that he had been told that my mother had been abroad and had contracted a highly contagious tropical disease. This, however, was said to be totally curable although the course of treatment involved rare herbs from other lands, and was therefore expensive."

My friend sighed, wearing a knowing expression. "Was a figure mentioned?"

"Indeed it was. The price was thirty thousand pounds."

I was appalled at the insensitivity and the audacity of the plot, for it was obviously nothing less. These people had somehow heard of Mr. Charles DeVille's infirmities, and his obsession, and were prepared to take full advantage of them for their own profit.

"It was on hearing this that the matter became clear to me," our host continued, "and I attempted to explain to my father, as gently as I could, the truth of the situation. I had barely spoken when he began to rave like a madman and I was forced to restrain him. Despite my efforts, his agitation increased to the point where I had no choice but to instruct Bidmead to summon a physician. Sadly my father's heart failed before this could be done."

"Tragic indeed," Holmes said. "You seem to have withstood the situation with great strength."

Mr. DeVille shook his head. "It may appear that way, Mr. Holmes, and doubtlessly some will think of me as having little compassion. The truth is, as I have mentioned, that I have long prepared myself for what I knew must eventually come to pass. Also, the knowledge that my father has escaped his suffering and is now in the same place, the place where my dear mother rests, is of some consolation."

#

I had many questions, but one begged for an answer before the others. Since leaving Warfield House my friend had said little, and by his expression I knew that he was giving great consideration to Mr. DeVille's words. We reclaimed the dog cart, Holmes handing a half-sovereign to the silent groom who touched his cap in acknowledgement. Some way towards the station we were halted by a farmer's boy, who held up his hand while his herd crossed the lane. It was then that I seized the opportunity to speak:

"Holmes, some of this situation is now clear to me, but I have a question."

He glanced back at me quickly as the last cow disappeared into the far field and the boy waved his thanks before following.

"Only one question, Watson?"

"I cannot see why Mrs. Cutts was used to impersonate the late Mrs. DeVille. Whoever is responsible for this could have used anyone, perhaps even someone willing, for the deception. As I see it, the identifying birthmark could just as easily have been reproduced on someone else."

"Indeed. But do you recall Mr. George DeVille's words, regarding his father's identification of Mrs. Cutts as his wife?"

I took a moment to consider. "I believe he said, 'the signs were there'."

"Precisely. He said 'Signs,' not 'Sign'."

"There were others?"

"One more unmistakable sign, at least." A crow flew out of a roadside tree, startling the horse, and Holmes allowed the animal to slow its pace. "Compare the portraits of Mrs. DeVille to your recollection of our client, and tell me what you see as a common factor."

"The style of the hair of each was unfashionably long, and similar," I replied after a moment.

"Bravo, Watson, your powers of observation increase. Now, do you remember asking me for an explanation of my discovery in the warehouse?"

"I saw your expression change as you held the chair for Mrs. Cutts."

"At that moment something unexpected came to my notice. It was something that would have convinced Mr. DeVille *absolutely*. I realised this later, as I inspected the portraits of his wife."

"I saw nothing."

"But you were in no position to. I saw, from my perspective then, that Mrs. Cutts' left ear was missing. It appeared that Nature, not surgery, was responsible."

"And you believe that this was true of Mrs DeVille also, and that the portraits deliberately concealed this?"

"Of course, since it is hardly an attractive feature. Nevertheless, Mr. Charles DeVille, must certainly have known of it. The birthmark was much more prominent, and he would have become so familiar with it over the years as to regard it simply as part of his wife's appearance. I would speculate that this woman Rebecca Daal either saw by accident that Mrs. Cutts' ear was missing and contrived the plot, or the plot was already in existence and a suitable substitute for Mrs. DeVille was needed and had been sought. In either case, it seems certain that an organised gang is behind this."

"So, aided by Mr. DeVille's infirmity and blindness, these criminals successfully convinced him that his wife still lived."

"A little more subtle, I think. They provided the opportunity for him to *discern for himself* that she lived. His eyes could tell him nothing. But his hands, their sensitivity increased by his constant reliance on his sense of touch, told him that the woman before him was indeed his wife, since she possessed both the birthmark and the missing ear. You will recall that Mrs. Cutts was warned not to speak or make any sound, probably because her voice would almost certainly be quite different from that of the lady she was being forced to impersonate. How this, or what must have seemed to him like her trance-like state was explained to Mr. DeVille, I have no way of knowing."

"To raise that poor man's hopes of an impossible reunion with the woman he so clearly still loved was a despicable act," I felt anger rising within me. "I have seldom been confronted with such callousness."

"Indeed." Holmes agreed. "The elderly Mr. DeVille's blindness and his rejection of his wife's death were the key factors in the plot, of course. Also the demand was for thirty thousand pounds, a vast sum but one the gang knew would be paid gladly, if it were believed that it was to be used for the cure of the fictional tropical disease. This tells us that they were familiar with the financial standing of the DeVille family, and suggests again that the plot was the result of much planning."

"So, we can now explain Mrs. Cutts" strange experience, but this gang of cheats and swindlers will probably turn their attention elsewhere as soon as the news of Mr. Charles DeVille's death reaches them."

"Undoubtedly," We arrived at the station and Holmes returned the dog cart to its owner, who accepted his payment with good grace. As we began a ten-minute wait on the platform, my friend mused sadly.

"The truth is, Watson, that this gang is indirectly responsible for the elder Mr. DeVille's death."

"Certainly there must be some doubt that he would have suffered such a seizure, had he not experienced renewed hope that was dashed so suddenly by his son. I cannot but think that Mr. George DeVille would have acted more carefully, had he anticipated the outcome."

Holmes nodded. "That may be so. As for the abductors of Mrs. Cutts, it is clear that such an organised group will quickly seek another situation with which to enrich themselves, as you have already realised."

"Unconcernedly causing more distress, without a doubt."

"I would be surprised to learn of that as a consideration for them. We will, I think, pay our friend Inspector Lestrade a visit. It may be possible to identify the gang from the files at Scotland Yard."

I recognised the altered tone of his voice, saw his eyes glitter, and was warned. "With what purpose, Holmes? I had assumed this affair to be over, since it can now be explained."

At that moment the train arrived. As we boarded he turned to me and said in a perfectly calm and unemotional voice.

"Not so. I am going to hunt down these brutes, and place them in the hands of the law."

Chapter Eight – A Face from the Past

I sat down to breakfast the next morning to find that Holmes had already finished eating. Lately he had taken to rising earlier than had previously been his custom, and I noticed at once that his eyes were alive with the thrill of the chase.

"I will ring for Mrs. Hudson," he said when greetings had been exchanged. "The bacon and kidneys are excellent today. When you have consumed yours and we have seen off a second pot of coffee, we have a busy day ahead of us."

Our good lady supplied me with a plate of steaming food, which I ate with relish. As my friend lit his first pipe of the day, I finished my coffee and asked:

"Are we to visit Scotland Yard, as you implied yesterday?"

Holmes breathed out a cloud of smoke. "When I last saw Lestrade he was about to embark on a case in Bristol. However, if things went as he expected he should have returned by now. Otherwise, I suppose Gregson or Hopkins might oblige us. As you can imagine, Watson, I am reluctant to enlist the Yard's help, but already this morning I have scoured my index, without result."

"Unusual, for you to have found nothing."

"Oh, I will not say that *absolutely.* There are three, possibly four unsolved cases that might well be the work of the gang we seek, but my newspaper clippings are sufficiently vague to make identification uncertain. You see how anonymous is our quarry, to have left so little imprint on the public perspective. These people are no amateurs, their experience is considerable."

"But I was under the impression that you have been confronted with three new cases."

Unusually, a puzzled expression crossed his face, but it was gone at once. "Watson, you surpass yourself. You noticed that I sorted my post into two piles before laying it aside. The one pile contains three envelopes, the other several more. You reasoned that the larger pile is of bills and the smaller of communications from prospective new clients, because it is my usual custom to arrange them in this way. Is that not so?"

"Again, Holmes, I believe you read my mind," I smiled.

"As I have said before, old fellow, my powers fall short of that. Otherwise you are quite correct, but the three new cases have none of the urgency that our current one promises and can therefore be postponed for the present."

"Your determination to see this gang behind bars is quite evident."

He nodded, and paused thoughtfully as he knocked out his pipe in the grate. "I cannot abide the prospect of a group with such an unfeeling disposition as to cheat a sick and elderly blind man, walking freely among us. Still less that they undoubtedly contributed to his death. Our success will remove this threat to other vulnerable victims."

"I expected no less of you."

We rose from the table together, and took up our hats and coats.

Holmes looked down from the window. "I see that a cab has just arrived opposite, and the passenger is searching his pockets for the fare. If we are quick we may get there before he finds it, and be on our way to Scotland Yard in a trice. Come, Watson!"

#

Lestrade had indeed returned from Bristol. Although it had been some time since he displayed the disapproval of Holmes that had

103

once been his usual attitude, I had never before seen him quite so amiable. I concluded that his latest case had ended well.

"So, Mr. Holmes," the little detective said lightly, "you have described a most interesting case. Unless I am much mistaken, you are here because you believe that our files can help you identify these criminals."

My friend shifted in his chair. "I am certain of it. A gang so organised is unlikely to have no history, and such a history would hardly go unnoticed. I would wager, Lestrade, that numerous unidentified crimes have been recorded, whether attributed to the same group of swindlers or not."

I allowed my eyes to roam around the inspector's dull and untidy office as he considered the matter. The stack of files upon his desk appeared to be no less high than the last time Holmes and I had sat here. From along the corridor I could hear a scuffle taking place and oaths shouted with feeling, presumably as a violent prisoner was brought in.

"Very well," Lestrade actually smiled, albeit thinly, "let us see what can be learned."

The walk down the dreary passageways was familiar to me, as this was not the first time we had visited these archives. The drab green-painted walls and uncarpeted floors lent the place the atmosphere of a tomb. This was where crime became history, always to be remembered in the annals of the Yard.

The inspector opened a heavy door and we followed him inside. Rows of shelves stretched the full length of the room, and many tall cabinets stood along one wall.

"Now, let me see." He walked slowly along the shelves. "Had you come to me a week or two ago, I would have had no hesitation in immediately selecting the Elias Borstein records."

"I understood that he and his associates reside in Pentonville, at present."

Lestrade had the good grace to suppress a sneer. "That is so, one of Gregson's dubious triumphs. Ah!" He pulled down a thick file and blew a sprinkling of dust from it. "In here are recorded crimes such as you describe. They go back several years and, I'm sorry to say, all are unsolved."

We seated ourselves around the rough wooden table at the centre of the room. Lestrade turned the pages quickly, hurrying through the oldest crimes. He stopped suddenly, turning the file so that Holmes and I could see its contents.

"These are the cases that I believe might be the work of the gang that you seek." He turned another page, to reveal several sepia photographs of a woman and three men. "We were certain, at one time, of the guilt of this pleasant little group in an affair involving a robbery and three murders. It could never be proven, and so we had to let them go. Where they are now, or if they are connected to your investigation, I am afraid I cannot say."

"Perhaps they...." Sherlock Holmes began, but ceased abruptly as I struggled to my feet with some surprise. "What is it, Watson?"

"I know this woman. I have seen her before."

Both men stared at me in surprise, and for a moment I doubted myself, feeling foolish for interrupting. Then I leaned over and looked more closely at the faded image, and was certain.

"Yes, it is she. A more alert expression, a little rouge on the cheeks it appears, and the hair is styled differently, but it is the same woman."

"You sound very certain, doctor," Lestrade commented.

"Pray enlighten us," said Holmes eagerly.

"That photograph is of a woman I saw briefly below stairs at Foley Grange. I would be prepared to swear to it. She was a kitchen maid, called Mary. The Squire described her as 'Something of a simpleton', as I recall."

Holmes leaned back in his chair with an air of enlightenment. "Thus is explained the drug in Squire Foley's wine, the mirror flashes and how Lance was aware of some of our activities. The full significance of these had eluded me until now. It seems that the Squire's judgement was rather hasty. Not all at Foley Grange perished in the fire, evidently."

Lestrade wore an expression of complete puzzlement, until Holmes explained to him the details of the case.

"I agree, gentlemen, that this is an experienced gang," the official detective said afterwards. "However, it does appear that there is a singular lack of proof with both the affair of Squire Foley and the more recent incident concerning the master of Warfield House. After all, one could not say with certainty that Mr. Charles DeVille would not have died from his infirmities, regardless."

"That may be," I said then, "But there is the abduction of Mrs. Cutts to consider. She can definitely identify the woman she knew as Miss Rebecca Daal."

Lestrade glanced again at the file. "Who is known to us as Mrs. Olga Stone. The bearded man, who I presume is the same as your client saw, is Alexander McIrwin. The remaining two men are unknown, and of course may have died or been replaced since their encounter with us. I really do not think, gentlemen, that there are grounds here for the Yard to proceed. Even if the gang were apprehended, they have only to avail themselves of an experienced lawyer who could get the evidence against them dismissed as vague and insufficient."

"Nevertheless, there is no reason that our investigation cannot continue." Holmes rose from his chair. "Thank you, Lestrade, for your most valuable assistance. We may yet supply you with the means to add these to your considerable record of arrests."

As we descended the steps to the street, it occurred to me that an aspect of this affair bore a similarity to that of William Lance.

"It would seem, Holmes, that once more we are to pursue the dead."

He smiled absently. "Or, again, someone who wished to be thought of as such. But the maid Mary, or Rebecca Daal, or Olga Stone, is very much alive and at liberty." He paused to hail a passing hansom. "At least, for the present."

We arrived back at our rooms in time for lunch. After a meal of roast lamb with mint sauce followed by a rich dessert, we repaired to our usual chairs around the fire. I was not surprised to see Holmes' preoccupied expression, for this was quite usual until a case was brought to a satisfactory end, and his words as he sat with his eyes closed surprised me still less:

"Pray do not interrupt my thoughts for at least an hour, Watson. I must give some consideration to how our investigation is to continue."

I nodded and picked up the mid-day edition of *The Standard.* After a while I lowered the pages and saw that he looked for all the world as if he slept.

It was more than an hour and a half later that his eyes suddenly opened.

"Are you all right, Holmes?" I asked on noticing his vacant expression.

"Watson, pray summon our page. I must send a telegram to Lestrade, at once."

I went out onto the landing and called to Mrs. Hudson, who sent the lad up to us at once. Holmes quickly took up a pen and wrote briefly, whereupon Billy took the form with some coins and left quickly.

"What message have you sent to the good inspector?" I asked my friend.

"I have requested, as a matter of urgency, that he has the photograph of Olga Stone copied, so that every officer on the streets of London can be aware of her appearance and constantly on the lookout. I will also call upon the Irregulars to maintain a constant watch. I can think of no more speedy method that will put us on their track."

With that he rose and went down into the street. From the window I saw him watch the passing crowd for some little time, until an urchin who was unfamiliar to me appeared. Doubtlessly Holmes averted the picking of a few pockets by calling to him, bringing an immediate response from the boy whom he apparently knew. A short conversation followed and some coins changed hands. After receiving a smart salute, Holmes turned away abruptly and I heard his footfalls on the stairs as the boy disappeared among the shifting throng.

"Regrettably I had no likeness to aid them," he said, once more sinking into his chair, "but the Irregulars are well-versed in the petty criminals of our city, and no less so in the gangs. If any recent newcomers are planning mischief, they will at least have heard a whisper."

"They rarely disappoint you," I agreed.

"They are my eyes and ears in the capital, often more valuable than the whole of the official force."

"So you have mentioned before. So now we await results?

"I have an experiment that awaits completion, and there are additional items to include in my index. I am sure that you can amuse yourself, Watson, until after dinner, when I am quite certain that the hook I have baited will have attracted some items of significance."

#

As it turned out, late evening had arrived by the time we heard. Wiggins, the leader of the Irregulars, reported that the capital had been scoured with but one result. After a short conversation he gave Holmes an address written on a scrap of paper, before accepting payment at the usual rate and leaving us.

"So, Watson, we are to visit Whitechapel, in the morning."

"Olga Stone has been found?"

He shrugged. "Perhaps. Wiggins said that the Irregulars searched every likely place known to them, with the result that four different women fitting her description were seen among the usual criminal classes. Two of these were too old and one had recently become a cripple, leaving us the remaining possibility to investigate. I am reluctant to set foot in Whitechapel tonight, because there is little guarantee that she will be at home, whereas we will certainly see her depart in the morning if we are there early enough. You will see then, old friend, whether she and your maid from Squire Foley's kitchen are one and the same."

So it was that we found ourselves in a hansom, well before eight o'clock the following morning. Holmes had instructed the driver to take us to a grim and dirty street with several vile alleys leading off, no doubt to similar thoroughfares. We waited for almost two hours opposite the house indicated by the Irregulars' information, during which time nothing occurred other than the brief appearance of the occasional shabby resident and the passing of constables on the beat. The horse had become restless more than once and had to be quieted by the driver, and was beginning to stamp its hooves again when two people emerged and stood in conversation briefly. They were a hulking, rough-looking man and a well-dressed woman, and even from here I could see her resemblance to the woman I remembered as a kitchen maid at Foley Grange. I craned my neck, in an effort to see her more clearly.

"Is that the woman you saw, Watson?" Holmes asked quietly from his half-shadowed position in the seat opposite.

"I am unsure, as yet."

Nothing more was said until the couple set off in different directions. Holmes waited until the man was almost out of sight.

"Driver!" he called. On hearing an acknowledgement, he continued. "Take us slowly past that woman as she nears the corner, so that we pass in front of her before she crosses the road. An extra half-sovereign, if you do it without attracting her attention."

The horse moved off immediately, quite slowly. We reached the end of the road with the woman still yards away from the junction, and by adjusting my position I was able to attain a good view from a frontal perspective.

"What do you say now, old fellow?"

"The similarity is strong, Holmes, but I have never seen this woman before."

"You are quite sure?"

"There is no doubt in my mind."

"Very well, we will return to Baker Street and explore other possibilities."

#

I felt that the morning had been wasted, and that we were both disappointed. When we were once more settled in our lodgings, Holmes called for tea. Shortly after, we were graced by the appearance of Inspector Lestrade.

"Ah, Lestrade," Holmes said by way of greeting, "I perceive from your expression that you have something to tell us."

"Indeed, – no thank you, Mr. Holmes, I won't take tea – but I have only a few minutes to spare. I am on my way to a new enquiry, and as I had to pass Baker Street on the way it seemed convenient to call in to tell you of a new development in that Olga Stone affair that you were interested in."

I saw that the inspector had Holmes' full attention at once.

"Pray enlighten us," my friend replied.

The little detective sat in the basket chair, at a gesture from Holmes. "I received your request to have the picture of Olga Stone copied, but it occurred to me that to first pass it around Scotland Yard might obtain a quicker result."

"And it evidently did, or you would not be relating this to us."

"No, indeed." Lestrade allowed himself a small smile of triumph. "One of our men, Constable Mullins, has been called to the National Gallery several times over the last few weeks, to eject a persistent troublemaker. Apparently, this man, always the worse for consuming excessive drink, has taken to staggering into the place to share rather loudly his views on various artists and their works."

Holmes nodded. "Evidently, he possesses something of a classical education. But the facts appertaining to this case please, Lestrade."

"Well, to get to this man, Mullins had to enter by the Trafalgar Square entrance which is on his beat, and pass through the building to the other side. In one of the exhibition rooms he noticed the same woman day after day, always sitting in the same position and staring at the same picture. He says he thought this peculiar at the time, but saw no harm in it and dismissed it from his mind. Later, when the photograph of Olga Stone was shown to him, he recognised her as the same woman."

"Has the Yard done anything to confirm this? Or taken any action?"

"We have many cases on hand at the moment, Mr. Holmes, and as usual we are undermanned. As I have said before, in the absence of sufficient proof there is little that we can bring against her in any case."

"So nothing has been done?"

An expression that might have been shame crossed the official detective's bulldog-like face. "Nothing."

"Capital!" Holmes rubbed his thin hands together with a delight that surprised me. "We will see if we can make anything of it. My thanks to you, Inspector, for bringing this to our attention."

Lestrade rose, and Holmes and I did likewise.

"And now I must bid you gentlemen good morning."

He was halfway to the door when Holmes called to him.

"One thing more if you please, Lestrade."

"Is there something else, Mr. Holmes?"

"Only the picture that this woman seemed so interested in. Do you recall its title?"

A notebook was produced, and read from aloud. "It was called 'Minerva in Repose,' by an unknown artist," Lestrade paused as a new thought occurred to him, "but now that you ask about it, something else comes to mind. Mullins swears that the woman and the girl in the picture looked alike. Do you think there's anything in that?"

Holmes gave a barely perceptible shrug.

"Who knows? But it is possible that we may find out soon."

#

Holmes said little for some time after the inspector left, but I could see that he was turning this new information over in his mind.

"Are we to visit the National Gallery this afternoon," I asked him as we finished our lunch. "It seems clear that this Olga Stone and her gang intend to make off with this painting, sooner or later."

"That is a possibility, certainly. There may be others."

"Shall I get our coats?"

"I will get one of mine, in a little while."

"You are going alone?"

He nodded. "If you recall, this woman, if she is indeed the same, has seen you before."

"Of course," I conceded.

"If this is the woman you saw at Foley Grange, we cannot risk her recognising you and becoming aware of our involvement," Holmes reiterated after a few moments of thought. "She has not seen me, but as a precaution I will go in disguise."

With that he vanished into his room, to emerge remarkably soon as a rather dignified older man who could easily be thought of as a student of the old masters.

"Well, Watson," he said in a voice most unlike his own, "I think this will be in keeping with the sort of gentleman you would expect to find spending his afternoons viewing portraits and landscapes. What do you say?"

"As usual, your new appearance is faultless."

He made a final appraisal of himself in a mirror. "It should serve. I will see you at dinner, when I hope to know much more."

After I helped him into the coat he carried, which suited well this new character, he picked up a gnarled and twisted walking-cane and was gone in an instant.

I spent the entire afternoon consumed by medical matters. First I completed the task of writing up my notes on several patients who suffered from persistent conditions, after which I retrieved the latest edition of *The Lancet* from my case and studied an article on an instance of scarlet fever which had unaccountably arisen in the north of Scotland. I knew that dinner time was approaching when the aroma of food crept in on my concentration. Soon after, the door slammed and I heard Holmes' footfalls on the stairs.

"Did it go well?" I asked the elderly gentleman who entered.

"It did indeed," he replied in his normal voice. "I perceive by the sounds and smells from the kitchen that Mrs. Hudson will soon be serving dinner. When we have fortified ourselves, I will elaborate."

He entered his room hurriedly, the door closing heavily behind him. I heard water being poured, and minutes later he was back restored to himself. A knock came at the door and he opened it to admit our housekeeper bearing a veal and ham pie large enough to satisfy both our appetites. After we emptied our plates and I had finished off a good helping of plums and custard that Holmes refused, our good lady brought a full coffee pot and we sat in conversation with the table between us.

"I must congratulate you, Watson," he began when our cups were full. "The woman in the National Gallery is indeed she who you recognised from Lestrade's photograph. This gang appears to roam the country in search of criminal opportunities, as with Squire Foley and Mrs. Evangeline Cutts. They must have a network of underworld contacts to alert them to whenever and wherever a suitable situation arises, for how else would they choose their victims? Be that as it may I watched her for a good while, at first while openly admiring another nearby work of art and then from concealment. She sat as Constable Mullins described to Lestrade, her eyes rarely straying from the picture and her position unmoving."

"Curious, that nothing seems to have changed since the constable first noticed her. I cannot imagine what the gang hopes to gain without making an attempt at theft."

"That I have yet to discover, old fellow. There was an air of expectancy about her at all times. She is quite plain, with no singular feature save a rose tattoo on her right palm. In the rare moments when she looked away it was as if she anticipated an imminent intrusion, since her glance settled briefly on both entrances to that room repeatedly. That someone is to meet her there at an undetermined time I am quite certain. I can see no other course at present, but to continue my observation in the hope that it will be soon."

I nodded, thoughtfully. "A pity that her current place of residence is unknown to us."

"Watson, you surely cannot think me so obtuse as to have neglected to discover that? I followed her, when she eventually left just before five o'clock. She is at the Nelson Hotel, near Charing Cross. I had no way of discovering whether any of the rest of the gang are staying there also since, with the exception of the bearded man whom Lestrade identified as Alexander McIrwin, they are unknown to me. Doubtlessly they will reveal themselves as we progress. For now, there is one more observation that I will share with you."

"Please do so." I drained my coffee cup and he did likewise.

"In the picture, the Roman goddess wore a necklace which was, as one would expect, of a most intricate and unusual design. Olga Stone, if that is the name she now uses, wore an identical one. This is no coincidence of course, but further evidence of the gang's meticulous advance planning. I am of the opinion that more than simple theft is their intention here."

"Most curious," I said again. "But what could be the object of that? Could they in some way be using the necklace as proof of a claim of ownership to the picture? Otherwise I confess to being confounded."

"As do I," Holmes admitted uncharacteristically. "But with a little perseverance, the waters may yet become clearer."

Chapter Nine – The Impressionable Victim

For the next eight days, Sherlock Holmes maintained his observation of Olga Stone. Every morning he would quickly consume a light breakfast before leaving for the National Gallery in the guise of an eccentric artist, a schoolmaster, a very elderly professor and – one of his standard characters - a befuddled priest, among others.

I became used to his returning to our rooms daily in such varying states, shortly after I had arrived there from my practice, and to the abrupt shaking of his head to signify that nothing new had occurred that day.

Then came the afternoon when he surprised me by appearing earlier, and still more by greeting me with a smile that bore a trace of smugness. I restrained my eagerness until he had shed his disguise of the day, that of a retired colonel, and we had eaten to our satisfaction.

"It is quite apparent, Holmes, that today has been different," I began when the coffee cups had been cleared away and we had repaired to our armchairs. "Your demeanour leaves me in no doubt. I do not need your considerable powers of observation to deduce that you have made some progress."

"Was it so obvious, Watson? You are right, of course. At last our investigation begins to move forward."

I leaned forward in my chair. "I am delighted to hear it. Allow me a moment to retrieve my notebook, and then I would be grateful for a full account."

"Which you will dramatize considerably and with your usual skill, I have no doubt. Very well, old fellow, I will relate the events of today as I remember them." He spent a moment in recollection as I waited with my pencil poised, then he began. "The first hour or so passed as all those before. The woman sat staring at the picture, and occasionally at the entrances, while a scant procession of the viewing public came and went. Then, quite suddenly, a sizeable brute with a straggling beard burst in on us as I pretended to scrutinize a nearby portrait of a pre-revolutionary French nobleman. With him was a much younger man, no more than twenty years of age I would say, to whom McIrwin, to give him the name that Lestrade supplied, pointed out 'Minerva in Repose' and began to elaborate on the skilfulness of the artist. I was surprised at how quickly the young man became fascinated with the picture, until I realised that he was a most nervous and impressionable fellow."

"If he was the intended victim," I ventured, "those qualities may well have been useful to the gang."

"In retrospect, I believe they were ascertained beforehand. Also, the days of waiting are explained, since the meeting had to be arranged in advance and its timing could not be guaranteed. From their conversation, I learned that the goddess in the picture closely resembles the younger sister of McIrwin's companion. She was a delicate girl who died of consumption late last year and the young man was hopelessly devoted to her. Presently I began to perceive the nature of the gang's intentions. Olga Stone took no part in the discussion, but altered her attention from the picture to the young man so that he could not fail to notice her. McIrwin practically had to drag him away eventually, such was his reluctance to leave. There can be no doubt of his intention to return to the picture soon. In fact, I expect him tomorrow and my surprise will be infinite if he does not arrive."

I put my notebook aside. "Did you discover the identity of this young man? It seems most likely that he must be someone of importance or of considerable wealth."

"It was for this purpose that I followed the pair from the gallery. Near Trafalgar Square they separated, McIrwin boarding a landau that appeared and the young man hailing a hansom. I did likewise and pursued him to Mayfair, where he has apartments. After he entered, a conversation with the *concierge* proved most illuminating."

"You discovered something of significance?"

"Several things. To begin, the young man is Henri Champonnier, the heir to a Parisian jewellery concern with branches in London. Though afflicted with a nervous disease and seemingly of little self-confidence, he is here to investigate the possibility of further representation. Possibly this is because his father wishes proof of his abilities. His twin sister, Monique, did indeed die of consumption and Henri was and is affected greatly by her loss, since they were inseparable."

"This gang then, is taking advantage of his vulnerability to somehow get their hands on some of the family's wealth."

"Precisely. It seems certain that they will attempt to create in Monsieur Champonnier some form of dependency upon them. How this will be accomplished, I have yet to ascertain."

"So you will continue to observe Olga Stone, in the hope of a further meeting with Champonnier?" I ventured.

"From his behaviour another liaison is a foregone conclusion, and that it will be tomorrow I am quite certain. I expect to learn much that will advance our enquiries."

#

Holmes departed later than before, the following morning. But first, after a breakfast of ham and eggs which he consumed in haste, he repaired to his room to quickly reappear as a one-armed ex-soldier.

"Things have begun to proceed satisfactorily, Watson," he said in his normal voice, "and as I have said, I am confident that this will continue today. I feel that some slight celebration would be appropriate, so what do you say to dinner at Simpson's? Pray tell Mrs. Hudson that she need not provide for us this evening, and I will meet you there at six o'clock."

"I will look forward to it. But Holmes, you surely will not attend in your present guise? Truthfully, I would find it embarrassing."

He laughed, the expression appearing strange on his altered features. "That never occurred to me, old fellow, but now that you have mentioned it I am tempted to do so in order to observe your behaviour." I believe he enjoyed the effect of this on me for a moment or two, before explaining. "You will recall that I keep several rooms across London, where I maintain a wardrobe and other necessities. A quick visit to the nearest of these will restore me to a respectable state in time for our meeting."

With that he was quickly gone, and I looked over the front page of the early edition of *The London News* before leaving a note for our housekeeper and setting off for my practice. The procession of patients that day offered nothing out of the ordinary, heavy colds and rheumatism being predominant, and the time passed slowly. I was glad to finally shut up my surgery, but I had almost two hours before my appointment with Holmes. I decided to smoke a pipe and examined for the last time a story of one of his adventures, before submitting it to my publisher. This completed, I pronounced it satisfactory and posted it in a thick envelope on my way to Simpson's.

The hansom delivered me to the door a few minutes early, but an enquiry revealed that Holmes was already waiting at a table on an upper floor. From the stairs, I entered a room of marble pillars and tall plants set in exotically shaped vases, a little breathless after my exertions. I had not thought to change my clothes as we were dining early, so it was with some self-consciousness that I saw he was clad resplendently in evening wear. No doubt this was because of my remark this morning which, I knew, he would not have forgotten. He rose as I approached.

"Watson, my dear fellow."

He greeted me, as was often his custom, as if much time had passed since our last meeting. From his enthusiasm as we shook hands, I deduced correctly that his activities this day had held no disappointments.

"It went well then, as you expected?" I asked as I took my seat at the opposite side of the table.

"It did, and what of your patients?"

"Unremarkable, all of them."

He smiled, knowing, I think, that I was both curious and anxious to hear of his progress.

"I see that a waiter is rapidly approaching. Are you ready to order now?"

"Of course," I said. "I confess to being more than a little hungry."

What followed was a superb meal appreciated, not surprisingly, more by myself than my companion. We had finished glasses of an excellent dessert wine, when he finally began his tale.

"I was right, of course," he said suddenly. "Monsieur Henri Champonnier did indeed reappear."

"You seemed extraordinarily confident of it."

"Had you seen the effect that the first sight of the picture had upon him, you would doubtless have reached an identical conclusion."

"But what came of it? I presume he was accompanied by McIrwin again."

Holmes shook his head. "No, but the woman was waiting. She was apparently transfixed by the picture as before and, after staring at it in like manner himself for a time, Champonnier sat not far from her and adopted a similar attitude. I will attempt to recall the conversation between them:

"Do not think me forward, sir," the woman ventured presently, "but I see that you share my fascination for this work of art. Pray tell me, if you will, has it any special significance for you?"

His answering look was suspicious, and his voice trembled. "The goddess is the image of my departed sister."

"I cannot believe it!" Her feigned surprise was most convincing, but a lesser effort would easily have sufficed. "You are he for whom I have been searching, for many months."

"What can you mean by that? Were you acquainted with Monique?"

"Not at all. Yet I know much of her. We have spoken many times, and she mentions you often with affection."

He studied her, curiously. "But you have stated that she was unknown to you. How can this be?"

Her reply was masterful, not least by its timing. After allowing a few moments for him to dwell upon his confusion, she explained. "I have received communications from the hereafter. Do not think me mad when I tell you that I have seen and conversed with the woman who was the model for the picture you see before you. She lived in the seventeenth century, her name was Fabienne Gerault, and your sister was a reincarnation in likeness and spirit."

"You surely cannot expect me to believe...." Monsieur Charponnier had leaned towards her, half-humorously, but now he drew away. "Are you then a spiritualist, someone who earns her living by speaking with the dead? I have always believed that those people are charlatans who profit from the desperation of the bereaved."

"I am no such thing. I have no connection with any such practice. These visions came upon me suddenly and without my bidding. I was told from the beyond that you would one day join me here, as I sat before the picture that is the image of Monique

Champonnier, if I exercised patience. I had faith, and it came to pass."

"No, it cannot be. I, too, would have been given a sign." He shook his head violently, in torment and confusion.

"But you have. I was instructed to make a pilgrimage to Paris, not to a church but to a place that I was shown. There I discovered a necklace which I purchased, this that I wear now. You will see that it is the same as that worn by Fabienne Gerault, in the picture. That was when I became convinced that the voice I heard in my head and the visions that came to me in the night were not madness, but real."

"That is a fantastical account, Holmes," I retorted as I realised that he had finished his recollections, "but it surely cannot have met with success. There are many such deceptions practiced in London these days, intended to defraud the gullible and broken-hearted. This is clever, but not the most ingenious I have heard. Some of my patients have related similar tales that are more convincing by far."

A grim smile altered his expression briefly. "But you are forgetting the disposition of the victim. Did I not say that this gang is meticulous in its planning and that its prey is carefully selected? Also, consider the necklace that had to be made in strict adherence to that in the picture. These people leave little, if anything, to chance."

"So Monsieur Champonnier was chosen not only because he is of a rich family, but because his insecure nature makes him susceptible to criminal schemes and unlikely suggestions?"

"Precisely. Anyone of a more steadfast disposition would have been much more difficult, or even impossible, to convince."

"We have experienced a similar situation before. I recall Lady Heminworth, who was tormented by a scoundrel who exploited her sensitive nature and beliefs."

"Quite so. There is usually a cold and callous mind behind such schemes. However, all that is necessary now is to find McIrwin and his associates and inform Lestrade of their whereabouts, but it must be done after the crime is committed as he himself implied. I fear that the young man will take it badly when his hopes for reunion with his sister are dashed."

"Did more transpire, before they parted today?"

"Almost all the remaining conversation consisted of Monsieur Champonnier reminiscing about his childhood with his sister and their later experiences together. I formed the impression that they were allowed few freedoms and had little contact with others of their own age. Hence their devotion to each other that bordered on obsession, and the ease with which this was used to cause him to believe what would normally be a ridiculous concept." After a moment, my friend added. "Olga Stone listened sympathetically of course, although I saw boredom cross her face several times. Nevertheless, she asked appropriate questions which were well-timed, and contributed more fiction to deepen her plausibility."

"You followed them, afterwards?"

Holmes nodded. "As I am now aware that Monsieur Champonnier resides in Mayfair, I had no need to pay him more attention. I pursued Olga Stone hoping she might lead me elsewhere, perhaps to others in the gang, but she returned to her rooms as before. However, they have agreed to meet once more tomorrow and I shall be in attendance."

#

Holmes returned much later, the following afternoon. Today he had concealed himself behind the guise of a retired naval captain, which he shed on his return.

Neither of us had any appetite that day, and so Mrs. Hudson had agreed to defer dinner for an hour or so. I had just finished a pipe of a Turkish mixture that had been recommended to me, and my friend lit up a cigar as we took our seats before the unlit fire.

"I perceive, Watson, that you have stood in the street near your practice, in conversation with an elderly grey-haired man who badly needs the attention of a barber," he said after scrutinizing my appearance.

"Good heavens, Holmes!" I retorted in surprise. "How could you possibly know that?"

He leaned back in his chair and blew out a ring of smoke, laughing at my perplexity. "Allow me to tell you how I spent my day, old fellow, and it will become clear to you."

"It appears that you have progressed further. I have my notebook, and you have my full attention."

"The conversation at the National Gallery went much as before, except that I had an unshakable feeling that I had somehow been discovered. When the pair left together I followed at a distance but worked my way nearer among the crowds in Trafalgar Square. I heard Monsieur Champonnier give his Mayfair address to the hansom driver, so I knew he was returning to his home as before. Olga Stone, having been left alone, walked for a while, possibly to determine whether she was observed, and then summoned a hansom of her own. I was fortunate inasmuch as I was standing near a tobacconist's at the time, for a hired brougham let off a passenger who entered the shop. Immediately, I replaced him and received a suspicious look from the driver when I instructed him to pursue Olga Stone's hansom which was by now almost out of sight. The man complied however, when I explained that he would receive an extra half-sovereign if the journey was completed successfully and undetected. He proved a quite competent temporary alley."

"Did you discover the whereabouts of other members of the gang?"

"Regrettably not. In fact I would swear that the hansom slowed down at times to allow us to catch up. I became worried and still more convinced that she was aware of my presence when the route taken was at first an erratic one, and absolutely certain when we approached Kensington and the street where your practice is situated."

I looked up from my notebook, shocked. "That is where you saw me?"

"Indeed. I imagine you had just closed your surgery for the day and chanced to meet a friend or patient nearby as you left."

"Exactly so. The man you have described is Mr. Francis Martland, who I have known for years. Despite his age he has an immense appetite and is one of my healthiest patients, since he requires my attention rarely." I put down my pencil as Holmes ground out his cigar. "Do you think this was coincidence that her hansom passed there?"

"I believe such things happen less than occasionally, as I have said before now. I fear more may come from this. It was most certainly a warning."

"To desist from our investigation?"

"Of course. I suspect that something in my movements may have been similar, from one disguise to another, for I seriously doubt that it was my appearance that aroused her suspicions. From there the hansom went straight to Charing Cross, and I saw Olga Stone leave it outside the Nelson Hotel."

"An expensive ride," I observed.

"With an unnecessary diversion."

Throughout our delayed dinner and during our conversation over brandy sometime later, I could tell that Holmes was distracted. Many of his thoughts, I have no doubt, were occupied with the investigation, and how he should now proceed. Several times I made suggestions, which were either politely refuted or met with a silent look of disapproval.

The evening wore on, and the hour drew near when I could decently excuse myself from my morose companion to take to my bed. I was about to rise and wish Holmes goodnight, when, out of the silence, the door-bell rang.

"A client," I speculated as we looked at each other in surprise, "at this hour?"

"Not for the first time." Holmes stood up quickly and went to the door to shout over the stair-rail to Mrs. Hudson, telling her that she should retire as he would attend to our caller himself. Moments later I heard footsteps on the stairs and he returned with an elderly lady who was clearly in some distress.

"A client indeed, Watson," he said. "But for you, not I." He turned to our visitor. "Pray be seated. Perhaps a brandy would help to settle your nerves as you consult with the good doctor?"

"No, no thank you, sir, for there is no time to lose. I have come to ask Doctor Watson to accompany me back to my home where my husband has been taken ill. I fear that he may be dying and wanted to call a cab to take him to hospital but he was most insistent that I call upon you. Please, come with me now. I have the cab waiting."

I looked at her sharply, for I sensed something more to this. "First, who are you, madam? I do not recall you as a patient."

"Indeed I am not, but my husband has long been so. I am Bertha Martland, and it is my husband Francis who is in grave need of you."

"This is the gentleman of this afternoon?" Holmes interrupted.

"The same. I must get my bag."

"I will accompany you."

"Holmes, there is no need." I replied with unnecessary firmness.

"As I mentioned earlier, I have little belief in coincidence."

Chapter Ten – A Warning

The dark streets were relatively quiet at this hour, and we found ourselves in Kensington before long. The house was a terraced building of the type usually considered to be the accommodation of the working classes as indeed this was, but the interior was spotless and well-maintained. Mrs. Martland took us through a dimly lit hallway to a parlour where her husband lay on a low chaise-longue clutching his stomach.

At my touch, he opened his eyes. "Doctor Watson, thank God."

"What has happened to you, Martland? How did this come about?"

"I took my wife to The Silver Crown," he gasped between sucking in great gulps of air, "for dinner. As we got home I felt as if my insides were on fire, and it's getting worse. Help me, please!"

"Open your mouth." As he did so I pressed a spatula onto his tongue. There were dark patches there and on the inside of his mouth, and his breath smelled strangely.

"Poison?" Holmes said from behind me.

"Definitely. We must induce vomiting, immediately."

I made to turn my patient over, but his body convulsed in a great heave and was still. An agonised expression was frozen on his face and his eyes had lost all animation. My stethoscope confirmed the obvious. After a while I lifted a blanket that was draped over an armchair and laid it over the body.

"I am so very sorry, Mrs. Martland," I said sincerely.

"My condolences, Madam." Holmes added.

She stared at me unbelievingly, then at Holmes, then back at me. If I expected her to become hysterical I was in error, for she appeared totally unmoved. Quite slowly and calmly she sat down, and I recognised the symptoms of deep shock. Moments later she began to shiver, unconsciously drawing her shawl tightly around her body.

I went to the kitchen and made her some sweet tea, while Holmes spoke to her in a low, comforting voice. Not for the first time, I witnessed an aspect of his character that rarely manifested itself.

Mrs. Martland drank and put the cup aside absently, and for later use I gave her laudanum from my bag. I explained to her that it would be necessary for us to inform the police, because of the nature of her husband's death.

She nodded her understanding, and spoke in a toneless voice. "Of course. I will get a neighbour to sit with me for a while."

We took our leave after we had ascertained that this had been done and that the lady was as comfortable as could be expected. Fortunately we found a cab nearby, its drunken passenger having staggered into a house at the end of the street.

"She took it rather well, I think." Holmes said as we turned a corner.

"The full realisation will come to her later. I have left her a sedative."

"Let us hope that it will help. However, she was able to furnish me with a full account of tonight's events, while you boiled the kettle."

I turned to him, astounded. "You questioned her, already? Holmes, I would rather you had spared her feelings, for now."

"She was perfectly lucid," he replied in a voice of mild surprise. "In fact, her calmness and presence of mind were admirable."

A moment of silence passed between us, then I asked: "What did you learn?"

"Exactly what I expected to learn. Francis Martland was murdered by a member of the gang we are pursuing. As to why, I am as yet unsure. Probably it was a warning that they are close and observing us, or that they are not to be trifled with."

"Mr. Martland said they ate at The Silver Crown."

"I doubt if the food at the inn is responsible. As they ate their dinner they were accosted by a short, shabbily dressed man who said that Martland was an old workmate. Martland replied that he'd never seen him before, and the man apologised saying he'd made a mistake. The couple then continued their meal and put the incident out of their minds."

"And you believe that this stranger poisoned Martland?"

"Undoubtedly. Probably by using some sort of sleight-of-hand to insert the substance into his food. Mrs. Martland was quite sure that no other unusual incident occurred throughout the evening."

We said little else until we reached Baker Street. I had hardly paid the cabby and ascended the stairs, before my friend wished me a curt goodnight and vanished into his room. During the dark hours I lay awake and heard him pacing, as he does when baffled or unsure as to how to proceed. Eventually I slept again, and awoke with the sun streaming through half-drawn curtains.

Holmes finished a scant breakfast with a grim expression. Two letters lay on the table near my place, both envelopes bearing the handwriting of colleagues. I put them away in a pocket, noticing that Holmes' post was more substantial. A small pile of paper and another of torn envelopes had been discarded near his half-empty coffee cup, but he held one sheet separately.

"I feared something of this sort, Watson," he said, handing me the paper.

I took it without a word, in unpleasant anticipation.

My Dear Mister Sherlock Holmes,

You will have realised by now how near we are. We are watching you but have no desire to repeat the unfortunate demonstration of last night. It would be in the interests of yourself and your friend, Doctor Watson, to leave us to our business which can be no concern of yours.

This will be the only warning.

We are everywhere.

It was unsigned.

"Not a cheerful message," I observed.

"Indeed not. Watson, if it is at all possible, I recommend that you leave London for a week or two."

I shook my head. "Never. We stand together, as always."

"Very well." The warmth in his quick smile did not escape me.

"What do you propose now, Holmes?"

"Since subterfuge is no longer effective or necessary, we will go together to the National Gallery and wait. If Monsieur Champonnier appears, we will explain to him about how he has been deceived."

"And if Olga Stone should be there?"

He considered for a moment. "We cannot arrest her, because in the eyes of Scotland Yard she has still committed no crime as yet. It would be unwise, I think, to attempt to continue our observation of her. An alternative course then, would be to converse with her if possible to see what can be learned."

We left immediately and arrived at the National Gallery early. After finding a nearby alcove in which to conceal ourselves, we spent an uncomfortable three hours in a fruitless vigil.

"It was no more than a possibility, now that she is aware of us." Holmes said at last.

We had exchanged scarcely a word, our concentration fixed on the entrances throughout.

"Olga Stone must have warned Monsieur Champonnier to stay away on some pretext, and possibly made other arrangements."

My friend was suddenly still. "Perhaps, but I fear more than that. We will call on him now at his apartments."

The hansom that we found nearby was slow, and I could feel Holmes' impatience. On arrival in Mayfair he strode swiftly into the building and immediately entered into conversation with a slight, balding man who I realised was the *concierge* he had spoken of beforehand. Presently, money changed hands and Holmes returned to the entrance hall where I had waited at his request.

"Will Monsieur Champonnier see us?" I asked.

"He is not here."

I studied his face. "Is this what you feared, before we left the National Gallery?"

"It is a situation that I should have anticipated. Two men, claiming to be inspectors from Scotland Yard, left with him earlier, after insisting that he settle his bill. My friend the *concierge*

133

described them well. One of them was a heavily-set man with an untrimmed beard."

"McIrwin, doubtlessly."

He nodded. "So it now appears that whatever plans they had to swindle Monsieur Charponnier's company out of some of its assets, have been replaced by a strategy of abduction. Regrettably, his room has already been cleaned and re-occupied, making examination useless."

His explanation would have been of greater length, I think, but it was halted as I raised a hand and pointed. "Holmes!"

He turned and looked where I had indicated. Three burly men, clearly roughs, were crossing the road at a half-run and on a course to intercept us. They drew heavy clubs from beneath their coats and approached rapidly.

"You should have listened, Mister Holmes." The first of them, a brute with a scarred face, swung his club viciously. Holmes quickly stepped aside but was not quite quick enough, sustaining a glancing blow to the shoulder. At once, he awkwardly raised his cane and stripped off the wooden scabbard to reveal a gleaming rapier. He was slowed by his numbed arm, but with a practised movement he thrust his weapon through the hand of his assailant, who screamed and retreated leaving a trail of blood.

I knew that my friend had taken precautions against such an attack, and as a result of his urging I also had prepared myself. My walking-cane was weighted with lead, which I used to advantage by bringing it down hard on the arm of the second man before he could swing his bludgeon at my head. I heard the bone break as he collapsed, leaving his remaining companion rather less assured and allowing me a few seconds in which to draw my service revolver from my pocket. We advanced upon him and at the last moment he swept his club aimlessly before him, more in desperation than aggression. Then, seeing the hopelessness of his position, he turned to flee, but was smartly tripped by Holmes.

"Tell your employers, whoever they are, that I am disinclined to surrender to threats. You retain your liberty now, only to give them this message."

Defeated, the man turned and ran, followed by the others who retreated as best they were able.

Holmes sheathed his sword, so that he held a walking-cane once more, and we continued along the road cautiously.

"We were fortunate," I remarked, "to have escaped so easily."

"Indeed." He rubbed his shoulder. "I am slightly bruised, and you are unharmed, but they are rather the worse for it."

"I had expected our adversaries to be of a more sophisticated type, but those men were common blackguards."

He signalled a passing hansom. "They were not part of the gang, but merely hirelings. I doubt if they knew any more of this affair than my name."

"We should report this to Lestrade."

"I hardly think an incident of common assault would interest him, even a murderous one since we have nothing more of those three but a vague description to offer. A visit to the Nelson Hotel will establish whether Olga Stone is still in residence."

We arrived to find that she had left, earlier. It seemed that the gang had fled, possibly together, with Monsieur Champonnier as their prisoner.

#

Upon our return to Baker Street I examined Holmes' arm, despite his protests.

"Severely bruised and swollen, but no permanent damage. Perhaps a hot poultice would relieve your discomfort."

"I thank you for your concern, Watson, but your attentions are quite unnecessary."

"Its function is unimpaired?"

"Absolutely."

"Very well." Reluctantly, I closed my bag.

Mrs. Hudson knocked our door and entered at Holmes' bidding. She held out a salver bearing a single envelope. "This has arrived for you, Mr. Holmes."

My friend took it and viewed it suspiciously.

"It was delivered by hand?"

Our housekeeper nodded. "Yes sir, before you returned. About an hour ago."

"Very good. Thank you, Mrs. Hudson."

As the door closed behind her, he turned the envelope over in his hands. It was unmarked except for his name, written with an exaggerated flourish.

"Good quality," he murmured, "and costing no less than sixpence a packet. Let us see what it contains."

He tore it open and extracted a single sheet of paper which, I noticed, was of the same colour and thickness.

"Apparently, the gang took the success of their hired brutes for granted. Their failure at their task was not reported back."

I looked over his shoulder, and saw the single sentence. *Mr. Holmes, you were warned.*

"I doubt if our friends with the clubs were paid for their work," I said.

He smiled, grimly. "Failure most likely had its own consequences that they would have wished to avoid. This is not a woman's hand. McIrwin or one of the others in the gang wrote this." He held the paper up to the light from the window. "Aha! But he was careless."

I saw at once what he had discovered. The sheet was not complete after all, but had been cut from a larger page. The left bottom corner was not quite a straight edge, and the words "...ton Hotel" were almost invisibly embossed.

"Not expensively purchased, but courtesy of a hotel," I corrected unnecessarily.

Holmes leaned forward quickly, reminding me of a hound when restrained on its leash. "Indeed, it seems I was premature. Perhaps this will tell us something."

I anticipated his next action, by plucking a slim volume from the bookshelf.

"Thank you, Watson. *The London Guide to Hostelries* should assist us." He opened it and scanned the pages, before placing it upon the table where we could both see more easily. "I am working, initially, on the presumption that the gang would have secured accommodations within reasonable distance from each other. I fear that we will have to inform our good lady that we will not be in for lunch. Our starting point will be the Nelson Hotel, in search of any traces left by Olga Stone."

"But, Holmes..."

He dismissed my objection impatiently. "I am aware that it cannot be there that this letter originates, because that name does not match what remains of the wording upon it. However, the place is worth investigating and I should have done so immediately we discovered that the gang had taken flight. Now, I see that Charing Cross has six hotels in the immediate vicinity with titles ending in "ton": the Norton, Atherton, Bridlington, Ellerton, Haverton and Carrington. After visiting the Nelson, from which I do not expect to learn much if Olga Stone is the careful type of criminal that I believe, we will take these others one by one. If this strategy produces nothing, we will spread our net wider."

"We must hope that the *concierge* or the manager of each establishment will be good enough to furnish some assistance."

"Not at all, dear fellow. In each hotel all we require is a few minutes in the foyer, where the customized notepaper is normally on display for the convenience of the guests. Having found similar paper, we will then look for the embossing, if any, and the printing style. It is only when we have succeeded in identifying these that we will need to approach the staff."

At the Nelson Hotel we were fortunate in finding a manager that was agreeable to allowing us to visit the room formerly occupied by Olga Stone. We were *un*fortunate, however, in discovering anything that would assist us. Holmes commented that apart from learning that she used henna on her hair, that her shoes were recently purchased and that she suffered from frequent indigestion, he could deduce nothing. It was much as he had expected.

We then began what I anticipated would be an arduous trek through the hotels that he had noted. As it happened, I was pleasantly surprised when our fourth attempt proved successful. In the foyer of the tiny and slightly distasteful Ellerton Hotel I watched as Holmes examined the stationery, and felt relief at his grunt of satisfaction. We then approached the rather red-faced reception clerk, who looked at us vacantly while we explained our presence. When my friend had concluded his request, the clerk crossed the room to the bottom of the staircase and shouted until a tall, bespectacled man appeared. This was the hotel manager, who was opposed to recognising our description of McIrwin or allowing us to examine the room in question, even at the proposal that he should receive a half-sovereign for his trouble. However, at the promise of twice that sum he relented and accompanied us to the second floor where he left us, after specifying that we should stay no more than half an hour.

"We were fortunate," I observed, "that it was McIrwin who stayed here, since his was the only description we could offer."

"I was fairly confident that he would stay nearest to Olga Stone," Holmes replied. "As we progress, it seems increasingly certain that those two form the inner core of this gang. They are essentially partners-in-crime while the remainder, as Lestrade observed, are probably viewed as expendable and replaceable."

I watched silently, as Holmes conducted a thorough examination of the room. Sounds of movement reached us from below, but otherwise he worked in silence.

"Obviously suffers considerably with dandruff," he muttered to himself at length, "and is a user of cheap tobacco. After peering into the wardrobe and beneath the bed, he took out his lens and kneeled to study the edges of the room, particularly the corners. "Halloa!" He cried at last. "We have something here, Watson."

I watched as he plucked a crumpled ball of paper from where it had evidently rolled after missing the waste-paper basket. "What does it tell us?"

"To begin with, that this establishment is rather slow in attending to its rooms after guests have departed, but more importantly that McIrwin, perhaps accompanied by Olga Stone, has left London by train. This is a fragment of a time-table, with the train leaving at eleven fifty-five circled in ink. It therefore remains to determine which station was the departure point. Come, we will enquire of our friend downstairs,"

We descended to the foyer, to find the florid clerk admitting a rather shabby-looking guest who parted with some coins before accepting the key to a room and taking the stairs. Holmes approached the clerk and described McIrwin again, before asking him to relate what he could about the bearded man's departure.

"I carried the gentleman's bag sir, after flagging down a four-wheeler for him."

"And did you perchance give the driver a destination, or hear your guest give one?"

"I did, sir." Here he hesitated, until my friend produced a half-sovereign. "It was Victoria Station. He said he was off for a few days by the sea."

"Capital!" Holmes relinquished the coin. "Many thanks for your help. Come, Watson."

We found a hansom quickly and went directly to the station. Holmes strode onto the nearest platform and we stood examining the time tables that were pinned to a notice board near the station manager's office, while trains came and went behind us amid screeching halts and billowing smoke.

"This, I think, is what we seek." With a long forefinger, he indicated the eleven fifty-five London & Brighton Railway train that left daily. "It stops twice on its forty-seven mile journey, but I believe we will not be unreasonable if we conclude that Olga Stone, McIrwin and however many accompanied them travelled to the terminus."

"Because the terminus is Brighton, and the hotel clerk mentioned McIrwin's comment about spending time by the sea?" I ventured.

"Precisely. You improve constantly, Watson."

From there we returned to Baker Street, and spent some time smoking before Mrs. Hudson served an excellent dinner.

"We have an advantage," I remarked when we had once more settled in our armchairs, "in that our pursuit is unexpected."

Holmes amazed me by laughing, as he knocked out his briar and put it aside. "Oh, Watson, have you not realised? We are being led by the hand by people who know my methods only too well, no doubt from a study of your literary efforts."

"My dear fellow, what can you mean?"

"Does it not seem to you, all too convenient? Part of the name of McIrwin's hotel 'accidentally' left at the bottom of the letter? The ball of paper containing the clue which led us to the Brighton train? You will recall that no indication was present at the Nelson Hotel, because that was not where we were to be led. It was not part of the trail we were intended to follow."

"Good heavens! We would have walked into a trap."

Holmes shrugged. "It is a situation we have faced before. We will play their little game, but we must be prepared for our adversaries to act first and at any time."

I resolved to check my service revolver again later, before taking to my bed. My friend's deduction that our pursuit was expected did not lie easily on my mind. We talked for an hour or two, Holmes diverting my attention and anxiety with excursions into various subjects, as was his custom. Finally, although he appeared unaffected, I felt the arms of sleep reaching out for me and rose to bid him good night.

"Sleep well, Watson," he replied. "We do not know what tomorrow may bring but, as always, old friend, we will face it together."

I nodded my agreement, and went to my room feeling a curious pride and pleasure.

Chapter Eleven – A Closer Encounter

It was a measure of Holmes' concern that he took an additional precaution from the first. With breakfast over and our landlady notified of our intended absence, we put on our hats and coats after ensuring that we were armed.

"Very well, Watson," he said as he looked down upon Baker Street. "From this window I will see the first hansom that delivers its passenger nearby. I will take it only if the cabby is of my previous acquaintance. When I am on my way to Victoria Station, you must follow but, as I have advised you before, having taken neither the first nor the second carriage that presents itself. I do not know the extent of the reach of this gang - we are aware that they know where we reside, so I cannot rule out the possibility of an attack at the outset." His posture altered suddenly. "Ah, but three hansoms have arrived and among them is my transportation. Tucker is an ex-army man who knows London well, and his cab awaits a new fare not far along the street. Take care, old fellow, observe all that is around you before you venture forth. I will meet you on the second platform shortly."

With that he was gone. Moments later I watched as he climbed into the hansom and disappeared from sight. No other hansom followed. I let ten minutes pass, carefully observing the outside scene as he had instructed. When I stepped into the street it was probably with exaggerated stealth, and I searched my surroundings for any sign that I was under scrutiny. I saw nothing and began to walk slowly, suspicious of every passing cart and coach. Very soon, a hansom paused alongside me, touting for a fare, but I kept my eyes to the front and strode on. When this happened a second time I felt the cabby's stare as he waited for some acknowledgement, but I ignored him also. I was fortunate in that the third hansom that came to a halt just ahead was carrying a man whom I knew slightly, and I therefore deemed it safe.

The station master's office was surrounded by a small crowd as I arrived. I glanced around me but Holmes was nowhere to be seen, until he appeared suddenly quite near to where I stood.

"You were not followed, Watson. From concealment I observed the entrance constantly, and it is certain that we are safe for the time being."

We repaired then to the overcrowded waiting room, where we continued for some time to observe the constant flow of waiting passengers and those alighting.

After a while I consulted my pocket-watch. "The next train to arrive will be ours," I remarked as I heard the first noises of its approach.

Holmes nodded. "We are still safe, but we should board quickly."

The train hurtled into the station, its brakes screeching. We hurried aboard, my friend having purchased the tickets previously.

"This way, Watson," he called over his shoulder as he preceded me along the corridor. "I have reserved a smoker."

We entered the compartment and he quickly closed the door behind us and drew down the blind. After placing our bags in the overhead rack we sat down opposite each other, and it was only then that he appeared to relax his caution. I said nothing as he sat with his head held to one side, listening carefully to the snatches of conversation as other passengers noisily moved along the corridor.

Finally, he seemed satisfied. "I do not think we were followed. Or if we were, we have certainly eluded them."

"Do you think our precautions were necessary? I saw no sign of any pursuit."

"Nor did I, but we must not underestimate this gang or their unscrupulousness. Let us not forget Foley Grange."

I could not dispute this, and took the issue no further. After the guard's shrill whistle, the train began to move.

"Brighton is forty-seven miles south of the capital," Holmes said then, "so our journey will not take long."

"How do you propose to trace these people, once we arrive? I cannot imagine that the local force is aware of every stranger in the district."

He leaned back in his seat. "Unless I am greatly mistaken, they will somehow accost us. We are following their trail according to their intentions, and I have no doubt that we will be observed as we find a place to stay. Remain vigilant therefore, at all times. Undoubtedly their plan is to murder us or take us prisoner, but to accomplish either they must reveal themselves."

"This is placing us in great danger," I retorted.

"Not for the first time," he said lightly. "We are no strangers to that, are we? Truthfully, Watson, it did not occur to me that you would pay it any mind."

My concerns evaporated as I realised that he had paid me an immense compliment by taking my services and my courage for granted. With a knowing smile, he then launched upon a series of observations and conclusions based upon the passing countryside and, not without difficulty, I listened.

He had concluded his oratory and lapsed into a short silence, by the time we reached Brighton. The signs announcing that we were nearing the station flashed past and then went by more slowly as we came to a halt.

We alighted and surrendered our tickets, and Holmes' earlier caution returned. I glanced around constantly but could see nothing but people from the train embracing those who waited for them on the platform, while others made off alone and silent. No one appeared to be observing our arrival.

"Through here." Holmes had led me away from the surging crowd and along the platform to its extremity. A rusty iron gate stood unattended and he opened it for us to pass through. Outside, we found ourselves confronted by a long lane overhung by leafy branches at both sides. The traps, dog-carts and hansoms that awaited arriving passengers were being quickly engaged, but Holmes placed a restraining hand on my arm.

"No, Watson, do not hail any of them. This fellow standing beside the landau near the entrance seems to be watching for us."

A tall young man, reminiscent of an undertaker by his dress, approached us. "Have I the pleasure of addressing Mr. Sherlock Holmes and Doctor Watson?"

"You have indeed," my friend replied.

The stranger took off his hat and bowed, with an air of relief. "I am John Leech, here to convey you to your destination."

Holmes and I looked at each other in surprise.

"And where is our destination, Mr. Leech?"

He looks at Holmes with a furrowed brow. "Why, I was told it was to be Mill House."

"Who gave you such an instruction?"

"The owner, Mr. Avery. I was told to meet every London train until I saw someone matching his description of you gentlemen. I have been here for hours."

"You are a local man?"

Mr. Leech threw out his chest proudly. "Born and bred, sir."

"You are to be commended for your patience." Holmes glanced at me again. "Very well, let us be on our way."

To my astonishment, he said nothing more and raised no questions or objections. We allowed our bags to be taken and put aboard the landau, which Mr. Leech drove away the moment we were seated.

"Holmes, this is an obvious trap," I said in a whisper so that our driver would not hear.

"Something of the sort, undoubtedly. Do not let your hand stray far from your revolver."

"Who can this Mr. Avery be?"

My friend shrugged his shoulders. "McIrwin probably, or one of the gang. Apparently, they no longer feel any need to conceal their plan of deliberately attracting us here. We will know more when we arrive at this Mill House, but do not drop your guard for a moment."

I spoke more quietly still, nodding towards Mr. Leech. "Do you think our new friend is in league with them?"

"He strikes me as an honest man. Nevertheless, we shall see."

The lane and the surrounding fields were soon left behind, and we had our first glimpse of the sea between the growing number of houses. After some narrow side-streets we came suddenly upon the long promenade. Traffic was slight, and I was able to pick out the Grand Hotel and the Metropole Hotel from the long row of impressive buildings facing the ocean. In the opposite direction, white-tipped waves lashed repeatedly against the sea wall and I heard the forlorn cries of gulls hanging motionless above them. We passed the West Pier where many people took leisurely exercise, and several statues that I did not recognise looked expressionlessly down at us. Not long after I saw the Brighton Palace Pier, extending from the shore like a long finger and with sellers of hot potatoes and chestnuts clustered around the entrance.

Holmes broke the long silence. "Have you been here before, Watson?"

"Never, this place is new to me."

"I was concerned here with a case of mistaken identity once, sometime before I made your acquaintance. It was a trifling affair, soon resolved, and I had almost forgotten about it. This place has changed little since, I think."

I saw that the promenade had now been left behind, and the buildings overlooking the sea were vanishing into the distance. Mr. Leech took us down a road with few houses, where trees and long expanses of grass were increasingly frequent. We turned onto an overgrown track with patches of rocky ground and eventually came upon a river.

"I believe it is known as the Whalesbone," Holmes said as if he'd read my thoughts.

The path and the river curved here, and a blackened, ruined building came into view. Much of the roof had long since crumbled, and the remains of a great water wheel hung awkwardly in the swirling torrent.

"Hence it is called Mill House," I observed.

"Not so," Holmes corrected. "Unless I am mistaken, the house is further on."

I peered in the direction that he had indicated and saw a long crumbling structure near the edge of a forest. As we drew nearer it was clear that whatever disaster had overtaken the mill had also struck here. The wings did not appear to be in a collapsed state, but most of the windows were gone and grass had grown tall around the door. Only the middle of the two-storey building, around the front entrance, appeared to be intact and showed signs of habitation. The landau came to halt in a small uneven courtyard that was overgrown with weeds in many places, and we alighted.

Holmes addressed Mr. Leech. "What occurred here, do you know?

"I do not, sir," he said from the driver's seat. "It happened before my lifetime. To me it has always been of this appearance, and deserted. I have never heard it spoken of."

My friend let his eyes pass over the house, before he spoke to Mr. Leech again. "Are you well acquainted with Mr. Avery?"

"Why no, sir. Until he approached me and paid me in advance at my pitch on Brighton sea-front, I had never seen the gentleman. His instructions were to meet you at the station and bring you here, nothing more."

"What of his appearance?"

"I recall little except his bushy beard, and that he was of a forthright nature."

"I see. Are you to wait for us?"

"It was never mentioned, but I received the impression that you were both to stay."

Holmes and I exchanged glances.

"It is a rather desolate spot," he pointed out. "If you would be so good as to wait, it would be better."

Mr. Leech touched his top hat. "I will let the horses drink and then return here to wait until I hear from you."

We thanked him and struck off towards the house as he jumped down from his seat and led the beasts towards the river.

"As I suspected, our Mr. Avery is McIrwin," Holmes confirmed as we avoided a clump of thistles.

"Further proof, if any were needed, of the intention to lure us here," said I.

We stood before the main entrance now, a massive iron-studded door of stout oak.

"We will not be using this door, I think." Holmes said.

I saw his meaning at once. Here too, vegetation had sprung up and grown high. In addition, layers of earth or dust had piled against the steps and wooden frame. The door, I could see, had been secured with iron staples.

"I would speculate that many years have passed since anyone entered. It seems to have been sealed, probably when the house was abandoned." I turned to my friend. "What awaits us here, Holmes?"

"That we will shortly discover, I have no doubt." He walked slowly along the front of the house, and I followed closely. "So, there must somewhere be…" He stopped suddenly. "Aha! This is where they gained entry. You see the disturbance in the gravel underfoot, and that the service passageway nearby has long since lost its door and been boarded over at a later time?"

"The planks are certainly not aged, and the nails are shiny and new."

He smiled briefly. "Excellent, Watson. You will have realised then, that whoever preceded us here has left, unless there is another entrance. I suggest we take a turn around the building, to establish this."

This we did immediately, and my impression of a dilapidated stone structure, beset by neglect and decay, was intensified. The rear of the building seemed to be in semi- darkness because of the closeness of the forest, and set in the walls were several empty plinths with their fallen statues in fragments on the ground below. We discovered three wide windows which Holmes

149

examined with his lens, only to confirm that the frames had not been disturbed for many a year.

"There are no other means of entry or exit," he confirmed as we regained the front of the building. "It is of course possible that the gang left someone behind to await our arrival."

"They were confident that you would follow them here."

"This is the work of someone who believes that he is sufficiently familiar with my methods to make predictions. I cannot but confess that he has been partially successful." He looked around us and reminded me once more. "Keep your weapon to hand, Watson."

With that, he tore away the planks covering the narrow passage that was the only entrance that we had been able to discover. Drawing his weapon, he advanced cautiously. As I followed I chanced to look up to a window on the upper floor, to see a crow perched and watching us like a sentinel. I had the fanciful notion then, which I quickly dismissed from my mind, that the bird was some sort of harbinger – a warning of evil to come.

We progressed slowly along the corridor, I imagined it to be originally a channel for delivering goods, or possibly a servants' entrance, with glass and stone fragments crunching under our boots. We froze into stillness abruptly, startled by birds fleeing from the naked rafters at our approach. To either side of us were doors, each hanging from its frame to reveal the strewn contents of rooms long disused. We peered into each in turn, not progressing further until we had ascertained their emptiness.

"This passage continues right through the house," Holmes observed as he stepped over a fallen beam. "There is a final corridor to the left."

With heightened caution we reached the corner and he peered around it. He became very still, studying the interior of the chamber beyond. He turned to me and nodded silently. Only then did we step forward.

Filtered sunlight streamed in from tall, discoloured windows. Cobwebs hung from chandeliers and from the fireplace, with dust much in evidence except where it had been disturbed by movement. Near the centre of the room was an old but well-preserved table with a baize-covered top, partially hidden by shadow. Dimly, I could make out faded portraits adorning the walls, while rusting breastplates and weapons were displayed above every doorway. Moments of silence passed then Holmes, having evidently decided that it was safe to proceed, pulled one of the ragged curtains back to its fullest extent and more light flooded in.

"Clearly, the gang used this room, possibly as temporary accommodation."

I was about to concur, but instead was shocked into silence. The shadows had receded to reveal two men sitting at the table, playing cards with coins scattered haphazardly around them. They sat statue-still, with expressions of great surprise frozen upon their faces.

"Good afternoon, gentlemen," Holmes broke the silence and his voice echoed faintly around us. They made no acknowledgement and did not move. For long moments, he scrutinized them, before we put our weapons away.

"How long since their deaths, Watson?" He asked.

I approached carefully and peered into each face in turn. I was able to make only a cursory examination.

"Less than a day, I would say. There is as yet no smell from them."

"And the cause of their deaths?"

"There is no indication of a wound of any sort, no blow or penetration is evident. I would say, supported by the shocked expressions, that a quick-acting poison was administered."

Holmes nodded. "That is my conclusion also. Again we have a demonstration of this gang's thoroughness, since the drinking vessels have been removed so that we may not determine the nature of the poison. However, they have not been so careful with their footprints."

At this he examined carefully the patterns in the dust. Speaking quietly to himself occasionally, he retraced our steps to the door before slowly recounting his observations.

"I am ignoring our own traces, which fortunately are mostly separate. Here is where five people entered the chamber, and here where the chairs were pulled back and two were seated." Pointing, he walked around the table. "This is where the remaining three stood briefly, probably serving drinks to the card-players. Then one of those remaining walked towards the wall, leaving some confusion which I will turn my attention to presently, and the last two returned to the door and left." He stopped to examine these footprints more closely. "Of these, one is certainly a woman, since the narrowness of the boot and the apparent style suggest it, while her companion, by the breadth of the imprint, is a heavily-built man. I believe, Watson, that these two, having disposed of their comrades, are what remains of our opponents."

"Unless more are added to the gang."

"Of course." He hesitated, but then his face lit up. "But I have missed something! What is this?"

While speaking he had walked slowly across the room, altering the angle from which he viewed the bodies. From his new position he had seen something that he now retrieved from a dead hand that had fallen into its owner's lap. It was an envelope, which he slit open with a thumb-nail. It contained a single sheet bearing but a few words that he held so that I could read:

Mr. Sherlock Holmes,

We give you these three.

"Three?" He questioned.

My eyes had adjusted, and I now saw the furthest parts of the room more clearly. My glance swept over the opposite wall and I was suddenly still.

"Holmes.....!"

He turned his head to follow my indication. Before one of the other doors was a dark, dry pool. Undoubtedly, it was blood.

"It appears as if their remaining comrade was wounded. He passed through that door, possibly attempting to escape the fate of the others. There may, however, be another explanation."

"Perhaps he still lives." Before he could say more I grasped the handle and wrenched the door open, too late to heed my friend's warning.

"Watson, no!"

I beheld for an instant the wreckage of another chamber. I had a glimpse of mouldered walls and collapsed floorboards below a sagging ceiling, surrounding a figure pinioned to a fallen beam by a knife protruding from its chest. The face was distorted in agony and the body drenched in its own blood, a scene that was immediately blotted out as rafters and slates came crashing down and my friend snatched the door from me and slammed it closed. Clouds of dust obscured our visibility like the fogs we were accustomed to in London, and we held onto each other as we stumbled, coughing, from the room. In the passage it was clearer, and we managed to stagger towards the open air struggling to breathe.

"What was that?" I asked Holmes when we were able to speak again. "What happened?"

"That little surprise was intended to bury us," he said as we began to slap the dust from our coats. "One of the gang, apparently McIrwin, had propped up the fragile ceiling with a number of fallen beams, which he arranged so that their only support would be pulled away when the door was opened. Then the first beam would dislodge the second, the second the third and so on, until the entire upper structure collapsed. The blood and the body of course, were the means of directing our attention to the trap and arousing our curiosity sufficiently to spring it. I must apologise, old fellow, for not realising what we were confronted with until you pulled the door open. I had a momentary view of a rope attached to the inner handle."

"If we had rushed into there, it would have been the end of us."

"Precisely their intention." He took me by the arm. "Come, let us seek out Mr. Leech."

More steadily now, we walked over to the waiting landau. Mr. Leech looked astonished at our appearance.

"Gentlemen, what has befallen you?"

"We experienced a rather unfriendly reception," my friend replied. "Pray take us to the local police station."

Presently we arrived at the town hall, the lower storey of which was the police station. Mr. Leech left us with a few coins from Holmes in his pocket, and after a short conversation with the desk sergeant we found ourselves in the cramped office of Inspector Barton.

"What has happened to you?" he asked brusquely after we had introduced ourselves and were seated.

Holmes related all that had occurred at Mill House, while the inspector listened in silence.

"Rather dramatic events for a stranger to the area to come upon, would you not say?" he commented as Holmes concluded his narrative.

"I have furnished you with an accurate account. My friend here will confirm it."

I nodded. The inspector was elderly and rather bent in stature. His attitude seemed to me rather smug, and I quickly formed the opinion that his retirement was near and that he was reluctant to exert himself.

"We have heard of you here, Mr. Sherlock Holmes," he said then. "I, myself, have read newspaper accounts of your interferences with Scotland Yard investigations and marvelled at their tolerance of you. I imagine that this gentleman," he gestured in my direction, "is responsible for the sensational literature portraying your exploits in the penny dreadful magazines?"

I felt myself growing hot with anger, but Holmes' voice was perfectly calm.

"As far as I am aware, none of those publications has featured my cases. As for Scotland Yard, I confess to having been of some trifling assistance from time to time."

"Perhaps you have, but I hope you are not intending to spread alarm within our town, with all this talk of murder."

Holmes sighed. We were not unfamiliar with officials of this temperament. "You have only to visit Mill House, to verify all that I have said."

"And what is the purpose of your presence in Brighton?"

"As I implied, I am here in the course of an investigation."

"With the authority of Scotland Yard?"

"Not on this occasion."

"I thought not. Very well, as you have made a statement I am bound to look into it. I will send a constable who will report presently. Until then I ask you to remain within these premises."

"That is outrageous, sir!" I retorted. "We are not criminals!"

Inspector Barton gave me a hard look, but Holmes spoke before he could retaliate.

"I would be grateful if you would extend our confinement to the nearest coffee shop or tea room, as we have not eaten since breakfast. Also, a telegram to Inspector Lestrade of Scotland Yard might reassure you as to our trustworthiness and validity."

This, I saw, made an immediate impression. "Very well," the inspector said again, "but you must remain nearby. I shall require you for a further interview, on the constable's return."

#

A short while later, we found ourselves taking coffee at a convenient establishment situated a short distance from the station. We had consumed a light lunch during which little was said.

"I am at a loss to understand why our adversaries found it necessary to cause us to journey to Brighton, in order to attempt to rid themselves of us," I remarked then. "Surely it would have been simpler to make such arrangements in London."

Holmes shrugged. "On that score we can only speculate. It may have been that another of their crimes was recently committed here and the gang met to arrange the division of the spoils, or perhaps Olga Stone and McIrwin's plan to reduce their number to two was designed specifically and in advance with Mill House in mind. It could be that our demise was planned at the same time, for the sake of convenience. My first thought was that the primary purpose was to induce us to leave the capital, but since their entire number, such as we know it, was evidently present here, I concluded that this was unlikely. There may, of course, have been additional or different reasons for this."

"Olga Stone, or perhaps it is McIrwin, seems intent on taunting us with the messages that accompany their activities."

"Thereby supplying us, intentionally or unintentionally, with further clues and incentives. They may well be paving the way to their own downfall. There is, however, a little more to be untangled here, yet."

"That inspector fellow will not prove helpful," I said as I pushed away my cup.

"I wager he will be a changed man, when he has spoken to Lestrade," Holmes smiled. "You observed how he received my suggestion that he send a message to the Yard. He seeks confirmation of his attitude towards us, but their reply will surprise him. I do not think we need to concern ourselves."

I nodded, as I peered beyond him. "Holmes, a constable has just entered the room. From the way he is examining the appearance of every diner, I think he may be looking for us."

My friend glanced over his shoulder and raised a hand. The constable approached at once.

"Mr. Sherlock Holmes?"

"Indeed."

The young man seemed uncomfortable. "Inspector Barton requests your presence back at the station, sir."

Holmes nodded. "Kindly tell the inspector that we will be with him in a few minutes."

With a polite acknowledgement, the constable left us.

157

"Inspector Barton has not fared well with Lestrade, I fancy," smiled Holmes, "and has taken out his anger on that young man. Also, notice how he now 'requests' our attendance, rather than orders it."

We returned to his office, to find Inspector Barton hurriedly filling in forms behind a pile of files which had been placed on his desk. He looked up and beckoned us through the open doorway, before inviting us to resume our seats with a polite gesture. From his expression, I deduced that he was greatly humbled.

"It appears," he avoided our eyes, "that I was hasty, gentlemen…"

"Has your constable returned from Mill House?" Holmes asked to interrupt the forthcoming apology.

"He has, sir. It was just as you said. I have made arrangements for the bodies to be transported to the mortuary, and for further examination of them."

"Excellent. The inner room will also need to be cleared."

"Instructions have already been issued. Also, since we have no indication that the pair whom you described as responsible have left the town, our constables will be on the look-out. Our detective force is small, but they will comb all likely areas. Be assured, gentlemen, that if they are still in Brighton, we will find them."

"I will be sure to tell Inspector Lestrade of your prompt action, when we return to London."

"I am obliged to you, sir."

#

"You can be surprisingly forgiving at times, Holmes," I said as our hansom drew near to the station. "That man's rudeness did not sit well with me."

He shrugged. "Once our credibility was established, the inspector acted in a satisfactory manner, I thought. It may be that his efforts will be rewarded with the capture of Olga Stone and McIrwin, but we cannot be sure that they have remained here. If they have made their way to the capital ahead of us, we may soon hear from them again. If that should happen, Watson, we must be ready."

Chapter Twelve – The Anxious Priest

So began, on our return to Baker Street, another few months without anything more of this affair. I returned to my practice, while Holmes was concerned with a number of cases which he later described as "trifling" or "insignificant". When I attempted to extract some details from him, I was met with the reply that none were worthy of my attention, or of publication, and he would say no more. During this period we saw little of Inspector Lestrade, save when he called to inform us of a single development. A corpse, he informed us, had been recovered from the Thames. Although the effects of weeks of exposure were apparent, Holmes identified the remains as those of Monsieur Champonnier. The only comment my friend made, on his return from the mortuary, was to the effect that the unfortunate Frenchman had probably become a threat to the gang, as he could readily identify both Olga Stone and Alexander McIrwin. Shortly after came the events which I have related elsewhere as "The Adventure of the Silent Sister", which Holmes swiftly brought to a successful conclusion. It was after a discussion of this case over breakfast one fine spring morning, that our housekeeper announced a new client.

"The Reverend Carlton Manfred, gentlemen."

Holmes rose and replied as she ushered in a stocky man in a dark pea-coat. "If you would bring us tea, Mrs. Hudson, I would be much obliged."

Our visitor was shown to an armchair, leaving his hat on a side-table. I saw that he wore a clerical collar as his occupation demanded, and put his age at about thirty. Long sideburns adorned his face, enclosing a rather sparse beard that was hardly discernible because of its light colour.

"My thanks to you for admitting me, although I have made no appointment," he said.

"No matter, sir." My friend bowed politely. "I am Sherlock Holmes, and this is my friend and colleague, Doctor John Watson."

"I am exceedingly glad to make the acquaintance of you gentlemen." The Reverend glanced briefly in my direction. "It was after reading an article in a periodical that I decided to consult you, Mr. Holmes. I have already been to Scotland Yard, but they would not agree with me that a crime has been committed."

"Perhaps it may turn out differently here," Holmes said as I rose to admit Mrs. Hudson with the tea tray. "But first let us have tea, and then you shall tell us all."

We sat and drank for a few minutes, saying little. When the cups had been emptied and replaced upon the tray, the reverend seemed settled.

"Pray tell us then how we can assist you," Holmes began. "I assume that your difficulty, whatever it may be, has arisen since your visit to India no more than a few months ago."

"Why yes, it was shortly after my return to England that...." Reverend Manfred ceased to speak and became still as confusion filled his face. "Mr. Holmes, how in the world.... Have we been acquainted previously, sir?"

"I do not believe so. But please do not look so astonished. I am not a wizard, but I learn much from observation."

I had seen Holmes cause such amazement many times. It was a small demonstration of his abilities, intended to instil faith in his clients and, on occasion, to provide him with some amusement.

"I do not see how you could have learned such things, for I have not referred to them as yet."

"No, indeed, but your appearance proclaims them."

Our visitor's eyes narrowed. "How so, sir?"

161

Holmes allowed himself a faint smile. "When I see a man wearing a signet ring embossed with a character of Hindu script, and his skin bears a brown tinge that would not yet have paled had his return from a tropical country been recent, I am forced to the conclusion that he has been in England for some time and that the country concerned was India. There is, you see, no mystery attached to it after all."

Enlightenment crept across our visitor's face. "Of course, I should have seen it at once. But how clever of you to notice, Mr. Holmes."

"The appreciation of details is often of much use, in my profession."

"Of course," the reverend repeated. "Of course."

"Then please, what is it that troubles you?"

Reverend Manfred cast his eyes downward and became quiet, as if searching for a place to begin. I made to offer a word of encouragement, but was instantly silenced by a gesture from Holmes.

"As you say, Mr. Holmes," our visitor began, "I returned from India about six months ago. I had lived there for two years, having felt the call to devote my time to the work of a missionary. Before that I served as a parish priest wherever the need was, usually at churches on the outskirts of the capital. This was after qualifying for my profession at Oxford, where this narrative should really have begun."

"Take your time, dear sir. Assemble your thoughts and recollections in their proper order and relate them accurately. Pray be precise as to details. There is no need to hurry."

"I thank you for your patience, gentlemen." He paused and, I thought, concentrated on expressing himself clearly. "At that time, during my studies, I became very close to four others who were similarly disposed. In fact, we spent so much time together that we were often jokingly referred to as 'The Band of Five' by our classmates. After completing our preparations and venturing into the world we corresponded regularly, and celebrated together when it became known that I had been accepted for a missionary post."

"Was this communication maintained, while you lived in India?"

The reverend nodded. "I received many letters during the first year, but after that they dwindled slowly. Finally I lost touch with my friends altogether, and my further attempts to encourage a response went unanswered. However, when I decided to return to England, I resolved at the same time to seek them out."

"May we know the reason for your return?" I asked.

"Of course. It came about that I had established a firmly rooted congregation in the south of Rajasthan. I knew that it would continue to thrive of its own accord, with the blessing of our Maker. Therefore, I was about to write to the church authorities to request a new post – I had for some time harboured a desire to answer the challenge that Delhi represented – when, quite unexpectedly, I became filled with a longing for England. Day and night I thought of her green fields and the coolness of a spring shower. Feeling thus, I wrote instead to the bishop, with whom I had a passing acquaintance. He was most understanding and saw to it that arrangements were made. I met my replacement briefly, before setting sail for home."

Holmes' eyes were half-closed, and Reverend Manfred saw this and looked at me questioningly, as often happens when my friend's attitude of deep concentration is misunderstood. I shook my head and made what I hoped was a reassuring gesture, a signal that he should attach no importance to this apparent disinterest.

"Naturally it took me a week or two to rearrange my life, after my arrival in the capital. When the day came that I learned I had been assigned to a new parish, I was overjoyed."

"The post you hold to this day, I assume?" Holmes ventured, without opening his eyes.

"Indeed. I now serve at St. Alvar's in St. John's Wood. I have been most fortunate."

"I am glad to hear of it, but pray continue."

"When things were settled, I realised that I had a full week before taking up my new duties. I seized this opportunity to renew my association with my former colleagues who had also been my friends, but I received a strange reception. I knew from our correspondence that they had taken to meeting regularly on the first Monday of each month in a room near St Uriah's, the church to which one of them, Reverend Godfrey Collett, had been assigned. I arrived and passed through the outer door without difficulty, thinking that my appearing unannounced would be as a pleasant surprise for them, but I was sadly disappointed. The inner door, a stout barrier with metal bands, was firmly locked so that I had to strike it with my walking-cane to attract the attention of those I could hear within. All sound ceased suddenly, and it seemed a long time before the door was cautiously opened a few inches. Godfrey admitted me to the others with a look upon his face that could have shown no more astonishment had I been a ghost. I was concerned at this, as I had fully expected my friends to surround me and to shake my hand one after another. Instead I was met with a cold indifference such as I would never have expected them to possess. The situation quickly worsened. I was viewed constantly with mistrustful, suspicious glances and some of my questions went unanswered. They spoke little to me and in whispers to each other, so that I felt surrounded by a conspiracy from which I was excluded."

"Did you make any attempt to discover the cause of this curious change in their attitude?" I enquired.

"I did, and several times, but after a while their rejection of me became so plain that I could bear it no longer. I asked, then pleaded with them to enlighten me if I had caused offence, or unwittingly been the instigator of any distress. Their replies were given in grudgingly few words, and the room seemed to turn colder as their acknowledgement of my presence became increasingly remote. Nothing would change them, and I left the place heavy of heart and hopelessly confused."

Holmes' eyes snapped open and he spoke in a gentle tone: "Reverend Manfred, you may believe me when I say that I sympathise greatly with you over the loss of your friends, and with the uncertainty that has attended the situation. However, you yourself have stated that Scotland Yard can discern no crime, and with that I must concur. I cannot see how, on this occasion, we can be of assistance to you."

"But, Mr. Holmes, there is more to this. A short time later, on the thirteenth of the month, news reached me that Godfrey Collett had been killed."

"And how did that come about?"

"He was hit by a passing horse and carriage, as far as can be made out, on his way to his church in the morning."

"An accident?"

"So it was believed, at first. The official force held no great hope of tracing the coach, since the incident was not witnessed. At the funeral, the remaining three of my former companions continued to ostracize me. I saw no more of them, but on the thirteenth of the following month another met his end."

At once, I saw Holmes" expression change. His eyes glittered as he recognised an aspect of the Reverend's tale that interested him.

"How did that occur, pray?"

"He was struck down in the street, after conducting the evening service."

"And robbed?"

165

"Not at all."

"At what church did he preside?"

"St. Thaddeus at Marylebone. He was the Reverend David Northman."

"And what did Scotland Yard make of that?"

"They would say only that their enquiries into the matter are continuing. I do not expect any result."

Holmes nodded. "Do you attach any significance to the fact that these crimes happened on the same day of the month?"

"Because the number thirteen is considered unlucky? I am aware of no connection."

"Did you attend the second funeral?"

"I did. It was no different."

"Is that the extent of the tale? But no, there has been another thirteenth since the second death, and I perceive from your demeanour that you have something else to tell us."

The Reverend Manfred closed his eyes for a moment, as if beset by a spasm of pain. "I wish it were the end, Mr. Holmes, but sadly you are correct. The Reverend William Fowke, of St. Bernard's, Woolwich, died then."

Holmes and I looked at each other. Scotland Yard could surely not have overlooked this.

"Surely it is clear that these are deliberate and calculated acts. What did Scotland Yard conclude on this occasion?"

"I pointed this out to Inspector Lestrade in no uncertain terms, but he would not have it that the situations held anything criminal. He held that the Reverend Collett being hit by a carriage and the Reverend Northman being attacked were separate incidents, and insisted there was no evidence to suggest otherwise."

Holmes smiled thinly. "And the death of the Reverend Fowke?"

"That was dismissed entirely. He fell down a flight of stone steps while returning from the bell-tower adjoining his church. He was in the habit of inspecting it after the ringers had finished their practice and left. Inspector Lestrade said there was no need of an investigation, since he had never seen a more obvious accident."

"His approach does not vary. Common factors, such as the date and the profession of the victims in this case, are invariably significant. Can you remember, Reverend Manfred, any similarity shared by your former friends but not by yourself?"

Our visitor spent several moments in consideration. "Only that I always felt that they took the entrance into the faith too lightly, compared to myself. Do not take this as a boast, gentlemen, for I assure you that is not the case. From my early years I was always a scholar, whereas each of the others had, as I formed the opinion from fragments of many overheard conversations between them, been at some time involved with the police. They were guilty of but mild breaches of the law as I understood, and the Church is forgiving. You will see however, why I sometimes felt that they had entered the profession as a refuge."

"That is most significant. Considering your account as a whole, are there any other unusual occurrences, or is there anything else that you wish to tell us?"

"Perhaps two things, but they can have no bearing on what I have told you."

"Pray let me decide that."

He reddened, and caught himself immediately. "My apologies. Of course you know your own business best. I was

167

referring to the fact that a grave was disturbed, the night before Reverend Collett's death, at the churchyard of one of the others of the four, Reverend Bulmer of St Silas, Kilburn. The earth had been mostly replaced, but it was obvious that there had been some interference. The incident was forgotten, with the events of the following day."

"Do you know whose grave it was?" Holmes enquired after a moment.

"It was that of a Mrs. Beth Eddicott, who had died two days before. A local woman, but unknown to me."

"And the other fact that you were about to mention?"

"Simply that my former friends seemed less dependent on the collection box, than previously. It is always hard to make ends meet as a priest, even with lodgings provided, yet my friends no longer showed such concerns. When I made a tentative enquiry as to this, David Northman replied that a priest soon learns to live a thrifty life, before directing our conversation elsewhere."

"Most interesting," my friend remarked. "But tell me, what has been done about the churches vacated by your deceased colleagues? Surely, replacement priests must be tending the flocks by now?"

Reverend Manfred looked surprised at the question, but answered immediately. "There are indeed temporary replacements, at both St Uriah's and St Thaddeus. As for Reverend Fowke's church, St Bernard's, I understand that it is closed at present."

"And there was no police investigation there, you have said?"

"None. My suggestion of foul play was, as I have mentioned, dismissed."

"Thank you. Watson and I will go to Woolwich when this interview is over."

"I will be pleased to accompany you."

"Please do not trouble yourself. There is no need."

"Then I will send a telegram to Mrs. Cowper, who lives in a nearby cottage and cleans the church regularly, requesting her to admit you."

"Capital! Now, Reverend Manfred, there is one other aspect of all this that we have so far neglected to discuss."

A confused expression flitted across his face momentarily, then his expression brightened. "The last of my companions!"

"Precisely. You stated that there were four."

He acknowledged this with a grave movement of his head. "The final one is the Reverend Mark Bulmer, of St Silas Church, Kilburn. That is where the grave that I referred to earlier was disturbed."

"And," Holmes added, "the thirteenth of this month falls one week from today."

#

Having concluded the interview and sent the good reverend on his way with a promise to inform him of the result of our enquiries, we partook of a luncheon of curried fowl before taking a hansom to Woolwich.

At my request we made but a single stop, for me to dispatch a telegram to a young locum who had replaced me several times before. In the early days of his profession, he was eager for the experience of running a practice and, as the appearance of new cases was unpredictable, I often had no choice but to summon him at short notice if I wished to accompany Holmes.

On our arrival the cabby reined in the horse at Holmes' direction, and we alighted. St Bernard's was a church built of pale stone, with a tall and tapering spire. It was an aging, dull building, in much evident need of repair. The surrounding churchyard was disproportionately large, I felt, with headstones leaning at all angles and a single discoloured stone angel conspicuous among them. Not far outside the lynch gate stood a stone cottage such as the Reverend Manfred had described, and on approaching Holmes rapped on the door with his cane. The grey woman who answered filled my expectations exactly. She was well into middle age, dressed in a drab and well-worn frock, and wore an expression of sombre detachment. She produced the key at Holmes' request, and in a sad voice instructed us to ensure its return as we left.

We entered after some little difficulty. I closed the massive door of the church behind us, and a dusty atmosphere of decay closed in before the echoes died away. This was a place long neglected, cavernous and old. The tattered state of the Bibles set before the pews confirmed this impression, and the light filtered through the stained-glass windows in shadowy patches upon hollowed flagstones that showed the use of many years.

"This way, Watson!" Holmes strode along the edge of the nave, beneath a long colonnade. He stopped suddenly, and drew the key from his pocket at a door that was half-concealed by the tall statue of a church dignitary from a previous century. "This appears to be the only entrance to the bell-tower, since the outer door is boarded up."

After some wrestling with the ancient lock, he admitted us into the interior of the narrow steeple. The tiny occasional windows in the steep spiral gave poor illumination, so that Holmes was forced to pluck a candle from its holder on the wall and light it with a vesta.

I watched as he paused to inspect the masonry, about halfway up the uneven stairs.

"If only we knew where the Reverend Fowke began his fall," said I.

"It cannot have been above this point," my friend deduced, "since there are no hand-rails from here upwards, and therefore no wooden supports for them."

"I cannot follow your reasoning, Holmes."

He made no reply but began to examine the first of the supports on both sides with his lens, and to move slowly downwards. "If this was murder, and if it was carried out in the way that I suspect, then the supports will confirm this for us."

"Do you intend to examine all of them, down to the entrance?"

For a moment I again received no answer, then excitement filled his face.

"Halloa! What is this? Yes, Watson, it is as I thought. These hard stone stairs would certainly be the cause of the death of a man unfortunate enough to lose his footing here." He turned and held his lens to another wooden support, opposite the first. "And here are fine splinters, from the tiny holes and marks where the nails were withdrawn, afterwards."

"Holmes, I am still uncertain….."

"No matter." He put away his lens and began to descend, and I followed. "Let us leave this dreary place before I explain."

We returned the key to Mrs. Cowper, whose expression never varied as she mumbled in a way that sounded more like the reciting of a prayer than an acknowledgement. After a short walk we encountered a hansom and my friend gave our destination as the Church of St Silas, Kilburn.

"What did you discover in that bell-tower?" I asked him the moment we were settled. "Was the Reverend Fowke murdered?"

He nodded. "Most definitely."

171

"Did the murderer hurl him down that flight of stone stairs?"

"There was no need."

I looked at him curiously. "Explain yourself, Holmes."

"In order for him to be pushed down the stairs, he had of course to be accompanied." My friend held onto the door-handle to steady himself, as the hansom bumped over the cobblestones of a narrow backstreet. "As we have as yet no indication of that, I decided to look first for signs of some sort of device intended to fulfil the same purpose."

"That was the discovery you made on examining the hand-rail supports?"

"It was. A trip-wire or cord would be the obvious method of causing the reverend to lose his balance, and such things need to be affixed firmly if they are to be effective. The stonework being out of the question, the wooden struts supporting the hand-rail seemed likely. My search for the holes where tacks or screws had been inserted were hampered at first by evidence of woodworm, but the marks where they had later been wrenched out by pliers or a similar tool guided me."

"So the murderer sought to cover his tracks?"

"As it happened, there was little need, since Lestrade dismissed the incident out of hand. There can be no doubt however, that the holes left by the fixtures were made recently. You will recall that I remarked upon the powdered and splintered wood fragments caused by their insertion."

After this, he lapsed into a long silence. He remained deep in thought with his head upon his chest until we entered a street that I recognised.

"We are almost there, Holmes. The church is just ahead."

He roused himself instantly. Minutes later we were once more passing through a lynch gate, this time approaching a church without a spire but boasting the battlements of a fortress.

"A church of the Norman style," my friend observed. "Of a condition that appears to be no better than St Bernard's."

"They both seem in need of funds," I agreed.

Around us were numerous headstones as before, but here were also many new graves covered in fresh flowers. Holmes took in the scene but said nothing, and the door opened as we neared the building. A young man, balding prematurely and wearing the dog-collar of a priest, emerged and stood before us.

"Reverend Bulmer, I presume," said my companion.

"You presume correctly, sir."

"Allow me to introduce my friend and colleague, Doctor John Watson. My name is Sherlock Holmes."

"I believe I have heard that name," the priest said after a bewildered moment, "but the connection escapes me."

"I am, by profession, a consulting detective."

To my surprise the reverend's eyes narrowed instantly, and his expression became furtive. There was a moment of silence, broken only by the passing of a brougham along the nearby road.

"What then, concerns you here?"

"We have reason to believe that your life may be in danger," I informed him.

His brow became furrowed, but the wariness remained. "How so, pray?"

Holmes explained at length, about the significance of the forthcoming thirteenth of the month, and our suspicions.

"I was greatly grieved," said Reverend Bulmer, "by the deaths of my friends. I understood, however, that the official police force has dismissed any notion that consistent crime was involved, and I therefore foresaw no danger to myself."

"Our investigations strongly suggest otherwise. It would be as well to exercise great care, I think."

The priest became very still, and avoided our eyes.

"I thank you gentlemen for warning me, and I will take care, but in the end my fate belongs to God. If need be, He will protect me."

"Let us hope it proves unnecessary," said I.

As we turned to take our leave, Holmes pointed to the numerous new graves with flowers heaped upon them.

"There have been many deaths hereabouts, it seems."

Anxiety, or doubt, returned to the Reverend's face at once. "Lately, we have been besieged with funerals."

Holmes turned to him, thoughtfully. "I perceive from the open grave over there, that another is to take place soon. Pray tell me, who is the local undertaker. I fully expect my family to have need of him soon."

This was met with some relief. "My condolences on your loss. Most of the burials here and those conducted at several nearby churches are overseen by Mr. George Larrimer's funeral company, who make the coffins and all the arrangements. They are situated in Murton Road, which is just off Kilburn High Street. It is less than half a mile away."

Holmes expressed his thanks and we left.

"I do not understand," I said to him as we regained the street and walked briskly. "You have no family other than Mycroft, and you mentioned only recently that he is in good health."

"Quite so, but to invent a relative who has recently passed over seemed the easiest way to induce Reverend Bulmer to divulge the name of the undertaker. A short walk should take us to his premises now."

"But what do you hope to learn?"

"Perhaps the answer, or part of it, to this curious affair. Mark my words, Watson, there is more to this than we have seen, as yet."

Chapter Thirteen – The Mercenary Undertaker

We reached Murton Road and found the undertaker's premises, sandwiched between that of an ear-trumpet manufacturer and a purveyor of exotic snuff. It was of dismal appearance, the plate-glass window smeared and the doors in much need of a coat of paint.

We stood a few yards along the street, watching a hearse that had seen much better days emerge from a crumbling archway that, presumably, led to a yard at the rear of the building. The black horses were unsettled and the coffin was jolted often as it bumped over the cobblestones, before the end of the street was reached and it passed out of our sight.

"Why are we here, Holmes?" I asked my friend.

He studied the window, where we could see a shiny coffin being placed on trestles as a display, before answering. "Surely, Watson, you cannot have failed to notice the Reverend Bulmer's concern, on learning of my profession. This puzzled me at first, but I then became convinced by his evasiveness that he is somehow involved in all this. The beginnings of a hypothesis then began to suggest itself, and I tested it by remarking on the recent burials. On observing the effect this had on him, I became certain. Unlikely, I grant you, that a man of the cloth would have dealings with criminals, but it was our client who informed us that his former friends were once among them."

"You believe that this George Larrimer is part of some sort of plot, then?"

"That is probable, if my theory is correct. When all is clear to me, I will tell you."

We entered the shop, a sparse place containing little more than several coffins in the centre of the room and a battered desk in one corner. We were approached at once by an exceedingly tall man, as tall as Holmes but even thinner. His eyes were sunk in his head, and it crossed my mind that he looked not unlike a cadaver himself. His black frock coat appeared draped upon his body and his face was bloodless. Never before had I seen a man more suited to his profession.

"Mr. George Larrimer?" enquired Holmes.

The man bowed gravely. "At your service, gentlemen."

"We have been recommended to you by the Reverend Bulmer. An uncle of mine has recently passed on, years before his time, and it has fallen to me to arrange the burial."

At once a spark of interest flared in Mr. Larrimer's eyes. "A young man, do you say, sir?"

"No, but he was hardly past his youth. He died suddenly."

"My condolences."

"Thank you," said my friend with a sombre expression. "Clearly, arrangements need to be made. I would appreciate a list of your services and charges."

"Of course, sir. Of course." Mr. Larrimer stepped quickly away from us and returned with a printed sheet from a desk drawer.

Holmes and I had hardly glanced at it, before he said: "I presume that building in your yard is where the coffins are made, since work appears to be taking place in there?"

"Indeed. We use only the finest timber."

"I expected no less. We would like to see the craftsmanship for ourselves, if that is possible."

Mr. Larrimer seemed rather taken aback, as if this were an unusual request from one bereaved, but he recovered himself instantly.

"Certainly. This way, gentlemen, please."

We followed him to a structure of the sort that could have once been used as a communal wash-house. Inside, five men were hard at work sawing and shaping wood that did indeed seem of a high quality. Brass handles were ready on a bench, to be added to the finished coffins later, and the smell of varnish was heavy in the air. Holmes and I listened to Mr. Larrimer's commentary on how funeral arrangements were conducted, "a complete service" as he put it proudly. I noticed that Holmes' eyes were everywhere, and a satisfied smile crossed his features briefly. The atmosphere, no doubt because of the limited space and the profusion of sawdust in the air, was fast becoming oppressive, and I was glad when my friend was satisfied and we returned to the shop.

"What have we learned, Holmes" I asked when we had bidden good day to Mr. Larrimer with the assurance that he would see us again.

"Exactly what I expected to learn."

"I saw some fine work, and some stout timber, but nothing more."

"Not even the rather excessive piles of sandbags, stacked against the wall and partially hidden behind the carpenter's benches?"

"Now that you draw my attention to it, their presence was rather strange. I cannot imagine that those premises, being situated nowhere near a river, are vulnerable to flooding."

"Nor are they. The purpose of the sandbags is quite different."

He would say no more. We walked for a while, mostly in companionable silence, until I was able to hail a passing hansom.

"Are you willing to accompany me, later?" Holmes enquired suddenly as we made our way back to Baker Street.

I hesitated, as the horse swerved to avoid a coal-wagon near a sharp corner. "Of course. Do I not always?"

"After dark, in this district?"

"If that proves necessary."

The beginnings of a smile lit up his face for a moment. "Excellent. I thought I knew my Watson."

"We are to return to the undertaker's, then?"

"Indeed. I noticed the deep doorway of one of the old houses, opposite. It should conceal us well."

I nodded. "But what are we looking for?"

"A visitor who seems certain to appear, during the hours of darkness. That will be the final confirmation of my theory."

#

We reached our lodgings with an hour to spare until dinner. I immediately lit my pipe and picked up one of the several second editions that Holmes had delivered daily. He busied himself with his index, although he did not enlighten me as to his purpose, until a knock on our door announced Mrs. Hudson with our dinner of beef and vegetables. After we had dined and the remains of our meal cleared away, we reminisced about those of Holmes' cases in which I had participated some years ago. It was rare to find him in such a reflective mood, and I made the most of it in order to gain information for the publication of stories as yet unwritten.

At last the light began to fade and we once again took up our hats and coats. The hansom that retraced our route from earlier in the day halted, at Holmes' request, a few streets away from our destination. I reminded him that it was dangerous to be on foot here at this hour, but he seemed not to be concerned.

"While we were visiting Mr. Larrimer," he remarked as we passed a noisy public house, "I took note of the funeral schedule on his desk. There are two due to take place tomorrow, and that is why, if I am correct in my further supposition, someone will call at his premises tonight. If they do not, I will conduct a similar vigil for the next few nights, but I will not ask you to accompany me."

"I will nevertheless, if you will allow me. My desire to assist you is equalled by my curiosity."

"Capital! I expect tonight to solve the mystery of the Reverend Bulmer's attitude on learning of my profession however, and tomorrow to remedy the situation with the help of Lestrade. But see, we are here, and as the undertaker's premises and the street appear to be deserted, we can safely step into the shadows of this doorway."

"Is this somehow connected to the murders of our client's friends?"

"I believe it to be directly connected, but again it is something I have yet to definitely establish."

We stood for more than an hour, speaking only in an occasional whisper. Then a short man in a bowler hat appeared and made his way cautiously along the street, often looking over his shoulder nervously. From a foot away, I could sense Holmes' smile of satisfaction.

The man came to a halt outside the undertaker's premises. Warily, he peered up and down the street then, apparently satisfied that he was unobserved, he rapped upon the door with his fist. A few moments passed, during which he was never still but shifted his weight constantly from foot to foot. Then a faint glow appeared in the window, soon followed by a shadowy form holding a candle. The meagre light revealed the features of Mr. Larrimer, as he pressed his face against the glass. We heard the dull sounds of bolts being withdrawn, before the door opened briefly to admit the visitor.

"As I thought," whispered Holmes.

"Have you now seen all that you expected?" I replied, in my anxiety to return to Baker Street.

"Not quite, Watson. Our little drama has one more act to play, I think."

About half of an hour passed, with no further happenings. I heard Holmes' movement, as he inclined his head to catch a far-off sound that steadily drew closer.

"Now, we shall see."

Before I could ask for an explanation, a cart drawn by two restless horses appeared at the corner. At a string of curses from the driver, the beasts slowed to a trot until he reined them in outside Mr. Larrimer's shop. Instantly, the gates beneath the archway swung open and two long bundles, wrapped in cloth, were loaded from the undertaker's shoulders and those of his visitor onto the cart. After a minimal exchange of words, the bowler-hatted man climbed up beside the driver and the cart left, leaving Mr. Larrimer to close the gates.

"Holmes!" I exclaimed when all was quiet again, "Those bundles looked like...."

"Bodies," he finished. "There can be no doubt, now."

"But this is appalling!" I could not conceal my distaste. "Who was that, the undertaker's visitor?"

"His name is Nicholas Waldren," he replied as we left our place of concealment and began to retrace our steps. "He is well-known at Scotland Yard."

"What were his crimes?"

"Just as they are now. He is a body-snatcher."

We emerged from those dark and empty streets fully prepared for a long walk. Fortunately we had travelled no more than half a mile, before encountering a mud-spattered brougham which eventually deposited us at our lodgings.

"Clearly, you have correctly identified the significance of all that we have seen, Holmes," I said as I poured us each a glass of port, "but I am still somewhat in the dark."

"It is quite simple, old fellow," he said as we seated ourselves. "The Reverend Bulmer, and probably the other former friends of our client also, have been guiding their parishioners to entrust their dead to Mr. Larrimer's establishment. As you saw, the bodies were then sold to Nicholas Waldren who, in turn, will sell them to a medical practice or hospital teaching school for the purposes of dissection by students of the healing profession."

"But I understood that a law was passed, years ago, regarding this. Time was when only the corpses of condemned men were used in this way."

"Yes, indeed. But the 1832 Act did little to increase the availability of fresh bodies for the study of anatomy. Hence the demand is great, and Waldron and his like flourish. Strangely, the stealing of bodies is not considered a serious crime, in law."

"But it is revolting!" I retorted. "And yet the science of medicine must progress. Nevertheless, that men of the cloth should be involved is deplorable."

"Quite so. The reverend will doubtlessly forfeit his livelihood when this becomes known to the church authorities, and it will leave a smear on the memory of his deceased cronies. For now, we know that there are to be funerals tomorrow morning at St Silas' Church. We will attend one of them, I think."

I took our empty glasses and replaced them on the tray. "It becomes clear to me now that the sandbags were to replace the weight of the bodies in the coffins. Am I correct?"

Holmes nodded. "We have no means of knowing how many times this substitution has been carried out. As our client observed, his former colleagues have made themselves richer indeed, from Messrs. Larrimer and Waldron."

"Will the reverend be arrested tomorrow?"

"That depends upon the events at the funeral, and upon Lestrade when he is made familiar with the situation. Get out your black cravat in readiness, Watson. As for me, I will wish you goodnight."

#

After an early breakfast, which Holmes ate with indifference, we engaged a hansom to deliver us again to the churchyard of St Silas. We interrupted our journey once, for my friend to send a telegram of which he would give no explanation. It proved to be an overcast day, befitting a funeral, and a small crowd of mourners already awaited the arrival of the cortege as we arrived. Standing among them I saw no one I recognised or of any particular note, while Holmes seemed to have a passing interest in a group of young men, top-hatted and dressed in black, who arrived late and breathless.

Then the hearse appeared, with Mr. Larrimer himself sitting beside the driver, and the crowd parted to clear the way to the church doors. Four men who had been appointed as pall-bearers shouldered the casket and took it inside with appropriate solemnity. We joined the procession and soon found ourselves sitting in a row of pews where women were already weeping and men sat with their heads bowed in silent prayer.

"Pay particular attention to events immediately after the service," Holmes whispered, and I nodded my acknowledgement.

Reverend Bulmer entered from a side door, in a flowing cassock. He reminded everyone, I thought with unnecessary vigour, of our purpose here today before the organist began to play and the first hymn was sung. Holmes, I noticed, did not sing but mimed the words as his gaze swept the nave. The music ceased and the reverend began a short review of the life of the deceased, which he interrupted momentarily as his eyes fell upon Holmes and myself. He attempted to recover himself, but our presence had obviously disturbed him since he faltered several times while intoning the remainder of the reminiscences. Then came the eulogy, during which he kept his eyes carefully averted, before a final hymn and prayer.

It was then that a curious happening caused some confusion. No more than a few minutes after the pause for silent contemplation was over, the priest turned and left to lead the procession to the graveside. The pall-bearers stood to resume their roles, but before they could approach the coffin four young men, I recognised them as the group that Holmes had watched arrive earlier, rushed before them and carried it to the head of the departing crowd. The pall-bearers stood confused, amazed and shaking their heads at this effrontery. They shrugged and followed as the last of the mourners left the church, probably assuming that the arrangements had been accidentally duplicated.

The procession slowly made its way along the gravel path that led to the open grave. Reverend Bulmer maintained a dull monotone that was punctuated by murmurs of 'amen' from those following, several times. Then the cavernous hole yawned in front of him, and he stood aside as the casket was brought to its edge. I saw that two gravediggers had appeared a short distance away, leaning on their shovels in readiness, and was vaguely aware that a landau had arrived from the opposite direction and had been turned around.

At a gesture from the reverend the replacement pall-bearers stood poised above the open grave. As a new prayer was begun the coffin was quickly tipped, not lowered, into it, and the dull impact and splintering of wood reached my ears at the same instant that the pall-bearers ran past me and hurriedly boarded the landau. Before anyone could collect themselves the horses broke into a gallop, retracing their route towards the gate at the rear of the churchyard.

A wave of outrage and confusion swept through the crowd. Somewhat shocked, I looked around me at a sea of astonished faces. Of them all, Holmes alone seemed unsurprised. Then some of the mourners looked into the grave and a new murmur of disbelief passed among them. The smashed casket lay on its side, with sandbags spilled out onto the moist earth.

Reverend Bulmer's face took on an ashen pallor. More, I thought, because of what had been exposed than by the actions of the pall-bearers.

"It appears that Mr. Larrimer's establishment uses rather inferior timber, after all," Holmes commented in what I considered to be rather bad taste.

"What is happening here?" I asked him with some confusion.

"Seemingly, those fellows were determined to reveal to everyone that body-snatchers have been at work. The reverend looks quite perturbed, at such a shameful revelation."

"But who would know…" I turned to stare at him, aghast, as the realisation of it struck me. "Holmes! Are you behind this?"

He adopted an expression that was a picture of innocence. "I fail to see how you could have arrived at such a conclusion, Watson. However, I will concede that those four young men could have been the same, or friends of, the obliging crowd that assisted me at Briony Lodge, during the episode that you published as 'A Scandal in Bohemia,' some time ago."

"Of course." I clapped a hand to my forehead. "The telegram you despatched earlier."

"How was that unusual? You know well that I often find it necessary to despatch telegrams."

"But to what end?"

"Well, I should think that many of the mourners here today would register some sort of complaint to Scotland Yard, after witnessing such events. Indeed, I have seen already at least two elderly gentlemen leaving in a manner that leaves little doubt as to their immediate intentions."

"This will put Reverend Bulmer in a precarious position."

"Nevertheless, I will ask Lestrade to delay his arrest, as I have another use for him. Now I think we should seek somewhere that serves a good luncheon. Let us see what Kilburn can provide."

#

After we had each consumed a veal and ham pie and a cup of strong coffee, we made our way to Scotland Yard. When we found ourselves sitting in Inspector Lestrade's office once more, it became apparent that Holmes' supposition at the churchyard was correct.

"I have already received several complaints about an appalling display during a burial at a church in Kilburn," the little detective began. "Is it coincidence that you gentlemen were present?"

"It was in fact a side-issue, brought to our attention during a current investigation. It seemed likely that we had stumbled upon the activities of body-snatchers, and we attended the funeral in the hope of securing some sort of proof to present to you."

Lestrade's eyes narrowed, and he gave us a wary look. "That sounds like rather a long shot, if you don't mind me saying so. However, Mr. Holmes, I would be obliged for any names or information you could provide me with."

Holmes shifted in his chair. "A look into the affairs of Larrimer's Burial Services, of Murton Road, Kilburn, would not go amiss. He is in the habit of selling bodies that have been entrusted to him to Nicholas Waldren, whom you already know."

186

"Indeed we do. He has been up before the magistrate before now, for this sort of thing. I warned him myself, last time, that if he continued his little game we would take a more serious view. It seems he took little heed."

"I should tell you, Lestrade, that I strongly suspect that the priest, Reverend Bulmer, is also involved. However, I can furnish you with no proof of that. It may be that things will alter, as my investigation progresses."

"That is highly distasteful, for a man of the cloth," Lestrade's bulldog-like expression became more serious still. "But they are not above the law. We will interview him of course, but if we cannot act I will wait to hear from you."

In the hansom that returned us to Baker Street, it crossed my mind that Lestrade would never have allowed Holmes to participate in any official investigation, in those early days of mistrust. It was a measure of how the relationship between them had changed for the better, that he now did so.

During the days that followed, Holmes would say little to me of the affair, although it was in my mind often. One evening as we took to our armchairs to smoke, I could contain my curiosity and frustration no longer.

"Holmes, you are doubtless aware that Reverend Manfred's case is still unresolved."

"You refer to the fact that the murderer of his former friends has not yet been apprehended?"

"Surely, it was Reverend Bulmer who was responsible?"

"You astound me, old fellow." A smile momentarily played around the corners of his mouth. "What then, do you deduce as his motive?"

I considered for a moment. "It occurs to me that, assuming that the payments from the body-snatchers were shared among the priests, Reverend Bulmer could have contrived to receive the entire amount by his colleagues' demise."

"An interesting theory. But what do you make of the grave that was apparently disturbed the night before the death of the first victim, Reverend Collett?"

"I had quite forgotten about that," I admitted.

"According to our client, it was the resting place of a Mrs. Beth Eddicot. Do you see how this is connected to all that we know?"

"I confess that I do not."

"Then perhaps tomorrow, which is again the thirteenth of the month, will bring some clarification. If Reverend Bulmer is not, in fact, the murderer, then that is the date when he will become the final victim."

#

During most of the following morning, Holmes busied himself with correspondence. He despatched both a letter and a telegram to the French police, and a well-wrapped packet to Leverton, the Pinkerton agent. He assured me that neither of these had any bearing on our current investigation.

"Holmes," I began when I saw that he had finished and was consulting his pocket-watch to see if the time for luncheon was nearing, "something has just occurred to me regarding Reverend Bulmer."

"Pray enlighten me."

"Has it crossed your mind that, if he is indeed to be a victim, the murderer may strike during the daytime, rather than wait for the hours after dark?"

He smiled at my realisation, and nodded. "It is for that reason that I have engaged Barker, the private enquiry agent who I have used before, to keep the reverend under observation until two o'clock. At that time I will relieve him and, if you are agreeable, you can join me at St Silas later after evening service is concluded."

He said little more during luncheon, save for some comments regarding the political situation in Germany. Immediately afterward, he disappeared into his bedroom and emerged shortly, disguised as an elderly working man with a drooping moustache.

"I will arouse little attention as a bereaved husband of the working class," he remarked. "On the way to the church I must remember to purchase flowers to adorn whatever grave I choose to loiter and pray beside."

I wished him well and he raised a hand in acknowledgement, as he left the room and descended the stairs. Moments later, I watched from the window as he engaged a passing hansom.

#

Evening came and, with some apprehension, I watched the light fade. Apprehension had robbed me of my appetite, and I had so informed our housekeeper. When it was fully dark, I made my way to the churchyard.

As I passed beneath the lynch gate I saw that the only light was a faint glow from the stained glass windows. I followed the path with the vague and shadowy shapes of tombstones ever beside me, inducing a feeling of unreasonable disquiet. Presently, I stopped to listen. The silence was disturbed only by the fluttering of a bird in a vaguely discernible nearby tree.

"Watson."

Holmes" whispered voice came so suddenly that I was startled. A hand grasped my arm and led me into the shadow of a tall bush.

By the time my heartbeat had returned to normal, my eyes had adjusted somewhat to the dark. I could just make out his shape, and saw that he still wore the disguise, as when he left Baker Street earlier.

"I see from the light in the windows that the Reverend Bulmer is still here," I said to cover my surprise at his unexpected appearance.

"I attended the evening service, earlier, and struck up a conversation with one of the congregation who was good enough to tell me that the Reverend stays late every night, in order to prepare for the next day's worship."

"But Holmes, why are we here? What are we watching for?"

"All in good time, old fellow. First I must rid myself of this, now that the light has failed." He peeled off the moustache. "Be so good as to watch the church entrance, and call me instantly if anyone appears. I will be but a moment."

With that he disappeared into the darkness. I watched the doors as he had instructed me, but quickly glanced over my shoulder once. In the light of the rising moon I saw him remove the flowers from a nearby grave, and wash his face in the water from the vase. He replaced the blooms and removed his cloth cap and wig, which he placed in a drawstring bag from his pocket. Restored to his usual appearance, he was beside me again in an instant.

"Nothing has changed," I reported.

"If the pattern is continued we will see a development at midnight, at the latest."

"What are we watching for?" I asked again.

In the pale moonlight, I saw him turn to face me quickly, before returning his attention to the scene before us.

"For the murderer of the former friends of our client, of course."

"But I thought...."

"I know, Watson, that you believed the Reverend Bulmer to be responsible, but when I enquired as to where the disturbed grave fitted into your theory you could not tell me. Ask yourself then, why would the Reverend treat a grave in such a manner? Certainly not in connection with the body-snatchers, who took their merchandise directly from Larrimer's shop, and to be seen to participate in such an outrage, accidentally perhaps, would have done nothing to enhance his reputation. Also, it was apparent that the grave, although disturbed, was restored in a considerate manner."

"You believe then, that the murders are unconnected to the crimes of the four priests?"

"I believe that the murders were committed *because* of their crimes. They brought destruction upon themselves as retribution for selling their deceased parishioners to the likes of Nicholas Waldren."

I was silent for a moment, watching the church but with my thoughts in turmoil.

"Then *who* is responsible?"

"If my suppositions are correct, we will discover that before the church clock strikes midnight."

Little else passed between us for some time. Thus began a vigil that was certainly not unique in my association with Holmes but was, for me, possibly the most puzzling. In such situations as we had faced previously our adversary, or at least the nature of our adversary, was known or suspected. I was certain only that my friend had deduced an element in this affair that had hitherto escaped me.

After a while the scene brightened as the moon rose higher. A breeze sprang up and disturbed the leaves of the nearby trees, causing me to imagine that we were observed by small creatures of the night. The silence was absolute, save for the occasional cry of an owl or the chime of the clock in the tower, and for the infrequent passing of a hansom along the road. Each time, after the sounds of the horses faded, I expected to hear the approaching footsteps of whoever had been transported here, and I saw that Holmes too, had inclined his head towards the lynch gate, but to no avail.

"Are you armed, Watson?" he asked suddenly.

"Surely, as ever."

"And I, also."

We listened, as the clock chimed at each quarter-hour. It seemed an eternity had passed since my arrival, and I moved my position to relieve the onset of cramp, when the chime for a quarter before midnight rang out. A rabbit or rat, I could not see which, ran among the gravestones not more than a few feet away, and I turned my head involuntarily. At the same instant, Holmes gripped my arm and whispered.

"There, Watson, at last."

I saw that someone with a steady tread was approaching from the opposite direction, from the other gate where the 'pall-bearers' had made their escape.

A tall man drew nearer quietly, moving like a shadow. He carried something over his shoulder, and the moonlight glinted on an axe-head. In front of the church he came to a halt, and looked up at the illuminated windows. He hesitated a moment more, then took the axe by the shaft and, slowly and silently, opened the door and entered.

Chapter Fourteen – A Crime of Pathos

Holmes leapt out of concealment as the door closed. "Quickly, Watson, we must be in time."

Try as I might, I could not match his speed, and so it was through the door that he had flung open before me that I ran breathlessly into the nave.

We stood with our revolvers drawn, confronting a terrible scene.

Reverend Bulmer crouched with an arm held up in a hopeless defence. "No! No! Spare me! Spare me in God's name!"

His assailant raised the axe higher, preparing to deliver a blow that would have split the head of his victim. Candles, arranged to illuminate the area around the lectern, cast grotesque shadows.

"Stop!" Holmes cried. "Lower the axe at once, or we will fire."

The man obeyed, but did not discard the weapon. Instead he clutched it to his chest and moved slowly towards us.

"I am aiming at your heart," I threatened. "Do not come any closer."

To my surprise, Holmes spoke calmly. "That will not be necessary, Watson. Observe his expression."

I did so, and was astounded to see tears streaming down the man's face. The axe rang against the floor and lay where it had been dropped, and the hands that had held it were placed over haunted eyes. His despairing sobs echoed faintly around the cavernous nave as he fell to his knees.

"Thank God you are here," Reverend Bulmer gasped in evident relief. "Another moment, and he would certainly have killed me."

"Undoubtedly," replied my friend, "and many men would have also, in his place."

"Who is he?" I asked.

The reverend appeared no less fearful than before, as he recovered his breath and answered. "His name is Andrew Eddicott."

"Is he one of your flock?"

"He is."

"In fact," Holmes suggested, "he is the husband of Mrs. Beth Eddicott, recently deceased. Is that not so?"

The priest opened his mouth to reply, but it was Eddicott who spoke first.

"He gave my poor Beth's body up for vile desecration. He and the others, they did it to many. May God damn them all!"

"My good fellow," I began, "there is no need…."

"Let him explain, Watson." Holmes stepped back and gestured to the nearest row of pews. "Reverend, sit over there, and I beg you not to interrupt or attempt to escape."

The priest, now with the look of a man cowed by guilt, slunk away from us and sat as Holmes had ordered. He placed his elbows on his knees and his head in his hands as Eddicott had done, and I recognised that he, too, was a man beset by despair.

I turned back to my friend, but was suddenly aware of sounds from outside. They were of men running, and approaching quickly.

"That will be Lestrade and his men," Holmes explained. "He is a little early. My telegram advised an appearance after midnight."

At that moment the church clock chimed midnight and the inspector and two constables burst into the nave.

"Good morning, Inspector," my friend lowered his revolver.

Lestrade's eyes narrowed as he took in the scene. "I see that you have the situation in hand, Mr. Holmes."

"You see before you the man responsible for the murder of three priests, and the attempted murder of Reverend Bulmer, here. The reverend is not an innocent victim, however, nor were the others. I suggest that you station your companions at the entrance to preclude the unlikely events of escape or any disturbance from without."

The little detective hesitated for no more than a moment, before gesturing to the constables to position themselves as Holmes had advised. His footsteps sounded loudly on the stone floor as he advanced on Eddicott.

"Now then, my lad, what have you to say for yourself?"

I swear that I have never seen a face as full of pain as that of Andrew Eddicott. The young man stood up and let his eyes fall upon all three of us in turn, as if he were confused as to who to address.

"Now is your chance," I advised him, "to tell all that you wish to be known of this affair."

The tears glistened on his face, and he spoke haltingly in the flickering light. "Not long ago, my wife passed from this Earth. She was my reason for living, though our life together was cruelly cut short by pneumonia. Reverend Bulmer presided over her burial and I tell you, gentlemen that until I stood by her grave I could not have imagined the agony of a broken heart. The following day I arrived early for the evening service, because I was still in great need of comfort and I thought I might speak to the reverend alone for a while,

195

before worship began. I entered the church and found it empty, but I heard voices from among the cloisters." He raised a hand to gesture towards the shadowy enclaves at the edge of the nave. "Not wishing to disturb the reverend and whoever it was that he was ministering to, I took a seat in a nearby pew. The conversation grew louder, and even contained loud laughter so that I was compelled by curiosity to move closer and to listen. I stood concealed by a pillar and saw that there were four of them, Reverend Bulmer and three others who I soon realised were priests also. Whatever I expected to overhear I cannot now say, but the words that reached my ears astonished me! I was witnessing a discussion about how the four would divide a sum of money among themselves, and had hardly recovered from my surprise when it became clear that they were speaking of money from resurrectionists!" Here he gave in again to grief, while Holmes and I waited and Lestrade made some effort to disguise his impatience. "I felt my blood run cold in my veins as they made light of the offences against the dead that they had committed so many times. Much of me could not believe the words I heard, not from men of the church, yet they were from the mouths of the priests standing before me. Then, as the awful shock began to pass, it was renewed a thousand times as it came to me that my Beth, her dear body, had been carved like mutton because of these men and their greed."

"But you could not rest until you were certain," Holmes anticipated.

Eddicott nodded sadly. "All the following day I suffered such torment as no man should. When evening came I watched darkness fall, and I knew what I must do. Very late, long after the service was over, I concealed myself in the churchyard until I saw the reverend leave. When I was alone I stood listening to the cries of roosting birds, and presently courage came to me. With the stout shovel I had brought, I dug Beth's grave until I had unearthed her coffin. It took me some time to prise off the lid, but when it lay beside me it was as if the devil gripped my heart. I looked upon the casket, filled only with sandbags, and knew at that moment that my worst fears were justified and that I would never know peace as long as those responsible lived!"

"So it was then that you planned the murders?" accused Lestrade.

After a silent moment, Eddicott bowed his head. "It did not seem like murder to me, for I have always held that a man has a right to his vengeance when a great wrong has been put upon him. I resolved that on the thirteenth of the next four months, the day my Beth was taken from me, each of these imposters would be sent to account for their actions to their Maker. My enquiries about them and their whereabouts were complete by the time the first date came around, and I drove the carriage that ran down the vicar of St Uriah's. Next came that of St Thaddeus a month later, when I struck him down in the street. The priest of Woolwich I caused to fall to his death in the tower of his own church, and," he pointed to the axe at his feet, "this was to have been the end of Reverend Bulmer."

"As good as any admission I have heard, in all my years in the force." Lestrade handcuffed Eddicott's unresisting hands, then signalled to the constables, who led their prisoner away.

"And yet I feel sorry for the man," I confessed.

The inspector looked at me in surprise. "Really, doctor, after what we have just heard? For the life of me, I cannot see why."

"Because, had it not been for the conspiracy of these priests, and for their pitiless greed, Eddicott would not have become a murderer. His crimes sprang from his grief, not from any intent to profit."

"That may be true, doctor, but we can't have people walking the streets of London killing whoever they wish, for any reason. I'd say the best he can hope for is to spend the rest of his days in an insane asylum, but the hangman is more likely."

"Let us now get to the root of this," Holmes interrupted. "We have not yet heard from the Reverend Bulmer."

197

We walked the few paces to where the priest sat unmoving, with his head bowed. At our approach, he looked up with eyes full of fear.

"We have proof that you have conspired with body-snatchers, from the prisoner Eddicott and from Mr. Holmes," Lestrade began. "Already, we have Larrimer and the resurrectionist, Waldren, in the cells. Although your crime is not considered serious, I cannot imagine that the church authorities will find your conduct favourable."

The Reverend shook his head hopelessly, and held his hands against his cassock as if to protect himself. "I am ruined."

"But it may go well with you in court, if you are honest with us. How did all this come about?"

Lestrade's question went unanswered for several moments, during which Holmes and I drew nearer so as to miss nothing.

"The four of us were known to each other, long before we decided to become priests," the Reverend began. "As you will no doubt have discovered, Inspector, we had each stepped outside the law at times. I doubt though, that the extent of our crimes is recorded at Scotland Yard. While at Oxford, we realised how our positions could be used to protect us from the consequences of any further criminal actions, and resolved to explore such a possibility later. We were at this time bound in friendship to a fifth priest, whom we judged not to be likely to participate."

"The Reverend Manfred," Holmes acknowledged.

"That was he, but he was posted to India, and so it was unnecessary to maintain our intentions in secrecy, as we had until then. We were already acquainted with both Larrimer and Waldren from our past lives, and so the notion of selling the bodies of the deceased took shape. I believe it was Godfrey Collett who thought of it at first, but each of us contributed until the process was honed into a workable plan. All went well, until Manfred showed signs of suspicion on his return from India. One of us, I honestly cannot remember which, suggested that he should meet with a fatal misfortune to ensure our future security, but this proposal was never acted upon. It was not until the interference of Andrew Eddicott that our scheme went astray."

"I cannot believe such things from men of the church," I said with undiminished dismay. "I find myself astounded."

"I believe that there may well be further charges, after all," Lestrade concluded.

"Did not any of you possess sufficient conscience to cause you to hesitate?" Holmes asked disapprovingly. "I would not have thought the betrayal of your trust and your flock would set lightly in your minds."

"Money does much to assuage guilt," the reverend replied, "and we were no strangers to crime. I, of us all, fared worse in that."

"You mean that you profited less?" enquired Lestrade. "If that is by way of a plea for clemency, it is doubtful that the court will consider it."

"Not at all, for I know I am beyond that. There is little I can do to help myself, so I am making a clean breast of things."

"Continue, then."

"After our dealings with Larrimer and Waldren had continued for some time, a woman came to see me at the church one evening, after the service was over. She made it clear to me that she had proof, I cannot to this day imagine how, of a serious incident I was connected with, years ago. It was quite possible, she explained, that she could be dissuaded from revealing her knowledge to the police, as long as a certain sum was handed to her on regular monthly visits. When my outrage and denials had subsided, she said that I had two days to consider the proposal. During that time I came to realise that I had little choice but to agree. My life would collapse, as indeed it has now, otherwise. At the appointed time she came again to receive the first payment, and every month after. That is why I had the least to show for our actions."

Lestrade's bulldog-like expression deepened. "This 'incident,' as you describe it, what was its nature?"

The reverend hesitated. "The worst. It was murder, although I had not intended it. In my criminal days it was my practice to follow gentlemen who appeared well-to-do as they emerged from a bank or, sometimes, a post office. I would wait until they passed through an alley or courtyard where my actions were unlikely to be observed, strike once with a club and make off with whatever money I could snatch. On one occasion I hit my victim too hard, or his skull was thin, and he died. How this woman knew of this I cannot tell."

"Had you an accomplice?" enquired Holmes.

"There was a boy who helped, so that we could watch in two places and double our chances, but he is long dead."

"Who was the woman?"

"I never knew or heard her name. She was always dressed plainly in a drab coat and bonnet."

"Has she returned recently, to extract her payment?"

"She has not, although it has been due for some days."

"Was there anything about her of unusual significance?"

He shook his head. "No – but wait, I once noticed something. There was a tattoo on her right hand. It was a rose."

I saw Holmes entire posture change. He took on a look which he often adopted, that of a terrier, restrained by a leash but eager for the pursuit.

"When she visited you at the church, was she alone?"

"Never. Always she was accompanied by a very large man with a thick beard. He stood a short distance away, as if looking to ward off any interference. He did not speak."

Holmes turned to meet my eyes, and I saw his thoughts. To the reverend, he said:

"And you know nothing of where this woman came from, nor where she went after her visits?"

"Indeed I do. One day, when I knew she would appear, I made certain preparations. I had an associate from the old days follow the woman to her lodgings, with the notion that I could find a reason to send the police there in the hope that they would discover evidence of some other crime. My only fear was that she would give me away while in custody."

"And as a result, what transpired?"

He sighed, tugging at his cassock. "Nothing. After the man reported back to me, I decided that the risk was too great."

"Where was this place?" From the sudden keenness in his eyes, it seemed that Lestrade too, had realised that Olga Stone and Alexander McIrwin were now the subjects of the conversation.

"It was a lodging house in Bermondsey. In the High Street, near the grocers and the Turkish baths."

"Very well. Have you anything more to tell us?"

The reverend shook his head without answering and stared at the floor, now a picture of misery and defeat.

"Do you have any further questions for the prisoner, Mr. Holmes?"

"I think not," my friend replied after a moment of consideration.

At a sign from the official detective, Reverend Bulmer also was removed.

"Well, Mr. Holmes," said Lestrade when only the three of us remained, "it seems we have crossed paths with our two old friends once again. If you are now going directly to Bermondsey I will be pleased to accompany you, as soon as I have instructed the constables to return with the prisoners to Scotland Yard."

Holmes turned to him with a thin smile. "My dear Lestrade, I have no such intention. If Olga Stone and McIrwin are still at that address, they will likely be there in the morning. If they have already left, then the trail will not be much colder than it is now. As I have explained to Watson before, this is, or was, a gang who travels the country while constantly seeking opportunities for crime. They doubtlessly have a widespread network of informers, and it was almost certainly by means of them that Reverend Bulmer's past crimes were discovered. I cannot think that he is their only blackmail victim, they are sure to have many, and it is inconceivable that these are their only current wrongdoings. No, I think we will pursue this first thing tomorrow morning. If you will be good enough to present yourself at Baker Street at nine o'clock we will, as you suggest, look into it together."

#

After an early breakfast, Holmes and I stood at the window looking down on Baker Street. Under a leaden sky many hansoms came and went, and gentlemen and beggars alike passed before our eyes.

"Lestrade is early," I remarked as a police four-wheeler came to rest outside our lodgings.

My friend nodded. "Let us save Mrs. Hudson the effort of answering the door, and go down to him."

We put on our hats and coats and were out in the street in moments. Lestrade opened the coach door and beckoned us to join him. We wished him good morning as we entered, and I noted that he seemed in good spirits.

"I have every confidence that I will have those two in handcuffs before the morning is out," he said as he made room on the long seat.

"Perhaps you will," Holmes agreed. "Certainly that is long overdue. But we must keep in mind they have worked together for a number of years, and are guilty of a multitude of crimes including several murders. This indicates that they are skilled in avoiding the law, for this cannot be the first time they have been close to capture, and that they will stick at nothing. Have you arranged for any reinforcements, Lestrade?"

The little detective's face broke into a smug smile. "Oh yes, Mr. Holmes, we are prepared, never fear. They have escaped the net before, but not this time. A coach containing four armed constables will be close at hand in Bermondsey, so that a whistle-blast will summon them quickly."

"Capital! Our advantage is that they are as yet unaware that we are drawing close, although they may by now have changed their place of residence as a precaution."

For the remainder of the journey Holmes was silent except for the occasional remark that contributed to the conversation between Lestrade and myself. For the most part my friend sat with his head upon his chest as was his habit, apparently deep in thought.

Once in Bermondsey Lestrade directed the driver to a side street, not far from but out of sight of our destination. We alighted outside a laundry, where open doors revealed several women with their hair caught up in turbans, already at work among clouds of steam.

"When we have turned the corner into the High Street, the lodging house is almost opposite," he said.

"Keep your hand on your revolver, Watson," warned Holmes.

When a landau and several hansoms had passed, we crossed the road and approached the house. It was a place that appeared to have seen better days, judging by the peeling paint and unpolished door-knocker, but through the curtained window was revealed a sitting-room that was tastefully decorated.

A rotund man in a morning suit answered our summons.

"Good morning," he looked uncertainly at each of us in turn. "My name is Walter Quince. How may I help you?"

Lestrade introduced himself, and described Olga Stone and McIrwin in detail. "I should make it clear that these are fugitives from the law, and are wanted for a number of serious crimes."

"One moment." Mr. Quince stepped back and turned to pluck a book, apparently a register, from a shelf. He turned a few pages and ran his finger down the entries. "Ah, here we are. I can think of none, save these, who correspond to your description. Mr. and Mrs. Stanley Clive, from Birmingham. They said they were here to visit elderly relatives."

"When did they leave?" asked Lestrade.

"Two weeks ago, all but a day."

"*How* did they leave?" Holmes enquired.

"A brougham was summoned to take them to the railway station. Mrs. Clive mentioned that they were returning home as their visits had been completed."

"By any chance," I asked then, "do you recall the name of the coach company, or of the driver?"

Holmes glanced at me approvingly.

Mr. Quince grinned broadly. "Oh, most definitely. His name is Mr. Charles Starrett."

"He is familiar to you, then?"

"He is my brother-in-law."

#

Mr. Starrett belonged to no company, but ran his business from his home near Clapham Common. In contrast to Mr. Quince he was exceedingly thin, but lacked height. His home and his appearance proclaimed him to be far from poor, and it struck me that his brougham was probably not his only source of income. We finally made his acquaintance after a wait of half an hour in an over-furnished parlour, during which his wife offered tea and assurances that he would be home before long.

He arrived abruptly, slamming the door behind him, and confronted us wearing a puzzled expression. Lestrade again introduced himself, and stated our business.

Mr. Starrett scratched his head and lowered himself into a chair. "It isn't easy to remember, after so many passengers since, but I think it comes back to me."

"Take your time, Mr. Starrett," Holmes advised. "There is no need to hurry."

Lestrade scowled and shifted in his chair at this, but said nothing.

"I believe I know who you refer to," recalled Mr. Starrett. "I remember, now. It was an early evening call. My brother-in-law sent a boy round here on a bicycle to fetch me for a fare. The strange thing was, the pair changed their minds a few minutes after we set off."

"They said at first that they were to catch a train," Lestrade prompted.

"Indeed they did, but they told me to take them to the Oriental Club instead."

"You did this?"

"Of course."

"You actually saw them enter the club?" Lestrade persisted.

"No," Mr. Starrett said after a moment, "They stood outside. I had the feeling that they were waiting for me to leave."

We left him soon after, expressing our thanks.

#

Lestrade wore a confused expression. "Where is this place?"

"Near Oxford Street," replied Holmes as we made our way back. "I will direct your driver further, when we arrive."

"What business could our friends have had there?"

Holmes shook his head. "Doubtlessly we will discover that, before long."

We returned to the four-wheeler, whereupon Lestrade left us for a short time, to find the armed constables and instruct them as to our new destination. When we were on our way once more, he repeated his assurance that they would be close at hand.

The journey seemed quickly over, as I was preoccupied with my own thoughts and with anticipation of what was to come, rather than the scant conversation between Holmes and Lestrade. When next I looked out, we were in the Borough of Westminster.

"We are approaching the point where Oxford Street meets Regent Street," Holmes called to the driver. "Pray turn into Hanover Square."

I heard a muffled acknowledgement, and the coach was altered in its course as my friend had directed. After a narrow street, mostly of solicitors or accountants' premises, some of which had recently been ravaged by fire, we were confronted with a fine Georgian building. The Oriental Club was indeed impressive. As we left our conveyance, I heard Lestrade instruct the driver to await the following coach and join the other constables to be on hand, should assistance be needed.

We strode up to the door, and Holmes rapped upon it with his cane. It was opened almost at once by a man in a butler's uniform, who stared at us doubtfully.

"This is an official police investigation," Lestrade announced before the man could speak. He then introduced us.

"My name is Smithers," the man replied seriously. "I am privileged to hold the position of head steward here. How can I assist you gentlemen?"

"We have reason to believe that two fugitives have either called here or taken refuge," the little detective paused and corrected himself. "No, more likely just one, since I imagine ladies are not permitted in the club."

Mr. Smithers looked affronted, at this statement of the obvious. "I should say *not*, sir!"

"Very well then. At this time of day most of your members in residence will be on hand, I take it?"

"Well, yes, many are in the Old Smoking Room, enjoying a late breakfast or taking coffee or tea..."

"Then we will interview these first," Lestrade interrupted. "Please stand aside."

"But....." Mr. Smithers" objections were cut short as we brushed past him with Lestrade in the lead. After a tiled hall, a wide staircase of gleaming oak stood before us and we ascended to the floor above with rapid steps. The low murmur of conversation ceased at once, and many of the members and attending waiters became very still, as we entered.

Both Holmes and Lestrade adopted a stance which reminded me of hunting dogs catching a scent, their eyes everywhere. Expressions of annoyance or outrage were strongly evident on the faces of the large group of well-to-do men before us, whose eating, drinking and conversation we had suddenly interrupted. I heard gasps of astonishment at our appearance, before glasses and cups were replaced noisily and speech was resumed in hushed phrases. The place held aromas of wood polish, cigars and brandy and I noticed an elaborate snuff box with a lid in the shape of a ram's head. From their bearing, I supposed that many here had military service, but it was not so. As has happened before, it was as if Holmes had read my mind.

"No, Watson, this club is mostly made up of ex-officers of the East India Company."

"I had made no such enquiry."

His half-smile acknowledged my perplexity. "Your expression as you took note of these men made the direction of your thoughts obvious."

"We will begin here." Lestrade approached the first table.

Some of the men, resplendent in their morning-suits, got to their feet aggressively, while others adopted furtive expressions or averted their eyes. The little detective began his questioning and received denials and shaken heads in reply. I saw that most of the members sitting at the far side of the room were less perturbed, puffing out clouds of cigar smoke while viewing the activity as would an audience in a theatre. Doubtless, not knowing the nature of the enquiry, they were preparing themselves to keep their various secrets hidden and to impart the minimum of information.

Holmes and I stood a little behind Lestrade, my friend paying close attention to the exchanges. At the same time his sharp eyes continually swept the chamber, as if awaiting some sign to light his way.

One of the most elderly members, a stout man with a tobacco-stained moustache, reacted violently to Lestrade's questions. He had concluded an animated outburst by striking the table with his fist, and threatening the official detective with the severe consequences that would result from a report of the incident to his superiors, when Holmes interrupted.

"Lestrade, look there!"

Several men at nearby tables had retreated to join those further off, hoping to postpone their questioning or intending that it should be over before they were reached. A large man, possessed of furtive glances in our direction and a secretive demeanour, slowly moved towards a door at the end of the room.

Holmes gripped my arm and directed Lestrade's attention. "There is McIrwin."

I looked at Holmes incredulously. Lestrade wore an uncertain expression.

"Holmes – that is not McIrwin. The fellow has no beard. He could have shaved it off of course, but his entire appearance is different."

"I'll wager he is our man, Watson. Granted he has altered his appearance, but his gait and the way he carries himself remain the same."

"Are you certain, Mr. Holmes?" asked Lestrade.

"Absolutely, but I see that he is very near the door now, and it seems he has noticed our interest in him."

We strode forward with Holmes in the lead, but too late. McIrwin, despite his size, moved quickly and disappeared, removing the key and slamming the door behind him.

"Back, at once!" Lestrade cried, as the key turned in the lock.

We turned and retraced our steps hurriedly. Holmes and Lestrade raced down the staircase before me, and I barely avoided stumbling by gripping the polished bannister in my haste. I was faintly aware of the alarmed conversation that had sprung up in the room as we left, steadily receding as we completed our descent.

Mr. Smithers stood like an open-mouthed statue near the entrance, and Lestrade confronted him immediately.

"Quickly, where does the door in the far wall of the room above lead to?"

"Well, I...."

"At once, man! This is vital!"

Obviously shaken, the head steward babbled a reply.

"It opens onto a flight of stairs that leads to Woburn Place."

"Is that the narrow approach to the club?"

"It is the *only* approach to the club."

Holmes had already left us behind. Lestrade and I ran into the street to find my friend awaiting us beside the exit.

"There is no immediate danger of his escape," he told us. "As you see, the coach containing our reinforcements is stationed towards the end of the street, so McIrwin is barred from leaving the area. His only options, when we have ascertained that he has indeed emerged from the club, are either to conceal himself within one of these office buildings or to seek refuge over there."

"In those burnt-out remains?" I looked where he had indicated.

Holmes nodded. "The recent fire has ravaged those buildings, and they are certain to be unsafe as a result. McIrwin, though, is a desperate man with much to lose, so he may well seek to hide among the devastation or try to pass through it."

Lestrade strode over to the door leading from the club, an anonymous exit set in a plain wall, and opened it. He stood peering upwards, before turning to us.

"There is no one here, now."

"Is the key in the lock of the door at the top?" my friend asked.

The little detective leaned further into the doorway. "I can barely see....yes, it is still there."

"Then most probably he has not doubled back. What lies beyond this wreckage? Is there a path leading from its rear?"

Lestrade held up an arm as a signal, and a constable detached himself from the others near the coach further along the street. He approached us quickly and saluted the inspector.

"Constable Redfern, sir."

"Are you familiar with this area, Constable?"

"Five years on this beat, sir."

"Excellent." Lestrade spoke in an even tone, but I could sense the restraint in his voice as excitement mounted within him. He knew the end of the chase was near. "What is at the other side of what remains of these buildings?"

"All along the backs of the offices on this side of Woburn Place is a high wall, topped with metal spikes. It must be about ten feet tall and is there because government buildings are situated on its other side. I don't think our man will get away through there, sir."

"Where does the end of the wall lie?" Holmes asked.

"I believe it ends behind a house in Regent Street."

"Thank you, Constable. Lestrade, I suggest that you despatch two constables to that place, and station the others here while we investigate within. I can see no other available concealment that McIrwin could have used."

"See to it, Redfern," the inspector said. "The fire has left little more of this place but scorched brick and cinders," he warned us. "Tread very carefully, gentlemen."

We soon discovered that such caution was justified. The interior still held a faint warmth from the recent flames, and the blackened floor retained pools of water from the attentions of the fire-brigade. Every pace proved perilous, the floorboards, what was

212

left of them, threatening to collapse under our weight. We advanced slowly, with much crackling and splitting underfoot. Twice Holmes steadied himself by gripping the edge of an empty window-frame or a door-handle, and I held onto Lestrade until he recovered his balance after trusting his weight to a treacherous joist. We soon found ourselves in a long corridor, with rafters hanging from the ceiling and doors reduced to the consistency of paper.

"I'll go this way, Mr. Holmes," the official detective said in a low voice.

Holmes nodded, and he and I crept away in the opposite direction. Every few minutes pieces of wood or masonry succumbed to the damage and fell to the floor. Here the smell of dampness was stronger, and the echoes of our movements deadened by the soaking masses that surrounded us. In the empty rooms on both sides, the desks and chairs were barely recognisable. Strips of panelling hung, all substance burned away, from seared walls.

Ahead of me, I saw Holmes" posture stiffen.

"Lestrade!" he called urgently.

I immediately heard the noisy approach of the inspector, as he trod upon charred embers and weakened floorboards. Then he stood beside us, continually glancing around warily.

"What have you found, Mr. Holmes?"

"Look there!" My friend indicated a hollow in the blackened mass that had once been a carpet.

Lestrade bent to examine the impression. "This could have resulted from the presence of the fire-brigade."

"I think not. Observe how it is relatively dry. The surrounding residual water has not yet had time to seep into the cavity made by a footprint, suggesting that it was made very recently. I would say no more than three or four minutes ago."

"Possibly." Lestrade still occasionally queried or denied Holmes" deductions only, more often than not, to conform to them later.

"But do you not agree….."

My friend was abruptly silenced as a shot rang out and we instinctively crouched. I felt the floor beneath us sag as I looked around with my revolver ready.

"Are you injured, Lestrade?" Holmes asked.

"No, the bullet hit the wall, I think."

"Watson?"

"I am unharmed."

We were now almost at the end of the corridor, where the remains of a staircase hung precariously. The meagre light glinted on the gun that McIrwin, his face red with fear and exhaustion, held aimed at us.

"Leave here," he cried, "or I will kill you all. I have sworn that I will never face the hangman."

"But you will," replied Lestrade. "That is long overdue. At the Yard we have been after you and Mrs. Stone, for some time."

"I tell you that I will not surrender." His voice held a note of hysteria, and because he was so desperate I feared for us in our position of no protection.

"McIrwin," Holmes called. "You cannot win, this time. We each have our revolvers trained upon you. How many times can you fire before we do?"

The fugitive was silent for a while, and the tension between us mounted as we waited, with our weapons levelled, for his response.

"Come on man!" shouted Lestrade. "How will you get away? Better to die later than now."

A further silence descended. As we waited, the creaks and shiftings within the house were the only sounds. I sensed Lestrade's growing impatience, and Holmes' cold determination that this man should either be apprehended or die.

Then McIrwin moved suddenly, in a frantic dash for the stairs. Pieces of debris, loosened by his actions, rained down on us. He was almost at the top before the weakened staircase collapsed. An avalanche of burned wood and loosened masonry plunged into the exposed cellar, as Lestrade left his position and made to dash forward into a blinding dust cloud.

"Wait!" Holmes gripped the little detective's shoulder, to prevent him from falling into the abyss.

For the next moments, I believe we all thought that McIrwin had perished. Holmes looked searchingly into the void left by the staircase, until we heard the echoes of running feet above us. They were sounds of urgent desperation. McIrwin ran from one end of the corridor to the other, frantically seeking a way out.

"We have him," Lestrade said triumphantly, an instant before the house shook around us and the upper floor began to crumble as the staircase had done.

"Quickly." Holmes pushed Lestrade and myself ahead of him, back into the passage while a threatening roar grew around us and the ground seemed to tremble. Again dust billowed everywhere, and we expected to be engulfed at any second as we ran for our lives. The way before us was obscured, as with a thick swirling fog, and I confess to being certain that our last moments had come, when a speck of light appeared and grew until it became the open outer doorway that led us back into the blessed sunlight.

We stood leaning against the wall of the adjacent building for what seemed a long time, coughing until the last of the dust was dispelled from our lungs while the constables looked on helplessly.

By the time we had recovered, all sounds within the building had ceased.

"Are any of you gentlemen injured?" Constable Redfern asked.

Lestrade shook his head and replied in a hoarse voice. "We have survived, thank you constable."

"Is our man still in there, sir?"

"He is, but he is dead. Now that the danger appears to be past, I must go back to verify that."

"We will accompany you again," Holmes affirmed.

The constables watched, as we again trod carefully into the building. Part of the corridor had collapsed, along with much of the floor above, and so it was easier to arrive at the site where McIrwin had met his end. As he and his associate, Mrs. Stone, had evaded Scotland Yard so many times in the past it was, I thought, to be expected that Lestrade would wish to be absolutely certain that he was no longer at large.

We saw at once that the chasm was much enlarged now. The masonry had settled in a pile, with spars of wood and metal projecting from the mound. The light was poor, enhanced only where one cellar wall was fractured, so that the three of us peered across the expanse for several minutes and saw nothing. Eventually the residual dust clouds thinned, and our vision improved.

Holmes stood beside me statue-like, his tall form bent as he peered into the wreckage. Lestrade scrutinized the scene carefully, and for a while we were silent, then Holmes pointed suddenly.

"There! Do you see, Watson?"

I held onto the remains of a heavy display cabinet, and leaned forward to a more advantageous position. "Over there, near that long chest?"

"Or what is left of it. Lestrade, look this way."

When our eyes finally adjusted, we beheld the full horror of the scene. McIrwin had been buried up to his waist by the avalanche, with his arms flung out as if to embrace it. The whites of his eyes appeared to shine in the semi-darkness, giving him the vacant expression of a marble sculpture. For the first instant I believed that he still lived, so unscathed did he seem, until I caught sight of the split beam that projected from the bloodied chest and appeared to have passed right through his body.

We turned away, and Lestrade was the first to speak.

"Well, it looks as if that's that, Mr. Holmes – this time."

Holmes nodded. "He will trouble us no more. Now I suggest that we leave here promptly, before we swallow more of this infernal dust."

Once outside, Lestrade instructed Constable Redfern as to the removal of the body and the erection of barriers to keep away curious onlookers. I could see that my friend was still concerned.

"This is not finished," he said as Lestrade came over to us. "There is still Olga Stone to be reckoned with."

"Indeed," the inspector agreed. "We still do not know of her whereabouts. McIrwin can hardly tell us now."

"Perhaps a further enquiry at the Oriental Club?" I ventured.

"A starting point, at least," Holmes acknowledged. "Let us seek out Mr. Smithers once again."

The head steward stood just inside the building, probably having watched the proceedings further along the street. He seemed rather subdued by the events he had witnessed, but made a valiant effort to disguise the fact.

"Is there more that I can do for you gentlemen? This has been a very worrying morning."

"We, too, have found little pleasure in it," Lestrade replied. "In order to complete our enquiries into this affair, we require to see the club records. The list of current members, to be precise."

"Surely, there can be no other…?"

"That is not our purpose. We wish to ascertain the name of whoever supplied the club with references, to admit Alexander McIrwin who has just met his demise during our pursuit in the building over there."

Mr. Smithers swallowed noisily. "This time, I regret that I have not the authority to accommodate you. However, Mr. Ernest York, the club secretary, has just returned from a meeting and will be glad to oblige, I am sure." He made a gesture, towards the innards of the building. "If you will be so good as to follow me."

He led us along a short passage, and knocked upon a door. In a moment he was bidden to enter and allowed us to precede him. A man dressed in immaculate grey and with a magnificent handlebar moustache rose from behind an ornate desk. Mr. Smithers introduced us and left, and we sat in comfortable chairs. I glanced around the room. It contained bookshelves and a row of portraits along one wall, which I presumed were of previous club secretaries and prominent past members.

"I will of course comply with any request from Scotland Yard," Mr. York replied after Lestrade had explained our presence. He stood and limped with the aid of a sturdy cane over to a glass-fronted cabinet and withdrew a leather-bound volume, which he opened when he had resumed his seat. He ran his finger down the lists on page after page.

"Gentlemen, I regret I cannot help you. There is no one of that name on the club register."

"He cannot have attended the club for long, and almost certainly under another name," Lestrade pointed out, after furnishing a concise description.

"Would you expect less than, for example, three months?"

"Most likely."

"Very well." The club secretary consulted the book again.

"Aha! Here is the only new member that I can recall, who seems to fit your description. I do believe that Mr Jasper Needham, is your man."

"And who recommended him?"

Mr. York looked up from the page and smiled. "He could hardly have had a better reference. I have a letter here from Mr. Bertram Torrent."

"The High Court Judge?" Lestrade queried with some amazement.

"The same. Mr. Justice Torrent has been a member here for some years, although we have not had the pleasure of seeing him of late."

"That is most unexpected!"

"Nevertheless, it is what is recorded here."

The inspector was clearly dumbfounded, and I saw the ghost of a smile in my friend's expression.

Holmes then requested Mr. York to provide his own recollection of Mr. Needham's appearance, which he seemed to find satisfactory. Lestrade wrote in his notebook during the few minutes of conversation that followed, before we bade Mr. York farewell.

#

As we walked to the waiting police carriage, the inspector was obviously perturbed.

"There is something peculiar here Mr. Holmes, if a High Court Judge is involved in this. I will return to Scotland Yard to see what I can discover."

"A very wise course of action, Lestrade."

The inspector left us, leaving the constables to continue their attentions to the burnt-out building. Holmes and I walked into Regent Street, where we easily found a waiting hansom.

"Are we on our way to visit Mr. Justice Torrent?" I asked him as the driver eased the horse into the traffic. I had not heard him state our destination.

He looked at me incredulously. "Why ever should we do that, old fellow?"

"Did not Mr. York identify him as the source of McIrwin's reference? I expected that we would visit the judge in an attempt to learn Olga Stone's whereabouts, if he is acquainted with her also."

"An interesting deduction, Watson, and quite logical were it not for the fact that Mr. Justice Torrent has no connection with this affair."

"I confess to being totally confused."

The hansom turned a sharp corner and we braced ourselves. Holmes scowled in the direction of the driver, before answering.

"It is all absurdly simple. The man who supplied the recommendation was not Mr. Justice Torrent, and the letter was a forgery."

"But Mr. York stated that the judge was a member of the club."

"That may well be, but I will wager that it was not he who assisted McIrwin, and possibly Olga Stone. You will recall that it was mentioned that his attendances are infrequent."

"I had thought our adversaries most unlikely associates of a man of such position. Who then, has falsified these things, and why was McIrwin in the club?"

"As to the reason, apart from being part of some new criminal scheme, I doubt if we will ever know unless Olga Stone can be persuaded to tell us when she is eventually captured. The perpetrator of these deceptions is the man who we are on our way to see now. He is a dishonest character, and well-known to Scotland Yard."

"Then perhaps Lestrade should have accompanied us."

"I think we will do better by ourselves, in this instance. I encouraged the good inspector, or rather did not contradict his belief that Mr. Justice Torrent was involved here, in order that he would return to the Yard to investigate and allow us to proceed alone."

"But proceed to *where*, Holmes?" I asked with growing frustration.

"To the home of one Cornelius Jack, known in criminal circles as 'The Impersonator'."

"I have never heard of him."

"That does not surprise me. If he were well-known, his activities would be severely curtailed."

Further than that, Holmes would not be drawn. All I could gather was that this Cornelius Jack somehow made his living from disguising himself, not unlike Holmes on occasion, but for unlawful purposes. With conversation denied me, I again gazed out at our surroundings. We passed through Regents Park and near to St James' Market. Entering Piccadilly, the driver turned into Castle Street.

"This will do," Holmes called to him.

Soon we stood watching the hansom drive away. I looked at my friend curiously, for this place was unfamiliar to me.

He looked around us, perhaps to ensure that we had not been followed. Several smaller streets led off from here, and after a moment of reflection he selected one of them.

"This way, Watson. Some years have passed since I last visited Mr. Jack, but I believe his residence to be unchanged."

We entered a narrow street with silver birch trees planted at intervals along the edge of the pavement. A succession of villas stretched away into the distance, each different in design from its neighbours and most of them showing the effects of age. Holmes strode past several with such speed and apparent enthusiasm that I could barely keep pace, then stopped abruptly and pointed with his cane.

"There, I think. The house with the domed roof and gold-painted door."

We crossed the street and approached the place. It struck me as a rather flamboyant example of the mock-Italian architecture that has sprung up in various parts of the capital, and it was not to my taste.

"We are here because you believe this man, who lives in this bohemian place, to have impersonated Mr. Justice Torrent?"

He rapped on the door with his cane. "No, I am certain of it."

"But how can that be? We have no evidence of his connection with this affair."

"I need none, in this instance. I know Jack is involved here because no one else could be. He is unique. Little is known of his origin, but I have documented some of his criminal exploits and been concerned with one. Strangely, he was innocent on that occasion."

Holmes inclined his head towards the door, and I did likewise. We had both heard a sound from within the house. Faint footfalls became louder, until the door opened no more than an inch and a single eye peered out as us.

"Good afternoon, Mr. Jack." Holmes said into the space.

For some moments there was no reply. We stood there in complete silence, without even the sound of a distant passing hansom. The street might have been uninhabited.

Holmes stepped back, doubtlessly intending that the man within should see him more clearly. I did this also.

Then the door swung fully open, to reveal a man of the most curious appearance, clad in a long garment cut from a single piece of cloth.

He fixed an odd gaze upon me, his eyes registering no recognition, and then upon my companion, before his face became animated.

"I had not thought ever to encounter you again," he said in a voice without accent or emphasis. "Come in, Mr. Sherlock Holmes."

Chapter Sixteen – The Heartless One

We entered a long, dim corridor. Despite the half-light, I could make out the lurid murals along its sides. Depictions of dragons and other mythological beasts glared and snarled at us, as did leopards and tigers from the ceiling above. From the wall at the end a coiled cobra watched, reminding me of my army days. At the sight of it, my skin crept.

We turned into a spacious room in which heavy curtains were drawn, though it was still afternoon. I saw that illumination was provided by a number of oil lamps, set on tables in each corner and elsewhere. Long couches, draped with rugs and blankets bearing designs that surely originated in China or India, stood around a rattan table. Holmes and I had removed our hats, and now sat opposite our host, as we were bidden.

Cornelius Jack arranged his robe-like garment around his body, as he lowered himself onto the cushions which all but covered the largest couch. He had about him an almost priestly air, and I seized the opportunity to study him before Holmes began his questioning. He was truly strange, of more than middle height but, I noticed, he seemed shorter because he walked in a hunched-up manner. He was completely bald, with a longish face and, to add to his peculiar appearance, a red spider tattoo graced the top of his head. Holmes had stated that this man's birthplace was unknown to him, but I would have wagered that he came into the world somewhere on the Asian continent, born of European parents.

Mr. Jack indicated a tall bottle that was set upon the table with several glasses. "This is a particularly fine vintage from the Hungarian Empire," he said in a rather high-pitched voice. "Perhaps you gentlemen would care to share it with me."

We both declined politely.

After taking a long draught, our host replaced his glass and scrutinized us for a long moment.

"Why have you sought me out, Mr. Holmes?" he asked then.

"You will recall," replied my friend, "my warning to you, at the time when I was able to extricate you from the Grantham Soames murder affair. I had accumulated evidence proving that your impersonation of the victim's father was instrumental to the success of the crime, yet I was not convinced that you were aware of the result of your actions. The lawyers for the prosecution would have it that you were an accomplice to the killing, but I suspected that you had been duped."

"I have forgotten none of this." Mr. Jack nodded his naked head slowly, and waited for Holmes to continue.

"I am glad to hear that. I learned then that you had a history of applying your considerable talent for disguise and impersonation to criminal purposes. Indeed, the files at Scotland Yard feature you often, although there has never been an arrest. I proposed that I should give evidence on your behalf, on condition that you gave your solemn word to cease all unlawful activities and take up my suggestion that you seek a career on the stage or in music halls."

"I have since appeared at the Gaiety, the Bijou and many provincial theatres, taking part in a variety of acts. I receive much less money for my skills than before, but I now have no fear of the official police. I have kept my word to you."

"I am prepared to accept that," Holmes leaned forward, watching Mr. Jack closely, "up to a point. But is it not a fact that you also take on impersonations, at dinners and parties, for members of London society who wish to play tricks on their guests by appearing to be on intimate terms with well-known figures?"

For the first time, I saw signs of disquiet in our host's expression. He nodded, warily.

"It has been known, on occasion, but there is no harm in it. I have caused loss or injury to no man."

"Perhaps you have, but again unwittingly."

Mr. Jack's frown deepened. "What can you mean, Mr. Holmes?"

"Simply that we called here on our way to see Mr. Justice Bertram Torrent. I wish to question him about a reference he gave to a certain Jasper Needham, at the Oriental Club. Regrettably, Mr. Needham, who we were pursuing in connection with a number of serious crimes, has recently met with a fatal accident."

"He is dead? That is certain?"

"We saw his remains," I volunteered. "There can be no mistake."

Mr. Jack's features relaxed, as if a great burden had been lifted from him. Holmes and I sat in silence. The repulsive red spider appeared to shine when caught by the light.

"Then I can speak freely. It is true that I created a document to ensure Needham's admission to the club. It is another of my practiced abilities. I have known him for much of my life, under such names as Simon Bourne-Markham, Gerald Noakes and Alexander McIrwin. I tell you gentlemen, that I have never made the acquaintance of a more formidable and deceptive scoundrel. When, for fear of bringing the law down upon me, I refused to aid him in an outrageous scheme of which he would tell me very little, he threatened me with The Heartless One. In the face of such a threat, I was powerless to refuse."

"That is the woman who usually accompanied him?" I ventured.

"That is the evil thing in the body of a woman with whom he shared his despicable deeds. Surely, no true member of the fair sex could contemplate such actions. I once saw her hack off a

226

woman's finger to take possession of her wedding ring, a poor widow who could not afford to pay for their so-called protection. She sold the young son of a Chinese trader in Limehouse to an Arab slaver, for the same reason. It was that family who first described her as having no heart, and the description has remained with her. I tell you, gentlemen, that is the truth. She has no compassion, no affection for anything in this world. She loves nothing but money."

"Certainly, all that we know confirms her cruelty," said Holmes, as I recalled the fate of Squire Foley and his household and others since.

Mr. Jack lowered his eyes. "She also I have known for many years. I could tell you much more. Had I refused McIrwin's demand, I have no doubt that I would now be dead or disfigured."

"It is about this woman that we are here. We know her as Olga Stone."

"She has used that name, before now."

"We believe that you have knowledge of her whereabouts."

His face changed. Fear and shock filled his expression as he realised what was about to be asked of him.

"No, Mr. Holmes, I have no way of...."

"Have either the man we knew as McIrwin or Olga Stone visited you here?" my friend interrupted.

"No, I would not...."

"Have you met them in some other place, apart from when the proposal was put to you?"

"No, I swear!"

"Then how did you cause the forged document, once you had completed it, to come into their possession?"

Mr. Jack's features moulded into a countenance of gloom and despair. "I despatched it from the post office."

"Then please furnish us with the address from the envelope."

"I cannot, but if I could I would not dare."

"If we capture her, and Scotland Yard is with us in this, you will be free of her threat forever. She has deserved the hangman many times over, and that will be the end of her."

I could see why Cornelius Jack was so afraid. Olga Stone clearly had a long history of vicious criminal activity. At Holmes' assurance hope crept into his face, to be dashed instantly by his recollections of her pitiless cruelty.

"But what if she eludes all of you? I know enough of her past to be able to say with confidence that she has succeeded in evading the law many times. She would find out the source of her betrayal. My life would be worthless."

"We will not fail," Holmes assured him. "My word upon it. It would distress me greatly to see you charged with forgery, after you had broken with the criminal classes so successfully."

"You would do this?"

"Not I, but the origin of the reference that the club received will surely be sought by Scotland Yard, when this affair becomes public. They are slow, but they often reach sound conclusions eventually. I would much rather represent you to them as the man who finally showed the way to this woman's arrest."

The hairless head shook slightly, and the eyes glazed as if in concentration. I had the impression that he fought an inner battle to prevent his body from trembling with fear. Presently, he looked at Holmes and spoke in a strained voice.

"Very well. You have convinced me that it would be for the best. I cannot give you directly the information that you seek for I have destroyed the note bearing the address, but I will tell you of someone who will know without question where Olga Stone is living. Her name is Gwendolyn Quenn. God help me, Mr. Holmes, if you are not successful."

#

We ate dinner mostly in silence, despite my efforts to introduce a conversation. Holmes had become reticent and said little more until the hour grew late.

"We rise early tomorrow, Watson," he said as we parted for the night. "No time must be lost in acting upon Jack's information."

True to his word, he had already finished his breakfast before I joined him. I hurriedly consumed my own, for his keenness to depart was evident. No sooner had I eaten my last slice of toast, than he sprang to his feet and put on his hat and coat. I did likewise and, with a call to Mrs. Hudson, followed him down the stairs. We were fortunate in finding a hansom near at hand and, after he had given the driver hurried instructions, were on our way at once.

"Holmes." I said as the hansom gathered speed, "Who is Gwendolyn Quenn?"

"A woman who is notorious throughout the ale-houses of much of the capital. A pickpocket by trade, she finishes a month-long sentence in Holloway prison this morning."

"And we are on our way there, now?"

He nodded. "To meet her as the gates close behind her. Mr. Jack was quite certain, old fellow, that if anyone knows the whereabouts of Olga Stone, it is most likely to be she."

"Assuming of course, that she will disclose such information."

"I have anticipated her refusal. It would not go well for her to decline to assist us, if that made it likely that Olga Stone would be informed otherwise."

"That would be like signing Gwendolyn Quenn's death warrant!" I exclaimed. "Holmes, I cannot believe that you would resort to that."

"Neither would I. But she will be unaware of my scruples."

I leaned back in my seat, and sighed. "Let us hope your deception convinces her."

Little more passed between us for a while. My friend's expression indicated that his thoughts were elsewhere, and I began to reflect upon the succession of events, beginning with the letter from Squire Foley, that had culminated in our hunt for this woman whose crimes seemed without number.

"We are almost there, Watson." His voice intruded upon my thoughts suddenly, bringing them back to our present purpose. "This is Camden Road, which leads onto Parkhurst Road where the prison is situated."

Minutes later, we were confronted with a grim sight. The building had two large wings which embraced the entrance, as if protecting it. A depressingly dark structure, it resembled nothing more than an ancient castle. In front of the massive doors iron railings ran the entire length of the prison, and before the gate a single uniformed guard stood watchfully. Holmes called to the driver to halt and to wait for us, and we alighted.

The guard was a tall, burly man. He fixed us with a suspicious glare that never wavered, as we approached.

"Good morning," said my friend. "I wonder if I might have a word with you. My name is Sherlock Holmes."

To my surprise, the man's face broke into a smile at once. "Mr. Holmes, I have read of you, sir. Your work is an example to us all. It is an honour to meet you."

"Thank you. May I know your name?"

"It is Harold Willis, sir. A prison guard for nigh on twenty-five years."

"Capital! You are just the man. I understand that it is customary here, to release prisoners at eight o'clock sharp?"

"That is so."

Holmes consulted his pocket-watch. "It is now five minutes before. Can we expect then, that Gwendolyn Quenn will pass through this gate shortly?"

"No, sir."

"Has her release been cancelled then, or postponed?" I interrupted.

If Mr. Willis wondered who I could be, or resented my entering the conversation, he gave no sign of it. "Not at all. We are awaiting the arrival of an unusually high number of new prisoners this morning, and it was thought best to dispense with her departure and other tasks beforehand."

"So she has gone?" Holmes asked.

"Not more than twenty minutes ago. She was met and driven away before I could close the gate."

My friend's brow furrowed. "Met, you say?"

"Indeed. The hansom had been waiting along the street, by that tree that you see there, for at least an hour. I began to grow suspicious, since most prisoners leave here on their own two feet, but then she appeared and was, as I say, driven away. It was most strange."

"What was it that made you consider it so?"

"The driver walked in an odd manner, suffers excessively in cold weather and is unable to speak."

Surprise such as I have seldom seen in him crossed Holmes' face, but was gone in an instant. "Pray explain how you formed these remarkable conclusions."

Mr. Willis' face reddened. "I have mentioned, sir, that I have read of your methods. The driver was clad in an unseasonably heavy coat and a wide-brimmed hat. He wore a thick muffler around his face so that little more than his eyes were visible. As he strode from the hansom to intercept Miss Quenn, I noticed that his steps were peculiar, short and quick like."

"Most interesting. And how did you deduce that the driver was without speech?"

"That was the most simple observation of all," the guard said proudly. "As they met, the cabbie made no explanation of his presence, nor did he enquire as to Miss Quenn's intended destination. He simply produced a sheet of paper and gave it to her. She read it and appeared to agree to whatever it contained, before entering the hansom. Moments later, they were gone."

"My congratulations on your powers of observation," Holmes said, handing the man a half-sovereign. "Am I correct in assuming that the hansom made off in that direction, continuing along Parkhurst Road?"

Mr. Willis touched his cap in acknowledgement. "Indeed you are, sir."

#

The prison receded quickly from our sight, as the horse broke into a trot.

"You are thinking that the driver was Olga Stone, Holmes?" I ventured.

"I am quite certain of it. The hat and muffler were an obvious disguise, the walk was that of a woman rather than a man, which was why it seemed odd to our friend Mr. Willis, and the medium of a written instruction was used to prevent both he and Miss Quenn identifying a female voice."

"Miss Quenn also? You believe then, that she was unaware of the identity of the driver?"

"I would wager that she would never have entered that hansom, otherwise. Some ploy was used, here. Remember that she knows Olga Stone and is familiar with her reputation. She would have realised that she was walking into a trap, had she recognised her."

"Olga Stone seeks to silence her because she could be a source of information to the official force?"

"And to us, also. Stone would never allow such a threat to her liberty to persist. Miss Quenn is in great danger."

Holmes urged our driver to increase our speed. He was determined to catch up with our quarry, but the effort quickly proved unnecessary. We rounded a bend in the road and came upon an inn. A sign, gently swinging in the breeze and bearing the likeness of a colourful figure, proclaimed the establishment to be The Cavalier. It was a low thatched-roofed building, with tables arranged across the open courtyard. These were well-occupied by early morning drinkers, judging by the temporarily abandoned tankards and glasses left upon them. Everyone, including the white-aproned innkeeper, had crowded around the table nearest the road. There appeared to be great excitement among them.

"Driver, stop at once!" Holmes ordered, and we jumped out before our conveyance had come to rest.

We approached the crowd, and I saw at once that the object of their concern was a stricken woman. It did not escape my notice also, that she wore a frock of the coarse material that is issued to prisoners in the absence or poor condition of their own clothing, during their confinement.

"Quickly, Watson!" We pushed our way through the confused group, vaguely aware of the words of sympathy, encouragement and pity from the onlookers.

The woman lay on the ground, close to a table that she had evidently occupied with another. She tore at the neck of her bodice, in such agony that prevented her even from screaming.

"I am a doctor," I told her, attempting some reassurance. "What has happened to you?"

Her words came out as a barely-understandable croak. "The drink!" She raised an arm briefly to point in the direction of the nearby table, then let it fall limply to her side.

"It is poison, Holmes," I said after smelling the liquid, but after a quick glance he forced his way up to her and placed his hands upon her shoulders.

"Are you Gwendolyn Quenn?" He asked her.

She made no reply but nodded frantically.

"You were left here by Olga Stone?" I felt that he could barely restrain himself from shaking her, such was his fear that she would pass from this world before answering his questions.

"Holmes!" I cried. "This woman needs assistance!"

He glanced at me quickly, over his shoulder. "Then give it to her, Watson, as I speak."

"I did not realise who had met me, until it was too late." She gasped with difficulty.

"Where is she now?" My friend insisted, as I called for a pitcher of water which was all I could do.

Her words were becoming more indistinct, so that he was forced to hold his head near to her face to hear her reply. "Ping Frost," she pronounced painfully, and then in a fainter voice still, "Heaven."

"Holmes, help me to turn her over," I called as the water arrived. "I am going to attempt to get the poison out of her."

He grasped her shoulder, intending to assist me, but Gwendolyn Quenn gave a sudden deep sigh and her body relaxed.

"She has gone," he said as we stood up. "The odour on her breath was identical to that of your patient, Martland."

I nodded sadly. "There can be no question, as to who is responsible for this poor woman's death. His also."

We left the body and Holmes examined the table. "Here we have a full glass, and another with the contents half-consumed. It appears that the two women sat down and Miss Quenn drank first, obviously after the concealed poison had been added to her ale. At that point, her purpose accomplished, there was no further need for Olga Stone to delay her departure. She then left, her drink untouched, as Miss Quenn writhed in her agony."

"The callousness of this woman has no bounds," I remarked.

"None. She may prove to be the most evil woman that I will encounter."

"I pray that we will meet none more so."

Holmes produced his notebook and scribbled a few words. He tore out the page and gave it to the innkeeper, who had been standing close by looking shocked. "If you have not already done so, send for a constable at once. Do not fail to give this note to him, and to convey that it is of the greatest importance that it reaches Inspector Lestrade of Scotland Yard without delay."

With that he turned abruptly, and I followed him back to the hansom. His face was grim as we set off back to Baker Street.

"There can be no chance of overtaking Olga Stone's carriage, now." I observed unnecessarily.

"She will be far from here, by now."

"But we still have not discovered her whereabouts."

"To the contrary, I now know exactly where she is currently living."

I glanced at him in surprise. "How can that be, Holmes? That unfortunate woman could say little that was understandable, before she died."

"You did not hear?"

I shook my head. "Only some words that meant nothing. They sounded to me, something like, 'Ping Frost', and 'heaven'."

"That is how it sounded, certainly, but I am more inclined to think that she was trying to answer my enquiry. I shall be most surprised if we do not discover that her words were meant to be, 'Epping Forest', and possibly 'The Haven'."

#

Presently, we arrived at our lodgings. After luncheon little more was said until we were well into the afternoon. I sat in my usual armchair, smoking and reading the mid-day edition of *The Standard,* occasionally looking up to see Holmes on his hands and knees, poring over a spread map of Epping Forest, the area described by our informant. Dusk was giving way to full darkness, by the time he finally rose and stretched his thin body.

"That will do, I think. I suggest we retire early, but not before Mrs. Hudson has served us with a late dinner. As before, an early start would be an advantage. However, there is one thing I must not fail to consider, since I can foresee a situation where our lives could depend upon it."

At that he picked up a pad of telegram forms and scribbled busily for some minutes. Before he could summon her, our housekeeper entered to ask if we were ready to eat. He assented, and gave her the form. I noted his altered tone, and concluded that he was impressing upon her the necessity to arrange for an urgent dispatch. We consumed a hearty meal, and took to our beds after conversation interspersed by long silences. Clearly his mind was elsewhere.

Morning came after a fitful night. After I had consumed a hasty breakfast, Holmes put on his ulster and ear-flapped travelling cap and we left early as he intended. He seemed pleased after receiving an answer to his telegram, and even more so when we easily procured a hansom. I heard him request the cabby to proceed with all speed.

"Why are we in such a hurry, Holmes?"

"The train leaves within the hour. It is imperative that we are on board. Arrangements have been made for later."

A cat scuttled across the cobblestones before us, narrowly avoiding a collision.

"This is not the way to Victoria."

"No, indeed. Today we leave from Liverpool Street."

I leaned back in my seat. The driver, I felt, was doing his best to comply with my friend's request. Several times we were forced to lose speed by thickening traffic, and once by a band of ragged urchins who reminded me of Holmes' unofficial force of

Irregulars, carrying bundles of unknown content across the street. The sun shone down at intervals, between fast-moving banks of cloud. We reached our destination in good time, and strode swiftly into the station after the hansom had departed.

We boarded the train with time to spare, and settled ourselves in a compartment of our own. As low buildings and warehouses passed out of sight, to be replaced by trees and fields, Holmes lapsed into conversation that was entirely unconnected with our current purpose. Before we arrived at our destination, the rural station of Wood Street, he had elaborated at some length on the subjects of Turkish history, species of English pond life and the prospects of a forthcoming war in South Africa.

The train lost speed as we approached, but he was already standing, peering through the smoke in search of a trap or cart to hire. We alighted and he strode along the platform purposefully with myself in his wake. In moments he had struck a bargain with a waiting local man, and we boarded a cart pulled by a sprightly young mare.

"That fellow will be waiting when we return here later," he said as the horse broke into a trot. "I do not anticipate that to be after mid-afternoon."

We took a road that passed through the village of Loughton. Afterwards we were quickly surrounded by the greenery of the forest and eventually found ourselves upon a narrow path. I had not rested well the night before, and the rhythm of the horse's hooves on the flat grassland was lulling me to sleep. I heard, between periods of semi-wakefulness, Holmes' references to Waltham Abbey, and Lee Valley. Many were the bogs and ponds that we passed as he droned on. Finally, I was shaken awake as he brought the cart to a sudden halt.

"I trust you are refreshed by now, Watson."

"My apologies, Holmes. I slept little, last night."

"As did I. This affair weighed heavily upon my mind, for this woman will doubtlessly cause untold further harm if we fail now."

"We will not fail. I have seen you triumph over worse than this."

"That is true, old fellow, but...." He interrupted himself as we rounded a bend to see a rough wooden dwelling beside the path. "Ah! The map was indeed accurate. We cannot now be far away. Here is a place where we may obtain directions."

Near the open door of the structure, an elderly man chopped logs and stacked them in piles. He wore an old pea-coat and a tweed cap and appeared rather portly. I imagined that this fellow made a living from selling firewood, living permanently here near the edge of the forest. Perhaps, I thought, it was to him that the forged document had been sent, to be held in care for McIrwin.

"Good day," Holmes called, handing me the reins as we got down from the cart. "You are the proprietor, I presume."

"I be he." He embedded his axe in a tree stump and came over to us, as I tethered the horse to a tree. "Are you here to buy wood?"

"Not on this occasion. We are from the Capital and Counties Insurance Company. A large policy has matured but we cannot discover the whereabouts of the holder. We are not sure of her name since she remarried, but information has come to us that she is in temporary residence in Epping Forest. If you have been here a good while, it may be that you are able to assist us."

The woodcutter made no answer for a few moments, he fingered his bushy moustache as he considered.

"There are a good many with cabins and the like, hereabouts. Some live in them all year round, but others come now and then for a day or two."

"This lady will not have been here long," Holmes said. "I believe she resides in The Havens."

Holmes described Olivia Stone but, I realised, she had probably made changes to her appearance since he had observed her at the National Gallery. While our new acquaintance listened I looked beyond him, at the makeshift structure that served him as living quarters. Through the open door I saw an unmade bunk, and a rough table holding a beer tankard and a large piece of cheese. The only unusual item, I thought, was the battered bugle hanging from a nail in the wall.

He took off his cap, revealing a thick shock of white hair, and scratched his head.

"I suppose there is one woman who it could be. I cannot remember her name. She came here with a man, her husband I dare say, but seems to be alone now. She hasn't a cabin though, they came by barge and moored it nearby." He stretched out a hand and pointed through the trees. "If you follow that path through the thicket, the River Roding is less than a mile away and that part of the woods is known as The Havens."

Holmes thanked him and received a nod of acknowledgement, though the man avoided our eyes. We set off in the direction that had been indicated to us, but walked for no more than a minute or two when he stopped, his body very still as he listened and held up a finger for silence.

"Holmes, what...."

"Quiet, Watson."

He put a restraining arm on my shoulder, and we stood like statues. All I could hear was a faint crackling and scuffling such as you would expect in the forest, apart from a quick blast of sound which I could not have identified. Then a smile of satisfaction spread over Holmes' face and he nodded.

"As I thought. I must mention that man to Lestrade, who might be interested in interviewing him as a possible accomplice."

"Who do you mean, Holmes? The woodcutter?"

"None other. His manner and expressions indicated that he knew more about our adversary than he was prepared to reveal. Doubtlessly he is paid to warn her of anyone who asks after her. Keep your hand on your revolver, for she is certainly expecting us now."

I nodded an acknowledgement in the half-light. Here the trees met overhead, casting shadows across the glade. His conclusion baffled me, but then I understood.

"Of course. That sound I heard briefly, moments ago. It was the bugle!"

"Precisely. Olivia Stone, or whatever she calls herself now, has ensured that she will not be taken by surprise."

He took out a pocket-compass, and changed our direction. We walked warily along this new path in silence, until I put a hand on his arm.

"What is it, Watson?"

I pointed ahead. "The earth, before us."

"I see that you have noticed the peculiar sheen on the vegetation there, and correctly identified it as a bog. I was aware of it, old fellow."

"We have seen the like of this, before now."

"Indeed. If we divert our course through this clump of silver birches and continue for a hundred yards or so, we may emerge on firm ground. Tread slowly and carefully."

We moved on considerably further, before we found ourselves on firm footing once more. Holmes consulted his compass often, and we diverted from our course several times. More than once I heard movement among the surrounding trees which seemed to match our own, since it halted as we did and then continued with us, but Holmes merely shook his head when I mentioned it.

We progressed through the undergrowth, pushing our way through prickly bushes when they obstructed us and avoiding any patches of suspicious ground. We encountered many smaller bogs, but were deceived by none.

I noticed that the trees were becoming more widely spaced after a while, then we found ourselves confronted by a pond. It was overrun with reeds and a kind of coarse grass, and branches and twigs floated on much of the surface, but the only signs of life here were the birds who fluttered among the branches high overhead, calling to each other.

"Not much further now, Watson."

"You seem to know where we are bound for," I replied in the same quiet tone.

"I have made the arrangements with care." He put away his compass. "Unless I am mistaken, our destination now lies straight ahead. Keep your weapon ready and look for a large clearing."

We came upon it soon after. The trees ceased suddenly on all sides of a natural circle. For some reason, I was reminded of an arena.

"It is now that we are in the greatest danger," Holmes warned. "The river, where we are told that Olga Stone's barge is moored, is a short distance between those beeches. This would be the most likely place where she would lie in wait."

"What puzzles me, Holmes, is how the woodcutter's bugle call could have been heard, from such a distance."

"That is easily explained. I deduced from the surrounding sounds, that a boy ran past us at some speed on a parallel course, shortly after we left the edge of the forest. I believe that it was he for whom the bugle call was intended, and that it is his function to act as messenger and warn our adversary, by pre-arrangement. Clearly, she has left little to chance."

I was about to voice my agreement, when a figure emerged from the trees. It was a woman, clad in dark clothing and holding a shotgun pointed in our direction.

"Good afternoon, Mrs. Stone," Holmes said, seemingly without surprise. "I am afraid your current name is unknown to me."

She moved towards us, out of the shadows, and despite some differences I saw that it was indeed the woman I had seen at Foley Grange, and in the file at Scotland Yard.

"I was warned that someone had asked after me, and knew it could only be you, Mr. Sherlock Holmes."

"You compliment me, Madam," said my friend. "You were not easy to find, but I believe that representatives of the official force are not far behind."

She smiled, a ghastly grimace. "Such a poor deception is not worthy of you. I had expected better. It is you I have to thank for another interference in our business, though it will be your last. Yes, I am aware of your previous activities against us." She took another step towards us and stopped, as if a new thought had come into her mind. "But wait! My partner, the bearded man whose name you are probably ignorant of, has failed to communicate with me. Tell me, Mr. Holmes, has he been apprehended?"

"He is dead."

Her face went grave for an instant, then her eyes settled on me. "You are the man I saw at Foley Grange!"

Despite my growing fears, for the tone of her voice had risen sharply, I replied civilly. "Doctor John Watson, at your service."

"So, you are both responsible for endangering my freedom and my activities. I cannot see the end of the damage you have caused. It is fitting that I should destroy you together."

The blast of both barrels made a dull echo around the clearing.

Chapter Seventeen – A Grim Conclusion

The sound died away. Above us, birds squawked in protest at this unwelcome intrusion. Holmes had seized me and pushed me before him to a place of safety behind the thick trunk of the nearest beech, and the thought flashed through my mind that once again I owed my life to my friend.

"Quickly, before she can reload." He drew a police whistle from his pocket, and its shrill sound pierced the silence.

I detached my body from the rough bark and stepped out beside him. Mrs. Stone, as we knew her, was frantically fumbling in the pocket of her long hooded coat for replacement cartridges. As we approached, she began voicing a manner of oaths that I never wish to hear again from any woman.

"Put down your weapon," I called. "Or we fire."

Then, to my surprise, Holmes lowered his revolver. In an instant, the reason became clear to me. I saw shadowy movement behind Mrs. Stone, before a burly constable emerged from the trees and plucked the shotgun from her unsuspecting fingers. She cried out and turned on him at once, clawing at his face, kicking and screaming, but he held her easily until another rushed up and secured her with handcuffs. Suddenly, there appeared uniformed men at almost every point of the circle, all with drawn weapons. Lestrade had been as good as his word, and had made her arrest certain.

Among their number was a sergeant, who promptly approached us and saluted.

"Inspector Lestrade's compliments, sir, and apologies for a slightly late arrival. I understand he was delayed."

"No matter, Sergeant. A timely intervention, nevertheless. You have your prisoner."

"Indeed we do, sir." With that he turned away and sent some of his men into the trees behind us, presumably to search the barge. The remainder he accompanied in another direction, taking Mrs. Stone with them. Holmes and I watched until they passed out of our sight, and her curses became lost to our ears.

Having experience of the pitfalls, we returned to the edge of the forest more speedily. Lestrade stood waiting beside a police coach, with the woodcutter in handcuffs. Apparently the inspector also had deduced the man's involvement with our adversary.

"I am glad to see that you are both safe, gentlemen," he began. "I acted in accordance with your suggestions, Mr. Holmes, but I was delayed by a summons from my superiors. The Cullington case again, I'm afraid. Apart from my own enquiries, both Gregson and MacDonald have made some small investigations, but we have made little progress. We believe some powerful figures are connected, and there is even a suspicion of someone on the fringes of royalty, but there is no proof of anything."

"Think nothing of it, Lestrade," Holmes smiled at the little detective's apologetic tone. "The constables arrived at the correct place and in good time. Everything occurred as I anticipated. Mrs. Stone is now in your hands. Pray do not mention me in your report, as to give evidence would seriously intrude upon my time and in dealing with any forthcoming problems." He hesitated. "Am I to take it that the men were from the Basingstoke Division?"

"It was the nearest station of sufficient size."

"And your prisoner is now on her way there?"

Lestrade nodded. "Until I have eaten a hearty lunch before collecting her for removal to Scotland Yard, which is where she will stay."

"May I make a request of you?"

The bulldog face took on a suspicious look. "I will accommodate you if I can, Mr. Holmes."

"Doctor Watson and myself are about to return to Baker Street. When you arrive at Liverpool Street Station with your prisoner, will you bring her first to us before delivering her to the Yard?"

The inspector looked thoughtful, for what seemed to us a long time.

"I don't know what my superiors would say to that suggestion," he said at last. "I assume your purpose is to learn more of her activities relating to your own business."

"It is."

"I should be taking on a heavy responsibility, for all the time she was in your rooms," he said indecisively.

"There is a precedent, if it assists your decision."

"If there is, I am unaware of it."

After a moment, Holmes said, "Some years ago your colleague, Inspector Athelney Jones, made a similar decision in my favour, because of my small assistance in an affair concerning a man known as Jonathan Small."

"I recall the case of the Agra Treasure."

"Then you will agree?"

"Very well, Mr. Holmes," Lestrade said resignedly. "You may expect us sometime this evening."

#

The hour had passed nine, by the time the inspector and Mrs. Stone, accompanied by a heavily built constable, arrived at our lodgings.

Showing them into our rooms, our housekeeper gave us an uncertain glance.

"Thank you, Mrs. Hudson," Holmes called to her as she closed the door. He was about to call her back to request refreshments, but Lestrade anticipated this and shook his head.

"Sit there," the inspector ordered Mrs. Stone, indicating the basket chair. "Capstone, stand behind and watch her closely."

They obeyed, and Lestrade lowered himself into the vacant armchair.

"A cigar, inspector?" Holmes offered.

"Not just now, Mr. Holmes, if you don't mind. To be truthful, I shall be very glad when this interview is over."

"Very well then," Holmes sat back in his chair. "Mrs. Stone, or whatever your name truly is, are you prepared to answer my questions?"

She spoke with a certain smugness, seemingly unaffected by her situation. "It can make no difference now, since my life will soon be over. I will tell you this at once. From my earliest days I have had a different view of the world, and felt deeply that there was an incompleteness about my existence, until I met the man you know as Alexander McIrwin, whose attitudes matched my own."

"How were your conceptions different?"

"They may be beyond your understanding. To most men and women, is it not growing to adulthood, marrying and producing children and working to keep them, that is their expectation? Of course it is, but I find such a prospect tedious in the extreme. We shunned such an existence, Alexander and I, in favour of a life of adventure."

"A life of dishonest pursuits and murder, would be more accurate," Lestrade interrupted.

Holmes shot him a look of disapproval, before returning his attention to the prisoner. The chains of her handcuffs clinked as she shifted in her chair, and Constable Capstone placed his hands upon her shoulders at once as a cautious form of restraint.

"How do you perceive 'adventure'?" Holmes asked.

She shrugged. "Perhaps I should have said that our lives were one long quest, or hunt. We discovered in each other a complete disregard for the lives and welfare of others, not so strange when you consider that much of Nature works in such a way. Does not one animal eat another? Our intentions were to roam the country, and perhaps other lands in the fullness of time, ensuring our continued survival and freedom by whatever means became necessary. We had no time, and indeed no regard, for the foolish restrictions of law and order." She glanced at Lestrade, then stared directly at my friend. "To us, much of life was a game and we have friends everywhere, so you may not have seen the last of this, Mr. Holmes."

I saw expressions of incredulity and anger darken the faces of both Lestrade and the constable, and wondered if my own appearance had been similarly affected. Only Holmes seemed unperturbed.

"This then, was your state of mind when you burned down Foley Grange, killing the Squire and his household?"

"It was a matter of concealing our activities, after your interference threatened to bring them to nothing. We had our own intentions towards Squire Foley, a scheme which would probably have ruined him but at the same time furnished us with a great deal of money. I went to considerable trouble to secure a position there, but when we saw that our efforts were doomed to failure it was important to leave no trace."

"How was William Lance involved?" I asked at the risk of a rebuke from Holmes. As it was, he merely waited for her answer.

Mrs. Stone laughed harshly. "Lance was an incompetent whom we were forced to include in our plans, before he could ruin everything. By the way, Mr. Holmes, it was not he who sent you the body of Nathaniel Barley, he would never have had the stomach for it, although it was intended as a warning on his behalf. My first thought was to arrange his demise, but that would have attracted unwelcome attention. He had his own rather inferior intentions towards the Foley estate, which he abandoned on throwing in his lot with us shortly before he met his end. We intended to dispose of him eventually in any case, had not you gentlemen helpfully intervened."

For the first time, my friend gave her an angry look, although his voice was unchanged. "No action of ours was intended as an aid to your purpose. Lance was killed while fleeing our pursuit. Inspector Grey of the local force has our full report and concurs with it."

I glimpsed Lestrade nodding his head, as Mrs. Stone looked at Holmes indifferently.

"There remains the questions of the incidents involving Mrs. Evangeline Cutts, the DeVille family and that of Reverend Bulmer," I reminded Mrs. Stone. "Not to mention the deaths of Monsieur Henri Champonnier, Francis Martland, Gwendolyn Quenn and others."

"And of a man called Cornelius Jack, whom we discovered murdered at his home early this morning," Lestrade added. "You were seen and identified from an official photograph."

Holmes and I glanced at each other, and I knew he was asking himself if Jack's death was a result of our visit.

She gave us all a haughty look, smiled crookedly and responded in a tired voice.

"They were no more than pawns in our plans, their disposals were precautionary measures. None of any importance." She glared at us, her eyes soulless black pools. "But I grow weary of this conversation, and of your company. I will say no more."

"No matter!" exclaimed Lestrade, eager to seize upon this to end the interview. "I have witnessed this evening as good a confession as I have ever heard. Take her out of here, Capstone."

The constable allowed his prisoner to rise, then bundled her out of the room. At the last moment she called over her shoulder. "One thing you can depend upon, Mr. Holmes – I will never face the hangman. I have sworn it."

I recalled McIrwin making a similar vow.

"We will see about that," said Lestrade to her retreating back as she and the constable began their descent. "Did you hear enough, Mr. Holmes?"

My friend shook his head. "Not so much as I would have liked, but it will do. Doubtless she will have more to say when she is interviewed at the Yard."

"You may depend upon it. They often speak freely, when their appointment with the scaffold gets near."

"I will be interested to hear your account of such a conversation, at a later date. Thank you for indulging me, Lestrade. Good night to you."

We said nothing until their footfalls died away. Holmes looked from the window as the waiting police coach departed.

"She, at least, will do no more harm," I remarked. "Heaven knows that her evil has tainted enough lives."

He nodded. "She is at the conclusion of a long and varied criminal career, but no more a threat."

"Thanks largely to you, Holmes. I believe I saw a spark of admiration in Lestrade's eyes."

251

He smiled briefly. "Let us now consider the matter closed, except perhaps for the account I shall one day have to give when you decide to add this to your published works."

"It could be interesting to many, I am sure."

"Let us postpone any further discussion of that to another time. As for now, a glass of port would suit us both, I think."

#

I had thought that this would be the last of this affair, but the conclusion was yet to come.

We had scarcely finished our breakfast the very next morning, when Holmes pricked up his ears like a gun-dog, as was his way when a coach drew up outside our lodgings.

"A new client?" I ventured.

He shook his head. The smoke from his old briar hung in a cloud above him. "It is Lestrade."

"So soon? Something important must have arisen, since last night."

"That is possible. It could be something new, but we shall see."

I made to reply, but then realised that I had missed something in his demeanour.

"Holmes, how did you know that our caller was the inspector? You did not move from your chair."

"That is true," he smiled at my perplexity, "but I did hear the reply of the official coachman, when he was told to wait. I recognised the voice of Mortimer, whose distinctive accent I have heard before, at the Yard."

Before I could comment, the door-bell rang and Mrs. Hudson showed in our visitor soon after.

"Good morning, Lestrade." Holmes finished his pipe and laid it aside, before gesturing that the inspector should take the armchair as he had the evening before.

"I didn't expect to come around here this morning, Mr. Holmes."

"And we did not expect you, although of course you are always welcome."

"Thank you." He hesitated, glancing away before speaking. "I have some news, regarding Olga Stone."

"Pray enlighten us."

"She has made good her boast. She will never face the hangman."

I looked at him in astonishment. "She has escaped!" I exclaimed.

"No, Doctor. Or perhaps so, in a way."

"Explain yourself, Lestrade," Holmes said.

"She cut her wrists, during the night. The blood from her opened veins made a pool in the cell. We found a rusty nail-file that she must have concealed upon her person. "

"She cheated the hangman then, as you say. But the result was the same."

Lestrade nodded. "She will not trouble us, or the people of this city, again."

There followed a silence, such as is often automatically observed after news of a death. Regardless that the deceased was fully deserving of her fate.

"Very well," Holmes said then. "Now this affair is truly behind us, and we can concentrate our efforts elsewhere."

Lestrade got to his feet. "We can indeed, Mr. Holmes. And now I must leave you, for I have much to do. I came only to inform you of this final development."

"My thanks to you for that, Inspector." I saw that Holmes had noticed the worry in the little detective's bulldog-like face, as I had. "Is it the case you mentioned beforehand, the Cullington affair I think you said, that is the cause of your concern?"

After an initial expression of surprise at my friend's perception, Lestrade replied. "There is too much to be taken into account. I cannot recall such a complicated case, before now."

Holmes rubbed his hands together, and sat upright in his chair. "I thought that you might care to share it with us. Nothing outstanding requires my immediate attention, so it occurred to me that perhaps I could be of some small assistance in the matter."

Also from MX Publishing

MX Publishing is the world's largest specialist Sherlock Holmes publisher, with over a hundred titles and fifty authors creating the latest in Sherlock Holmes fiction and non-fiction.

From traditional short stories and novels to travel guides and quiz books, MX Publishing cater for all Holmes fans.

The collection includes leading titles such as _Benedict Cumberbatch In Transition_ and _The Norwood Author_ which won the 2011 Howlett Award (Sherlock Holmes Book of the Year).

MX Publishing also has one of the largest communities of Holmes fans on Facebook with regular contributions from dozens of authors.

www.mxpublishing.com

Also From MX Publishing

Traditional Canonical Holmes Adventures by
David Marcum

Creator and editor of
The MX Book of New Sherlock Holmes Stories

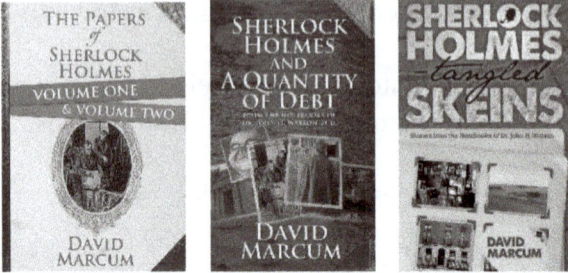

The Papers of Sherlock Holmes

"The Papers of Sherlock Holmes by David Marcum contains nine intriguing mysteries . . . very much in the classic tradition . . . He writes well, too." – Roger Johnson, Editor, *The Sherlock Holmes Journal,*
The Sherlock Holmes Society of London

"Marcum offers nine clever pastiches."
– Steven Rothman, Editor, *The Baker Street Journal*

Sherlock Holmes and A Quantity of Debt

"This is a welcome addendum to Sherlock lore that respectfully fleshes out
Doyle's legendary crime-solving couple in the context of new escapades . . . ." – Peter Roche, Examiner.com

"David Marcum is known to Sherlockians as the author of two short story collections . . . In Sherlock Holmes and A Quantity of Debt, *he demonstrates mastery of the longer form as well."*
– Dan Andriacco, Sherlockian and Author of the Cody and McCabe Series

Sherlock Holmes – Tangled Skeins

(Included in Randall Stock's, 2015 Top Five Sherlock Holmes Books – Fiction)
"Marcum's collection will appeal to those who like the traditional elements of the Holmes tales."– Randall Stock, BSI

"There are good pastiche writers, there are great ones, and then there is David Marcum who ranks among the very best . . . I cannot recommend this book enough."
– Derrick Belanger, Author and Publisher of Belanger Books

256

Also from MX Publishing

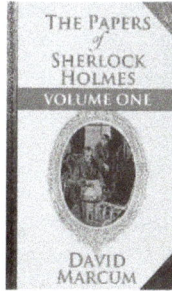

Our bestselling books are our short story collections;

'Lost Stories of Sherlock Holmes' , 'The Outstanding Mysteries of Sherlock Holmes', The Papers of Sherlock Holmes Volume 1 and 2, 'Untold Adventures of Sherlock Holmes' (and the sequel 'Studies in Legacy) and 'Sherlock Holmes in Pursuit', 'The Cotswold Werewolf and Other Stories of Sherlock Holmes' – and many more……

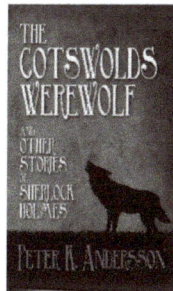

www.mxpublishing.com

Also from MX Publishing

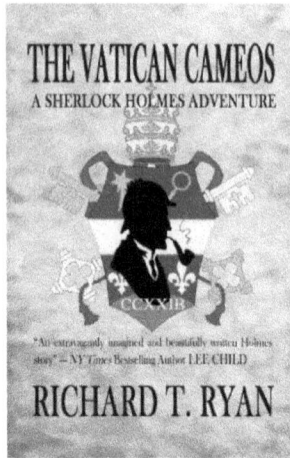

When the papal apartments are burgled in 1901, Sherlock Holmes is summoned to Rome by Pope Leo XII. After learning from the pontiff that several priceless cameos that could prove compromising to the church, and perhaps determine the future of the newly unified Italy, have been stolen, Holmes is asked to recover them. In a parallel story, Michelangelo, the toast of Rome in 1501 after the unveiling of his Pieta, is commissioned by Pope Alexander VI, the last of the Borgia pontiffs, with creating the cameos that will bedevil Holmes and the papacy four centuries later. For fans of Conan Doyle's immortal detective, the game is always afoot. However, the great detective has never encountered an adversary quite like the one with whom he crosses swords in "The Vatican Cameos.."

"An extravagantly imagined and beautifully written Holmes story"
(**Lee Child**, NY Times Bestselling author, Jack Reacher series)

9 781787 054172